JOE COLTON'S JOURNAL

A lot has happened since I last wrote. Turns out, my father, Teddy, had got himself hitched to another woman just before he married my mother. Pretty shocking to learn that your parents' marriage wasn't legitimate—and neither are you. On the bright side, I have a wonderful new family to add to our brood. The Coltons of Black Arrow, Oklahoma, are the descendants of my father's legal wife, Gloria WhiteBear. They are a remarkable bunch of people and I'm delighted to meet all of them at my newfound nephew's holiday wedding in Washington, D.C. Although trouble always seems to follow the Coltons no matter where we're from, I just hope <u>this</u> wedding goes off without a hitch....

THE COLTONS:
COMANCHE BLOOD

JUDY CHRISTENBERRY

has been writing romances for over fifteen years because she loves happy endings as much as her readers do. She's a bestselling author for Silhouette and Harlequin Books. A former high school French teacher, Judy now devotes herself to writing full-time. She spends her spare time reading, watching her favorite sports teams and keeping track of her two adult daughters.

LINDA TURNER

began reading romances in high school and began writing them one night when she had nothing else to read. She's been writing ever since. Single and living in Texas, she recently bought her first house, which was built in 1920, and plans to spend the rest of her life restoring it. She had the 2000-square-foot home moved forty miles from San Antonio to the Texas Hill Country. When she's not at the computer typing her next book, she's likely to have a hammer in her hands.

CAROLYN ZANE

lives with her husband, Matt, their daughter, Madeline, and their latest addition, daughter Olivia, in the rolling countryside near Portland, Oregon's Willamette River. Like Chevy Chase's character in the movie *Funny Farm,* Carolyn finally decided to trade in a decade of city dwelling and producing local television commercials for the quaint country life of a novelist.

Judy Christenberry
Linda Turner
Carolyn Zane

A Colton Family Christmas

Silhouette Books

Published by Silhouette Books

America's Publisher of Contemporary Romance

Special thanks and acknowledgment are given to
Judy Christenberry, Linda Turner and Carolyn Zane
for their contributions to A COLTON FAMILY CHRISTMAS.

SILHOUETTE BOOKS

A COLTON FAMILY CHRISTMAS

Copyright © 2002 by Harlequin Books S.A.

ISBN 0-373-48478-X

The publisher acknowledges the copyright holders
of the individual works as follows:

THE DIPLOMAT'S DAUGHTER
Copyright © 2002 by Judy Russell Christenberry

TAKE NO PRISONERS
Copyright © 2002 by Linda Turner

JULIET OF THE NIGHT
Copyright © 2002 by Carolyn Suzanne Pizzuti

This edition published by arrangement with Harlequin Books S.A.

® and TM are trademarks of Harlequin Books S.A., used under
license. Trademarks indicated with ® are registered in the United States
Patent and Trademark Office, the Canadian Trade Marks Office and in
other countries.

Visit Silhouette at www.eHarlequin.com

Printed in U.S.A.

CONTENTS

THE COLTONS:
COMANCHE BLOOD

Meet the Oklahoma Coltons—a proud, passionate clan who will risk everything for love and honor. As the two Colton dynasties reunite for a wedding, new romances are sparked from a near-tragic event. After all, passion and drama come with being a Colton....

Billy Colton:
The military man is disciplined in everything but women. But when he's called on to save beautiful Eva Ritka from ruthless terrorists, can he save his own heart, too?

Julianna Stevens:
The criminal psychologist hasn't seen her cop ex-husband in three years. But when they are forced to work together to resolve a hostage situation, she realizes that second chances only come once....

Ian Rafferty:
When he heard the gunshots ring out at the wedding, the quick-thinking entrepreneur pulled the woman next to him to safety into a closet...and into his life forever.

Joe Colton:
He's overcome the shock that he's not the legal Colton heir. But the happy reunion with the Coltons of Oklahoma is cut short when madmen threaten to rip the family apart once again.

THE DIPLOMAT'S DAUGHTER
Judy Christenberry

Chapter 1

Major William Colton sat up in the luxurious bed and stretched. He definitely wasn't in St. Petersburg, Russia, anymore. He'd returned to Washington D.C. a couple of days ago. He was glad to be back in the States, especially because so much had changed. Although he secretly wished he was at his great-grandfather George WhiteBear's ranch in his family's hometown of Black Arrow, Oklahoma.

Now that some of his siblings had flown the nest, it wasn't often that they all assembled in one place. But today, Christmas Eve, they were celebrating the marriage of his brother, Jesse. And they were doing so in Georgetown, an historic, high-class section of

Washington D.C., in a mansion that had recently come into their family. It had been rented for years by the Chekagovian government and used as their embassy and, later, a diplomatic residence.

Strangely enough, it was left to them by a grandfather they never knew, along with a trust fund of ten million dollars. Jesse, who did very well for himself as one of the top operatives for the National Security Agency, had used his share of the money and some of his own to purchase the mansion for his bride, Samantha. After all, he was the only family member living in Washington, D.C., and he could entertain the country's political elite in the house, in addition to raising a big family of his own.

Right now, of course, the mansion was filled with family, but after everyone went home, Jesse and Samantha would have to produce a lot of babies to fill this big a place. Billy grinned at that thought. He'd like a lot of nieces and nephews, but not any children of his own. He wasn't cut out for that.

He pulled on warm-up pants and a T-shirt and headed down a flight of stairs to find the kitchen. He could smell the coffee already. When he reached the large kitchen, he found his brother Jesse sitting at a big round table alone. "If I join you, will you share your coffee?" he asked.

"I think I'd better. You don't look like you're awake yet, Billy."

"Probably not. I think I'm still adjusting my inner clock to U.S. time. I need caffeine. Where is everyone?"

"They're all still asleep. It's only six-thirty here. Which makes it five-thirty in Oklahoma," Jesse said.

Billy grinned. "I forgot. When we were kids growing up, I thought we always got up too early. But the Army cured me of those thoughts."

A lot of things had changed over the years. As children, they had all resembled each other, but now differences were more apparent. Billy looked more like his Irish mother, with his hazel eyes and easy manner. Jesse took after his father, who was half-Comanche Indian, with his dark brown eyes and stern features.

"They've cured you of a lot of things, brother," Jesse said with a laugh. "I can't believe they're going to let you in the Pentagon. How did you get such a cushy job?"

"Cushy? I'll have you know my assignment may bring about world peace! I certainly made headway in Russia with my training school." He laughed, thinking about some of his early struggles to adjust to Russian culture.

"Well, go to it, brother. I'm all in favor of world peace."

"Yeah. I'm actually going to design more training sessions based on what I did in Russia. It is a pretty cushy job," he added with a grin. "At least compared to working in Russia. And it might be a little warmer here."

"As long as you keep 'em fooled about your talents," Jesse said with a laugh.

Billy was used to the teasing. He'd gone from an unruly, headstrong boy to a spit-and-polish, well-disciplined soldier. He'd seen the world, able to use all the languages he spoke. And he'd made a good living for himself. He'd been raised in Black Arrow, Oklahoma, with his four brothers and sister by their parents Alice and Thomas. His father had served his country in the military for more than twenty years, and his wife and children followed him wherever he had to go. But Oklahoma was home.

Billy took a sip of coffee, then said, "We had a good life as kids, didn't we?"

"Yeah," Jesse agreed, a smile on his lips.

"Stop thinking of Samantha," Billy ordered.

Jesse looked up in surprise. "How did you—"

"You always get this silly grin when your mind's on her. You're worse than anyone I know."

Jesse chuckled. "One day you'll understand."

"I doubt it."

"What do you mean? Aren't you going to marry and have a family?" Jesse asked, concern on his face.

"Easy, brother. You don't have to worry about me. The army life doesn't encourage having a little woman and 2.5 children, along with all their belongings. Hell, it would've taken me months to move us back to the States, instead of a couple of hours."

"But you're going to be settled here for quite a while, aren't you? Long enough to put down roots? Dad thought it might be permanent. He said once they got you in the Pentagon, they'd keep you."

"Mom and Dad are wishful thinkers."

"Yeah, 'cause they asked me to find you a nice lady."

Billy stared at his brother in horror. "They didn't!"

"They did. In fact, Samantha promised to help me— Hey! I forgot. We met the perfect lady for you a couple of weeks ago."

Billy held up his hands. "Don't even think such a thing. You got anything to eat? My stomach is uneasy about your plans."

Jesse got up from the table and took down a plate from the cabinet. Then he opened a box on the counter and filled the plate with iced doughnuts.

Bringing them to the table, he put them in front of his brother. "Don't eat yet. Samantha has trained me." He returned to the counter and opened other cabinets. He came back with two saucers and napkins. "Now you can eat, in a civilized manner."

"Man, it's just the two of us. She'd never know. You are already trained. None of that for me."

"Oh, yeah? The day will come when I'll remind you of your words, and you'll have to eat them."

"What makes you so sure? Just because we're brothers doesn't mean we do everything alike," Billy pointed out.

"It's a human condition, brother. Man is attracted to woman. Some more than others. And then one day, smack in the face, he falls in love. And it's over. No more prowling around, no more chasing other women. I've found my special lady, and I want to make her happy. You'll see."

"Well, she's certainly made a good catch. This place is first class. Sure you can afford it?"

"I'm sure. But it's funny, isn't it? Living where our grandfather Teddy Colton was raised?" Jesse reached over for a doughnut and munched on it for a few minutes. "I can afford it, and I like the fact that we're connected to all this elegance. It's a bit different from our home in Oklahoma."

"Yeah. I thought you all had gone crazy when I got the news. Grandma Gloria. Hard to believe some man made her rich. Ten million. That's a lot of money. She knew about it, though, and never touched it. That's what blows my mind.''

"She was a disciplined woman. A strong woman. I don't think we inherited much worthwhile from our unknown grandfather."

"You found out much about him?" Billy asked. He hadn't been here for the initial discovery, and the meetings with their grandfather's other children and grandchildren.

"He didn't tell his other wife about Gloria. But I guess he felt guilty enough about Gloria to provide for her and the twins." Their father, Thomas, was one of those twins. The other, Trevor, had died in a plane crash with his wife Sally Sharpstone, who was also half Comanche. Their five children had been taken in by Gloria.

"Dad said one of them is an ex-senator. Must've been a shock to him to find out he's illegitimate," Billy surmised.

"Not really. Joe's cool. It's his brother, Graham, who's on the shady side. Joe knows his brother makes mistakes, but he doesn't believe his brother is as bad as he is. Rand and I agree on that."

"Who's Rand?"

"I'll introduce you. He's Joe's oldest, a great guy. We're all meeting here because of Rand. He's an attorney here in D.C. He helped us work everything out with the house and the trust fund.''

''Sounds like a good guy.''

Billy got up to refill his cup and did the same for his brother. ''Not that you needed your share of the money, but I'm glad Mom and Pop have the extra income. Maybe they'll travel now.''

Jesse chuckled. ''Yeah. They'll travel, all right. To wherever the grandkids are. They know what's important.''

''You mean if I don't produce grandkids, they won't come see me?''

''Oh, you know they'll come, though they'd rather not go as far as Russia. With you here in D.C., they'll come see you. But they'd like it if there were grandchildren.''

''You've got babies on your mind, brother. Are you and Samantha going to start a family pretty soon?''

''We've talked about it. Among other things.'' Jesse added, ''Rand and his wife are expecting their first any time now.'' His eyes were twinkling at Billy. Then he sobered. ''I couldn't have found a better partner than Samantha. I want to experience everything with her. We make each other better.''

''It's a good thing you're getting married today. I don't think you could wait much longer.'' Billy slapped his brother on the shoulder. "You've been practicing celibacy too long!"

"You think all I'm talking about is sex? It's a lot more than that," Jesse assured him. "Some day you'll know, whether it sneaks up on you or smacks you in the face. There's a woman out there who will suddenly change your life...for the better." He looked off into space, a dreamy look in his eyes. "You'll see. In fact, I'm going to suggest to Samantha we invite this woman we met over to meet you. After all, you're new to town."

"Brother, I don't have difficulty meeting women, wherever I am. In fact, sometimes I have trouble getting them to let me go. They may get that forever feeling, but I don't."

Billy took another doughnut, eyeing Jesse. His brother was getting married tonight. It was normal that he'd feel that way. But it didn't happen that way for everyone. Billy had stood by some friends who'd received "Dear John" letters. And he'd known others who cheated on their wives, still chasing skirts while some little woman waited faithfully at home.

That was why he didn't think marriage was for him. He was in the Army. It was his chosen career. The two didn't mix well. His father had been able to pull it off, but he wasn't his father. He wouldn't set himself up for failure. But he was happy for Jesse.

Chapter 2

Several hours later, Billy emerged from his bedroom dressed in his khaki uniform. The creases in his pants were sharp and precise. He wore a tan nylon jacket with thick lining to protect him from the winter cold. His shoes were brilliantly polished.

He again encountered Jesse.

"Ah. There's my brother the major," Jesse said. "This morning I thought maybe you'd given up some of the pomp and circumstance."

"No way, brother. And I'm off to pick up my full dress uniform so I'll be dressed for the wedding this afternoon in formal military tradition. Hey, I don't want to embarrass you."

Jesse's grin disappeared, and he reached out to take hold of Billy's shoulder. "Never, my brother."

Billy almost felt tears. When he'd struggled to find his way as a young man, his brother had always been there for him, as he would be there for Jesse this evening. Whatever else his parents had taught them, they'd shown them the importance of family.

"I know. You've always been there for me. It's a family tradition I don't intend to let go of." He clapped Jesse on the shoulder in return.

"Billy," his father called, coming down the hall with their mother, Alice. "Jesse said you were up early. Are you going out?"

"Yeah, Pop. I took my dress uniform to the cleaners yesterday morning. I need to get it before the wedding."

Alice frowned. "Are you sure it will be open? It's Christmas Eve, you know."

"I know, Mom," he said and leaned over to kiss her cheek. "But I checked the hours yesterday. They're open until four today."

"All right, dear, go ahead. But when you get back, your father and I want to have a long talk with you. We think it's time you settle down, like Jesse."

Billy rolled his eyes at Jesse. "Mom, I'm an army man. I have to be able to pick up and go. That's not what happens when you're married."

"We'll talk when you get back," she repeated. "Dad?"

His father, a handsome man with stern features twinkling eyes, simply said, "Go on, boy. You're going to need that uniform."

Billy left, muttering to himself that the entire world had gone marriage mad.

Outside, Billy zipped his jacket against the cold. He slid his hands in his pockets and started walking to the corner where he could hail a taxi. Georgetown was well-populated. Lots of taxis came and went.

But when he reached the corner, he kept walking. It was only a few blocks to the cleaners. The walk would be good for him. There was definitely no danger. Georgetown was upscale, a place for diplomats, high government officials and the wealthy who wanted to influence any of the above.

He was glad he was in the military. He hated the games the politicians played. And just about every four years, a new horde of politicians moved into Georgetown and other neighborhoods around D.C., ready to change the direction of the government.

Billy noticed a number of pretty ladies as he walked. In Russia, there were some lovely ladies, but they were hardened by the political and economic turmoil their country was struggling with since the fall of communism. Here, the women seemed softer, more bright-eyed.

As he checked out the "scenery," he couldn't help but remember Jesse's words this morning. But he really didn't understand what Jesse had been saying. He saw some pretty ladies, a number of whom responded to his smile with an inviting look. But two minutes later, he'd find another lady just as attractive.

In spite of being brothers, he didn't think he was like Jesse. He didn't have the potential of finding that special woman who would knock him for a loop. It was Jesse who didn't understand. Billy had never found someone to whom he wanted to promise forever. He felt they were passing ships in the night. Enjoyed for a few minutes, then it was over.

He wouldn't want to promise forever and *not* feel like Jesse did about Samantha.

He reached the block where the cleaners were located before he even realized it. Then, out of the corner of his eye, he caught movement from the other side of the street. A beautiful blond woman crossed the street in the middle of the block, dashing between cars stopped at the light. "Definitely a risk-taker," he said beneath his breath. "A beautiful risk-taker."

He'd like a closer look, but he'd have to race down the sidewalk, and she'd think he was crazy.

He smiled at his ridiculous thoughts until he saw her go into the cleaners.

"This is my lucky day." He jogged to the cleaner's door. Then, after taking a deep breath, he entered the small business.

She was at the counter, his risk-taker. She turned around, as if making sure there was no danger. She was a tall blonde, with big blue eyes that were framed by full lashes touched by mascara. Her cheeks were rosy, making him want to warm his hands against her beautiful skin. Her cheekbones carved her face from an oval to a heart-shape, reminding him of his father's people.

She flashed him a smile, innocent and friendly, then turned her attention back to the man behind the counter. "Would you please look again? My father brought them in two days ago. He'll need one of the suits for tomorrow."

Her father. Not her husband. He was amazed at the relief that filled him. What was wrong with him? Why should it matter to him? But he noted how elegant, yet soft, her voice sounded, pure and fresh. An urge to ask her to say his name filled him.

The man behind the counter looked at him. "I'll be with you in a moment, sir."

"I'm in no hurry," he said, smiling at the woman as she looked at him again.

She murmured a sweet thank-you, and the urge

to kiss her shocked him. Her lips were full, soft, and covered in a luscious red lipstick. He wanted to taste her, to make contact with her, lasting contact. Man, he'd been thinking too much about what Jesse had said. It was Jesse's power of persuasion. That's all it was. He didn't really feel overcome by her nearness.

Did he?

Eva Ritka was distracted from her errand by the handsome man in military uniform. He was tall, broad-shouldered, the picture of health, of strength. The perfect hero. She found her breathing speeding up. This is ridiculous! But those words didn't settle down her reaction.

His smile when she looked at him after he'd come in left her wishing she could reach out and touch him. Had she lost her mind?

"Miss, I've got one more place to look. It'll take me a minute if you both don't mind waiting."

Eva risked another look at the handsome stranger. "I hope you don't mind?"

"Of course not. I'm not in a hurry."

She smiled at him again. "Thank you for being so considerate."

The man behind the counter nodded to both of them and rushed away.

"Do you use these cleaners often?" he asked.

"I'm new to town and it's my first time bringing my clothes here."

She realized her hands were trembling, so she clutched them together. "Y-Yes, I come here frequently. Are—are you living here now? Where did you come from?"

"Yes, I'm stationed here now. At the Pentagon. And I moved here from St. Petersburg, Russia."

"Oh, it's a beautiful city."

"You've been there?"

"Yes. I'm from Chekagovia. You've probably never heard of it but—"

"Yes, I have. I know quite a bit about it."

Her eyebrows went up and she smiled.

"After he finds your clothes, we could go next door for a cup of coffee and we could compare our experiences in St. Petersburg."

"I'm sure that would be interesting, but I have a number of errands to do before the stores close. It is Christmas Eve, you know."

"Right. I should have wished you Merry Christmas. Do you have plans for tonight?"

"Yes, of course. Georgetown is a huge party place during the holidays."

His gaze, gorgeous hazel eyes, remained fixed on her face, and she felt heat rise in her cheeks. "Is it a friendly city?" he finally asked.

She licked her dry lips and thought she heard him

groan. "Yes, I think Georgetown is friendly. You're not here all alone, are you?" Her voice rose in growing horror, as if he were being tortured. But the thought of this man being alone at the holiday disturbed her for some reason.

"I hope you're not alone for the holidays," she said.

"No, my family is here with me."

The man behind the counter arrived with the suits Eva waited for, and she quickly paid her bill. "Thank you for finding them," she said. Turning and looking at the handsome man she said, "Merry Christmas! I hope you enjoy the holidays." Then she stepped out of the shop.

She felt relief when she went outside. This stranger aroused a new feeling, one that scared her. It was so intense it worried her. She didn't know him, so how could she have these feelings about him?

The cold air helped ease the intensity, but in its place she felt an inexplicable longing.

Billy watched her walk away. Something about her made him stare after her.

"Sir?"

"Uh, yes. I need to pick up my dress uniform."

His uniform was easy to find. He paid and carried

his hanger out the door. She was gone, already on her way to another errand.

How would he find her? Would he even see her again? He needed to see her again. He *wanted* to see her again.

He could ask the man at the cleaners if he knew her name. Although he knew she was Chekagovian. He could find her name from army sources, perhaps. As soon as Christmas was over, he made a promise to himself to find this beautiful mystery woman.

He started back down the street, his thoughts on the woman of his dreams rather than the sparkling Christmas decorations in the shop windows. He imagined them discussing the beauty of St. Petersburg. He felt like he knew her already and he'd only spent minutes with her. Maybe Jesse was right after all.

He came to an abrupt halt after he had walked past a sign offering a town house for sale. He turned back slowly, consideringly, knowing he couldn't pass it by.

It was only a couple of blocks from Jesse's house, a great location. He wouldn't have a long commute to the Pentagon. Shopping surrounded it, and they'd be close to Jesse and Samantha. He opened the door and stepped into the dim hallway that led up the stairs.

As he reached the top of the stairs, a lady Realtor met him. "Good afternoon. May I show you around the town house we have for sale? It's a real bargain."

He took the printed sheet she offered and followed her around it. In every room, he saw the elegant blond woman from the cleaners, reading in the sitting room, baking cookies in the large kitchen with a child beside her, wearing a negligee in the bedroom. Warm and welcoming. Was he going crazy?

In the end, he offered earnest money to hold the town house for him until the day after Christmas. Somehow he believed by then he'd know if this feeling would fade.

But it felt right to him.

By the time he got to Jesse's house, he had rationalized his action, buying a town house on impulse. He explained to his parents that he had plans for the near future, but he couldn't tell them anything right now. Surprisingly enough, they seemed satisfied with his words.

He felt different. Maybe he looked different, too. He only knew that his world had changed since he ran into a certain lady from Chekagovia.

Chapter 3

After he donned his dress uniform, Billy wandered down to Jesse's room. It seemed to him there were some chores the best man had to perform, but he wasn't sure what they were. He rapped on the door.

Jesse swung the door open, calling out their sister Sky's name.

Billy felt a little confused. He looked over his shoulder, but no one was there. "You expecting Sky? Is she here?"

"She's supposed to be here. But her plane was canceled. But she got on the next plane out of Oklahoma City and made it to D.C. She called, but you know how traffic is."

"Don't worry, Sky will make it on time. Is there anything else to worry about?"

Jesse charged back into his room and Billy followed him in. "Yes, there is! Sky made Samantha's wedding present for me."

"You haven't given it to Samantha yet?"

"No! I wanted it to be special. I wanted Sky to make it. It's a diamond necklace." Jesse was already dressed in the pants and shirt of his tuxedo, and he returned to pacing the floor. "She's got to get here before the wedding begins."

"You know Sky will do the best she can," Billy assured him. Sky had become quite talented at jewelry design and had had to come to the wedding so late because she was opening another jewelry store in Houston. "Jesse, just be patient."

"You don't understand! I want everything to be perfect for Samantha," Jesse almost shouted.

"Actually, I do understand, though I'm not sure I'll go for the formal wedding routine when—if— it's ever my turn. Will Mom and Dad mind?"

"Probably not," Jesse said, frowning curiously. "You sound like you actually have someone in mind."

"I do. It happened, just like you said."

"Who is she? Do we know her? Are you sure?"

"I think I'm sure."

"So, who is she?"

"I don't know."

"Damn it, Billy, now's not the time to tease me! I'm worried about—"

When they both heard a knock, Jesse leaped across the room, abandoning their conversation, to pull the door open again. This time Sky stood on the other side of it. He crushed her in an embrace, then asked for his gift.

"Here it is. I thought you would be worried about it." She handed it to Jesse and he sprung open the black box to look at the gorgeous diamond necklace, a small circle of diamonds with a larger diamond in the center. "It's perfect," Jesse murmured as Billy came to look over his shoulder. "See," he added, "it's to show Samantha that she's at the center of my world."

Billy whistled. "Yes, it's beautiful…and pricey, too, right, little sister?"

"Jesse only wanted the best," she assured Billy with a smile.

"I'm so glad you're here," Jesse said. "I'm sorry you couldn't convince Great-Grandfather to come. But I know how he hates flying. So no words of wisdom or omens from him?"

"Something about a house of dreams has many windows to the past, whatever that means," Sky said.

"Great-Grandfather WhiteBear has always been

a mystery in many ways. I wish he could have made it, but he wasn't feeling well enough to make the long trip.''

Jesse then turned to Billy. ''Billy, can you go to the church? Samantha is in the Bride's room. I want you to give her the necklace with my love. I'd have Sky give it to her, but she has to get dressed. And I have our trusty brothers Grey, Shane and Seth running other errands.''

''Don't you want to give it to her?''

''I'm not allowed to see her before the wedding. It's considered bad luck.''

''You're kidding!''

''Just go, Billy. It would actually mean a lot to have you present it to her. Please give it to her with my love. I'll be along behind you. The wedding starts in half an hour.''

Billy closed his hand around the black leather box. ''Okay, but I feel kind of strange giving this to Samantha. What if she decides she wants to marry me instead?''

Jesse noted the big grin on his brother's face and shoved him out of the room. ''I'm pretty sure Samantha won't change her mind.''

Billy knew she wouldn't either. The bond between her and his brother was clear for everyone to see. ''All right, I'll see you both at the church.''

The church was only a couple of streets over, so

Billy briskly walked there. He knew the Bride's room was in the front of the church. In the meantime, he thought he should think about how he wanted his wedding to look. Because he didn't want to wait too long to claim his bride. He laughed as he had that thought. That would make Jesse laugh out loud. This morning, Billy hadn't even wanted to consider getting married. Now he was planning his big day.

Guests had already begun to arrive and he saw his twin brothers, Shane and Seth, seating them in the church. Seth came up and whispered, "Aren't you supposed to be at the other end of the aisle?"

"Yeah, but I have to deliver something to the bride. Did you know Jesse wouldn't bring it because he's not supposed to see her before the wedding?"

"Sure. It's against the rules."

"I don't think I like those rules."

"They don't matter if you're never going to marry. That's what you told us yesterday," Seth reminded him.

"A lot of things can change in one day's time. I'm not only going to marry, I've already picked out my bride." He shouldn't be telling everyone since he didn't even know her name. They'd think he was crazy. But he felt so different. He'd thought yesterday he'd feel sad about Jesse's marriage even though he knew it was what Jesse wanted. But yesterday, he hadn't understood how Jesse felt. Now he was starting to get it.

Would he be following in Jesse's footsteps next? He gave himself a quick shake. All of this wedding stuff was really going to his head. He had to get hold of himself.

He stepped over to the door to the Bride's room and rapped on it. An older woman opened the door a crack.

"Yes?"

"I need to speak to the bride," Billy said, an ingratiating grin on his face.

"I'm sorry, the bride is incommunicado."

He tried again. "I'm the best man, Billy, brother to Jesse. I was late to the rehearsal dinner last night and didn't get to meet you. You must be Samantha's mother, Ellen Cosgrove. Please, Jesse sent me here with a very important message for Samantha."

Obviously, Samantha was listening, because she immediately called out, "Let him in."

The door fell open and Ellen Cosgrove waited until Billy had come in before she closed it again. All Billy could see, however, was Samantha. He considered her a beautiful woman, but he'd never seen her look so beautiful as she did today. Her long, white wedding gown was simple but elegant. Unlike a lot of gowns, it didn't have bows or lace or pearls or anything extra. Classic Samantha, as Jesse always said.

"You look beautiful, Samantha. Jesse is a lucky guy." He leaned forward to kiss her cheek.

"Thank you, Billy. Is everything all right?"

"You afraid Jesse is backing out on you?" he teased.

"That's not funny!" a pretty brunette said, folding her arms over her chest and glaring at him.

"Samantha knows Jesse isn't going to do that," Billy returned. "Right, Samantha?"

"Right, Billy. My sister Juliet is apparently more nervous than I am." Samantha glanced at the woman who still had her arms folded tightly. "But what did Jesse send you here for? Isn't it almost time for you to meet the minister in the back?"

"Sure is. That's why I'd better give you this." He held out the leather box toward Samantha.

"What is it?" Samantha asked, not taking the box, as if she believed it held a trick.

"It's Jesse's wedding gift to you. He had our sister Sky make it special just for you." Billy reached for Samantha's hand and found it trembling.

"What's wrong, Samantha? Didn't you expect a gift from Jesse?"

"I—I'm surprised, that's all. He didn't need to get me a special present."

"Jesse wants everything special for your wedding, because he doesn't intend to do this ever again." Billy pulled both her hands into his and pressed them around the box. "He wants you to open it now."

"Now?"

"Now," Billy said firmly. "And no tears. I don't want to be accused of ruining your makeup."

Samantha sniffed and smiled. Then she slowly, agonizingly pried open the box.

And drew in a deep breath!

Her sister, who'd protested earlier, exclaimed, "It's gorgeous! I've never seen a necklace quite like that!"

Samantha's mother looked over Samantha's shoulder. "My, that is quite beautiful. It is real, isn't it?"

Billy looked at her, offended. Before he could say anything, however, Samantha said, "Sky only works with real stones and Jesse wouldn't give me anything fake."

"Right," Billy said emphatically.

"It's the loveliest thing I own," Samantha said softly. "Billy, would you fasten it around my neck?"

"Sure."

"Don't step on her dress!" her mother warned, but Samantha lifted up her hair and said nothing.

Billy stood behind her, fastening the fragile necklace in place. Then he looked in the mirror as Samantha stared at the necklace, reaching out one finger to gently touch it.

"Will you tell him how much I love it…and how much I love him?" Samantha said softly.

"He already knows, sweetheart, but I'll tell him," Billy said in return.

"Thank you, Billy," Samantha said.

"I don't mean to rush you, but we're supposed to start down the aisle in five minutes. I think you should be in place by now," Ellen Cosgrove said.

He nodded at the woman and moved to the door. "I'll see you at the altar, with Jesse, Samantha." He nodded to the two other ladies.

Then he was back in the lobby of the church, among the guests. More and more people were arriving. He saw his parents standing over in one corner, waiting until the wedding started to be shown to their seats.

He stepped to their side. "Are you enjoying all this mess?"

"Billy," his mother fussed at him. "This is what the Cosgroves wanted. After all, Jesse is an important man."

"I know but, if you had a choice, would you want this big a wedding?"

Thomas smiled. "We would want whatever kind

of wedding makes our child and his or her partner happy. If you don't want a big wedding, then don't have one. But you'd better wait until you pick a bride. They tend to have an opinion of their own.''

"I'll remember that," Billy promised. He kissed his mom's cheek and told them both he'd see them at the reception and slipped to the room behind the altar where he was to meet Jesse and the minister.

Jesse eagerly greeted Billy. "Did she like it?"

"Of course she did," Billy assured him. "And it looks wonderful on her. You're a lucky man, brother."

"Yeah," Jesse said, his eyes holding that dreamy look that announced he was thinking of Samantha.

Yesterday Billy would have asked Jesse if he was nervous, but he understood Jesse's feelings today.

Five minutes later, the minister led them out to the altar. Billy looked out at the large audience. The reception at the house would be full of people, but many of them would be family, even if he didn't know them yet. The West Coast Coltons had a lot of members. Joe Colton and his wife Meredith had not only had five children themselves, but they also had adopted several children, as well as being foster parents. The only obvious member of the Colton clan not there, besides Great-Grandfather George WhiteBear, was Joe Colton's brother, Graham. He wasn't on anyone's good side these days.

Though the wedding was taking place in a church and included a lot of guests, the wedding party was going to be small. Just Jesse and Samantha, and Juliet and Billy.

The music changed. Then Shane brought his mom and dad to their seats on the right side of the church. They looked distinguished and happy. Then Seth escorted Mrs. Cosgrove down the left aisle to her seat, taking her place where her husband would join her after he gave their daughter away.

The music changed again and Juliet appeared to walk alone down the aisle. Billy didn't really know her, but he guessed she was nice. She was dressed in a floor-length gown in burgundy. The color flattered her golden-brown hair. She moved up to stand on the other side of the minister. Billy wished it was a certain Chekagovian blonde.

He could feel Jesse tense beside him. It was time for the bride. The music rose and the audience rose with it, everyone staring at the back of the church.

Jesse's face relaxed into a sublime smile that seemed to flow through him. No one could ever doubt his love for Samantha. Just as none of the children had ever doubted Thomas's love for Alice.

Just as his lady would never doubt his love for her. He pictured the tall elegant blonde coming down the aisle to him, ready to unite her life with him. The joy that filled him was almost overpowering. Again, he had to shake himself.

Jesse took Samantha's hand and turned to the minister. Billy suddenly remembered he was supposed to move to their side and give Jesse the ring at the right time. He'd best stop thinking crazy ideas about his own wedding, or he'd mess up Jesse's.

When the vows were spoken and Jesse had kissed the bride, they turned to meet their family and friends for the first time as a married couple.

Billy was so happy for Jesse and Samantha. Taking Juliet's arm, he followed Jesse and Samantha down the church aisle, ready to help them celebrate their new life together.

Chapter 4

Eva Ritka stared at herself in the mirror. Her father would hate it. He never objected to her buying expensive gowns. But they should always be appropriate for her position, hostess to him, the former ambassador and a high-ranking Chekagovian diplomat.

In other words, stuffy! But she was twenty-eight, for heaven's sake! She wanted her life to contain a little excitement. It was Christmas Eve, but she wasn't playing hostess. She was going to a friend's party tonight. And she wanted to look her age.

And maybe meet someone who didn't know how proper she was. Someone who might kiss her under the mistletoe. Someone like the soldier in the cleaners this afternoon. He'd stayed in her mind all day. She wished now she'd gone to have coffee with him. She sighed. She'd dated other men, but none of them had meant anything to her. Yet, she'd spent ten minutes with the handsome soldier and she couldn't get him out of her mind. There had been one other man she'd gotten serious about. But she'd been more in love with love than with him.

She looked at the gown again. It was black and white, with a scarlet rose at the low vee neckline. To draw attention to her bosom. Most unladylike, according to her papa. Eye-catching, she thought. She nodded abruptly. She'd made her decision. Her gift to herself this year would be freedom, at least for a few days.

She redressed and stepped out into the main room of the store.

"Miss Ritka? Have you decided?" the saleswoman asked.

"Yes, I have, Sally. I'll take this one."

The lady's eyebrows shot up. "Really? A great choice," she hurriedly added.

"Yes, thank you."

Once she'd left the shop, Eva pictured herself dressed in the gown, being stared at by the young men at the party. But she wished, most of all, to see and be seen by one man in particular. Could she be so lucky? She gave a cynical smile. Of course, that was impossible. Her hostess was a snob. She only invited people with the best pedigrees. But she wasn't interested in the boring, aspiring politicians that would be at the party tonight. She wanted a strong man, well-built, like the soldier today, picking up his cleaning. Good heavens, she'd forgotten to see if he was married! He was exactly what she wanted, dark hair, hazel eyes, the total opposite of her blond, blue-eyed self.

Not a silly man more interested in counting his money than in telling his woman he loved her.

She shouldn't blame her father for not being a hero. If her mother hadn't died so early, she was sure her father would have been a loving husband. But with a baby and a country to serve, he'd given his life to that country.

Eva spent a great deal of time on her appearance that night, wearing more makeup than usual. She wanted someone to notice her blue eyes tonight. Eva paused on the doorstep of her first stop, drew a deep breath and reached out to ring the doorbell of the elegant Georgetown house where she'd spent twenty-four of her twenty-eight years. The original owner had died recently and the people who inherited it wanted to move in. She didn't blame them because it was a lovely home, but it created a lot of chaos in her life.

She sighed. She'd been her father's hostess since she was sixteen. Maybe she was tired of the role. Lately, life had seemed boring. She gave a half laugh. She should be ashamed of that thought, but she wanted more in her life which included day-dreams about the soldier. Or maybe she just wanted a life. Hence, the semi-scandalous gown. Shaking off her thoughts, she finally rang the doorbell.

She drew a deep breath as the door swung open. She gasped. It was him! The man she'd seen in the cleaners. This couldn't be happening! The man stood there staring at her, as if he found her appearance a welcome surprise. The gorgeous man she'd longed for. Was she imagining him?

He was dressed in full military dress, looking more handsome than ever. In a deep voice he said, "I guess it *does* pay to get the door. You must be Cinderella? I should've recognized you this morning."

Billy stepped back in surprise at seeing the woman of his daydreams today standing right in front of him. She looked like a princess. But she'd looked beautiful this morning, too. His dream girl…in a very sexy dress. There was a split that ran right up her very firm thighs. It invited thoughts for which his mom would've washed out his mouth. And the curve of her breasts, visible in the low neckline, were creamy, inviting and he wanted to touch them.

What luck that he'd been standing in the hall when the doorbell rang and he'd told William, one of the caterers at the wedding reception, that he'd help out by answering the doorbell.

Billy had a hundred questions to ask her, but he had to remember to go slow. She might not have thought about him as much as he'd thought about her.

Eva blushed when her soldier noticed her flattering stare. Her dream man. Of course she was staring. As much as she'd hoped to see him tonight, she hadn't really thought the impossible could happen. And he was as perfect as she remembered. Maybe that explained why her body had lit up at the sight of him. "No," she said, answering his question of her identity. "I'm Eva Ritka. I apologize for disturbing your evening." She could hear beautiful music in the ballroom.

"You could never be an unwelcome interruption, Cinderella. Tell me, will I do as the handsome prince?"

If only she could forget her reason for being there, and pretend with him. She quickly squeezed her eyes shut and imagined him with his chest bare, exposing his beautiful muscles. She desperately wanted to touch his skin, to be sure he was real. But now? Here? She hadn't thought she would meet the gorgeous stranger here, among people she'd met. She wanted to smile and throw herself into his arms. Instead, she pulled herself together. "You're certainly handsome, sir, but a major in the U.S. Army might be a little overcommitted. I've heard Uncle Sam is very demanding."

He seemed surprised that she recognized his rank from his military uniform. Obviously he knew nothing about diplomatic training.

"Hmm. Well, the least I can do is ask you in. Perhaps you're a long-lost cousin I haven't met yet."

She blinked in surprise, and gave a sudden thank-you that she wasn't kin to the handsome man. Not that it mattered. She'd probably never see him again. It amazed her how her heart ached at that thought. What was wrong with her?

"No, I don't think so. My name is Eva Ritka," she said again, "a former resident of this house."

"Are you interested in moving back in? I have space in my room. Or I'm planning on moving into a town house soon. There will be plenty of room there."

She laughed and he smiled in return. Ah, someone who didn't take himself so seriously…unlike her father. This man's smooth flirtation didn't disturb her. As a diplomat's daughter, she'd had a lot of experience with flirtatious young men. But most of them took themselves so seriously. "I appreciate your sacrifice, but I don't think it will be necessary. Actually, I simply want to retrieve a personal object I left behind."

His hazel eyes narrowed. "You certainly dress well for such a mundane errand."

She couldn't hold back another blush. Her pale skin that accompanied her blond hair and blue eyes was part of her heritage. Her country, Chekagovia, was a middle-European state that had evolved from the unrest after World War Two. It was a good thing she didn't know any state secrets. She'd be under his spell in no time and tell him anything he wanted to know. "Thank you for the compliment, but I am on my way to another party."

"Ah. Are you sure a fairy godmother didn't dress you?"

Before she could think of an answer in response to his charming silliness, someone else entered the hall. "Miss Eva! What are you doing here?"

"William! How are you?"

"Fine, miss, but the Coltons have moved in. I don't know what—"

"It's nothing really, William. I didn't know the Coltons used the same caterers as my father." She turned to Billy. "May I run upstairs to retrieve something I forgot?'' Then she could put this bothersome chore behind her.

The caterer bid her goodbye and continued with his duties, serving the guests. The handsome military man said, ''Of course. I'll accompany you to be sure you don't steal the family silver.''

Eva had no choice in the matter, apparently.

''Thank you,'' she said softly, moving forward to take his extended hand. The strength of his grip gave her second thought. He would not be easily led.

''Now, Cinderella, where shall we begin our search?''

''Major Colton, I promise you can trust me not to steal anything.''

''Probably,'' he said agreeably, ''but I refuse to abandon you now that I have you in my clutches.''

His playacting of a villain was admirable and brought a smile to her lips. ''Very well, sir, you have me in your clutches. Shall I lead the way to the attic?''

''*Après vous, princesse,*'' he said with a deep bow.

Billy held his pose until the beautiful lady passed him on her way to the stairs. He had teased her by calling her Cinderella, but her beauty was more than sufficient for that role. He guessed, however, she'd never scrubbed the kitchen floors. She moved with the elegance and grace of a true princess. He'd already recognized that quality in her.

He was used to beautiful women. Not only did his rank provide opportunity to meet important people, but also his broad shoulders and good looks worked wonders in his favor. But there was something almost overpowering about this woman, as if danger lay in being close to her. But he had already discovered her power that morning. Never one to resist a challenge, Billy studied her even more as he followed her to the second floor.

There was something unusual about her reason for being there. She said she'd forgotten something in the attic.

If it was worth a great deal, he thought, as he imagined a royal crown covered with rubies and emeralds and diamonds, it shouldn't have slipped her mind. After all, as beautiful as she was, he'd also noticed the intelligence visible in her beautiful blue eyes.

If it was a toy she'd loved as a child, why hadn't she kept it closer to her, in her bedroom?

If it was neither of those, why was it so important to retrieve it on Christmas Eve?

The thought of a mystery, involving a beautiful woman, was as enticing as her gown. But the most important thing about her arriving this evening, was that he now knew her name. He now knew who he intended to marry.

He'd just returned a few days ago from St. Petersburg. He'd been staying at his brother Jesse's new home, but he realized now that he'd scarcely seen any of it. Certainly he hadn't been to the attic. But why hadn't Jesse or his new wife Samantha checked out the attic before they moved in? Why did Eva think whatever she was looking for was still there?

"Where do you now reside, Miss Ritka?" he asked casually, as if her place of residence didn't matter at all. In actual fact, his heart beat faster.

As she reached the second floor, she paused to smile at him over her shoulder. Unfortunately, her cashmere coat covered her shoulder, distracting him. "May I take your coat? We don't want you to grow overheated."

She thought about his offer before she slowly agreed and slipped from the heavy covering. He folded it over his arm as his gaze appreciated the soft, pale skin of her shoulders and arms.

"Thank you."

"Why is this object located in the attic?"

"I used to play there as a child."

He walked the length of the hall and hung her coat in a large closet. "No one will touch your coat here and we can pick it up on our way down."

Again she hesitated, but then she nodded and smiled that glorious smile again.

He closed the closet door and extended his arm. When she laid her hand on his arm, he felt as if he'd been given the highest award.

They climbed to the third floor and she led him directly to another door that appeared to lead to a generous closet. However, when the door was opened, they discovered stairs that led up. Billy found the switch that lighted the stairs all the way to the top and another door.

"You seem quite sure of your destination. Why did you forget it?" Somehow, he had the feeling this object had a lot of significance. Her casual story didn't fit.

"We moved quickly and I forgot it in all the hustle and bustle." She smiled again. Then she hurried up the stairs.

By the time Billy had reached the large attic space, the elegant lady was standing before one of the dormer windows. She was slowly counting the windows.

"Have you forgotten?" he asked as he reached her side.

"No. I always had to count. There are twelve windows, you see."

"What is the significance?"

"The sixth window has a hiding place that I discovered accidentally. I bragged about my hiding place to Papa. He gave me a present but he asked me to keep it in my hiding place. As I grew older, I didn't visit the attic as much. That is why I forgot it when we moved. I had too much to do. I came back shortly after, but I think I checked under the wrong window. As I said, I was a little harried back then.''

So she hid the object because her father requested her to do so. Why would he ask her to hide her gift? Billy watched as she slid a panel under the window to the left, revealing an empty space in the wall. ''Is it gone?'' he asked, not wanting her to be upset.

''No,'' she said confidently as she reached into the darkness. Then she pulled forth a small item. ''Here it is!''

Billy stared at the small golden box. It was a nativity scene with the traditional figures, including three wise men. Several palm trees framed the scene, and resting on the highest one was a star.

''It's charming. Does it play music?'' he asked.

''Oh, yes,'' she said in reverent tones as she pulled out a key that fit perfectly into the base of the music box, so smoothly that he would never know it was there, surprising Billy. She inserted the key into a small hole and turned it. Immediately a beautiful sound filled the attic, the song ''Silent

Night,'' which seemed so appropriate in the darkness of the attic on Christmas Eve.

''No wonder you returned for it. It is beautiful.''

''Yes. I would hate to lose it. But I have to confess. I lied to my father. I told him I had it safe even though I knew I had forgotten it.'' She gave him a wry smile that charmed him. ''Papa would be horrified if he knew I was here.''

He leaned closer. ''Are the Coltons not good enough for the Ritkas?''

She didn't show any fear at his closeness. ''Don't be silly. Of course it's not that. You have money, that is the devisor these days, you know. Money, not blood.''

''You are more cynical than I would have expected, princess.'' But she was good, he reminded himself. Her words took interest away from the music box, yet she hadn't explained why her father would be horrified that she had forgotten it.

''I am no more a princess than you are a prince.''

He smiled but took the cloth bag from her in which the music box had been wrapped. ''Shall we rewrap it?'' He thought it would be interesting to hold the music box.

''Yes, please. I must take it home before I can go to my party.''

''Why don't I drive you home and then to your party. It will save you time.''

"Oh, no, I couldn't impose on you to such an extent." She smiled again and he wanted to tell her she could demand anything of him if she smiled.

"It's not a problem. I'll be happy to serve you, if you'll dance with me first. After all, I will be saving you at least half an hour. That's assuming you can get another taxi. After all it is Christmas Eve."

And it would give him more time with the beautiful princess and her mystery music box.

"Oh! I asked my driver to wait! Good heavens, I'll owe him a fortune."

"I'll go pay the bill and send him away, while you powder your nose. Deal?"

"Well, OK, but I won't be able to stay long. My father—he wouldn't want me to be careless with the music box, you see. It is a family treasure."

"So are you, princess," he assured her, his hazel eyes intent.

She smiled. "I can take care of myself, but the music box is defenseless. Anyone could steal it."

"I don't believe in taking chances with the most precious things and people," he said. But she'd given him another clue. The music box was connected to the Ritka family fortunes. Taking her hand, he led her to the stairs. He turned off the light, leaving the attic filled with shadows. The stars and moonlight turned the room into a magical place, and he hated to take her back into the real world.

When they reached the second floor, Eva intended to retrieve her cashmere coat, but Billy suggested they leave it there with the music box in its pocket, away from their guests, so it wouldn't be disturbed.

When they reached the bottom floor Billy sent her off to powder her nose while he took care of her driver. Before separating, she said, "The driver works for us frequently. His name is Jerry. Tell him I requested his departure."

Billy nodded and watched as she walked away, finding her words strange. He didn't like the sound of this guy Jerry.

Billy approached the white limo while he reached for his billfold, glad he carried a substantial amount of money at all times. He found it eased situations much better than words.

"Jerry? Miss Ritka thanks you for your services, but she won't be needing you any longer," he said with a calm smile and reached into the warm limo, its heater going full blast, with a hundred-dollar bill.

The driver immediately reached out to take the bill, but he didn't put it away. He stared at Billy before he said, "I don't believe you."

"She said you probably wouldn't. But she had

to powder her nose. I swear I'll see her home safely. I know her father guards her well. I don't blame him." This time, Billy used a friendly smile.

"Her father told me to see her to the party. I wasn't supposed to bring her here."

Billy sighed, pretending exasperation with Jerry's stubbornness, but his alert heightened. "But she didn't know I was home. I just got back." He opened his wallet and drew out another bill. "For your troubles. And it means Eva won't tell her father that you helped her." The man's eyes widened. Then he reached for the second bill. Almost before Billy could get his arm back from the window, the limo peeled out of the quiet, expensive neighborhood. "Hmm, dear old dad must be tough," Billy muttered to himself. Not that he was intimidated. Not enough to abandon his Cinderella. With a smile, he headed back inside to find her.

Chapter 5

Billy entered the warmth of the house and immediately looked for Eva. When he discovered her standing by the door to the ballroom, watching the couples inside, waiting for him, his heart tightened. Waiting wasn't something he did well. Nor, he'd discovered, something women did well. But his Cinderella was waiting, though he could name ten or twelve men in the room, unattached and quite willing to show her around. In fact, he watched as one of his twin brothers approached her, clearly offering an invitation. She refused.

He slipped up behind her and whispered, "Good decision," in her ear.

She jumped and whirled around, her skin turning pink again.

"Your skin is like a blooming rose. *Möchten Sie tanzen?*" he asked and slid his arm around her small waist and nudged her into his arms. It amazed him how well she fit against him.

"*Ja,*" she answered softly without any comment about his switching to German, one of Chekagovia's formal languages. He guessed she was five feet ten inches, about four inches shorter than him. He'd danced with too many short ladies and spent his evening unable to carry on a conversation because he couldn't duck and waltz at the same time.

"You dance well, Major. I imagine dancing is part of your duties." She leaned back to smile at him as she watched his reaction.

"*Et vous aussi, mademoiselle,*" he said. Then he added, "My partner makes it easy, princess." His lips seemed to move closer to those luscious soft lips until she turned away.

"Don't like me?" he asked softly.

"I don't even know your first name, Major."

"Billy!" A man across the ballroom floor called.

She didn't react to the name so he added an explanation that would let her know she had her answer.

"There you have it. Everyone calls me Billy." He turned to acknowledge the person who had

called his name as he'd answered her question. Joe
Colton was a tall man and a voice with authority.
And respect. He was just getting to know him.
"Evening, Joe." He stopped dancing but kept his
arm around Eva's small waist.

Joe looked at Eva and Billy's arm. "I would
guess this young lady was from your side of the
family if she weren't so fair. Introduce me, please."

"May I present Cinderella. I found her scrubbing
the floors in the kitchen and begged her to keep me
from being lonely."

"Ah, kitchen maid uniforms have changed con-
siderably. Thank you for gracing our wedding
party."

Eva took his story in stride. "Thank you, Senator
Colton. A Christmas wedding is a lovely thought.
I'm Eva Ritka." And offered her hand.

Joe brought her hand to his lips and Billy was
surprised to discover jealousy in himself. He was
never jealous. Until now.

Joe added, "You are the former resident. Is your
husband here also?"

"She's not married," Billy interrupted, perhaps
a bit too brusquely. But he hoped he was right.
Only her father had been mentioned.

"My father leased the house, Senator. We were
sorry to leave because it is a delightful house, but

we were planning to move to our new residence anyway, for security reasons.''

"So I heard from my son, Rand. I want my wife to meet you. There she is across the room. I'll go get her. Keep her here, Billy."

Billy glared at him.

Before he could decide what to do, several tall, handsome men surrounded them. Eva had no doubt that these men were connected to Billy because of their likeness, though she still thought he was the most handsome. Before either of them said anything, they began talking in a language she didn't recognize. She loved languages and learned them easily, but this one she couldn't identify.

Billy felt Eva's stare. His brothers had been asking questions in their native Comanche. Though they used English most of the time, they used Comanche if they didn't want to be understood.

"I'll make apologies for my brothers and cousin, Eva. This is my cousin Logan, and my brothers Grey, Shane and Seth."

She nodded and smiled. A family. She'd always longed for brothers and sisters. Billy was surprised by the question that followed.

"I didn't recognize the language you were speaking. What was it?"

Grey, Billy's oldest brother, laughed. "You seem perfect for Billy. He's a natural linguist and a new language gets him more excited than girls.'' Everyone laughed except Billy. ''That's Comanche,'' Grey continued.

She turned to Billy. ''Could you teach it to me?''

''It's hard. How many languages do you speak now?''

She ducked her head, and he was learning fast she either didn't want to answer the questions or her answer was less than the truth. ''Five or six, but I'd love to learn Comanche.''

''We'll talk about it.'' Carefully promising her nothing.

''You boys doing all right?'' Thomas Colton asked, probably sent by Alice, his wife, to make peace, as he had many times in their childhood.

''Yeah, Dad,'' Billy said. ''Dad, I'd like you to meet Eva Ritka. She and her father were the tenants until we got here.''

''I see. I hope we didn't inconvenience you too much, Miss Ritka.''

''Of course not, sir. We understood,'' she assured the distinguished man.

Before anything else could be said, Joe returned with both his wife, Meredith, and Alice, Billy's mother, introducing them.

In a beautiful, mellow voice, Alice said, ''I hope my boys are behaving themselves.''

''Mom!'' several voices protested.

"Your children are lovely gentlemen, especially Billy." For the first time since she'd met him, Eva could see the slightest hint of a flush on Billy's tanned skin.

"Did you meet our son Jesse and his bride, Samantha?" Alice asked, pride in her voice.

When Eva said she had briefly met them a couple of months ago when they were out visiting the house, Alice insisted Billy take her across the room to say hello to the wedding couple. He was grateful. It meant he could escape all of them.

Billy led Eva over to Jesse and Samantha. They'd just been having a visit with some of their new Colton cousins. When Jesse looked around and discovered Billy, he greeted him, but his gaze continued to check out the woman.

"Jesse, Samantha, this is Eva Ritka."

"Eva!" Samantha exclaimed, reaching out to take Eva's hand.

Billy stared at his new sister-in-law. "You act like you know her!"

"But I do," Samantha agreed.

Jesse clapped his brother on his shoulder. "Remember, I told you we'd met a lady just perfect for you. This is her!"

Eva's cheeks turned red, which made her even prettier in Billy's eyes. "I'm glad I talked Eva into joining me tonight. You see," Billy continued, "she came here looking for something she left behind. It was a terrific surprise since I ran into her this morning at the dry cleaners."

Samantha leaned forward. "Oh, can I help you find it Eva? We haven't noticed anything but—"

"Oh, no," Eva said. "Billy had already helped me, thank you. I'm sorry I crashed your wedding reception. I tried to skip in unnoticed, but Billy wouldn't let me." Then she flashed Billy a smile.

"We're delighted you're here," Samantha said.

"Thank you," Eva said. "Samantha, that necklace is beautiful. I've never seen one like it."

"Why thank you," Samantha said glowing. "It's Jesse's present to me for our wedding. His sister, Sky, made it for me."

Eva turned her gaze to Billy and Jesse. "You have a sister who can make such wonderful things?"

"Yes," Billy said. "You'll meet her later."

Samantha asked Eva a question and Billy leaned over to his brother. "You're right. She's the one for me."

"You mean you've fallen for her? That's pretty fast."

"I fell in love with her the moment I first saw her this morning. But I didn't find out her name until tonight."

"That's going to make Samantha happy. She liked Eva when we met in October."

"Even better, I put down money on a town house two blocks away today. But don't tell Eva yet." Billy grinned at his brother, knowing the warning was necessary.

"You what?" Jesse demanded. "Are you crazy?"

"Jesse, what's wrong?" Samantha asked, but both ladies were staring at them.

"Your husband is telling me I don't know what I'm doing, Sam." He looked at Eva. "You believe I know what I'm doing, don't you?"

"I suppose, Billy, but I don't really know what you're talking about," Eva said.

"I made a real estate deal this morning. It's a pretty town house only two blocks away, Samantha, so you'll have me for a neighbor," Billy commented.

"Oh, I'm sure it's a great buy. Houses sell quickly in this neighborhood."

"Good. Maybe I'll take you to see it next week, Eva. You can give me your opinion about decorating it."

"Well, I want to see it, too," Samantha said.

"Don't forget me," Jesse said. "But we'll see it when we get back from our honeymoon, my love. Not before."

They all laughed.

* * *

The next half hour didn't go the way Billy had envisioned. Meredith Colton began introducing Eva to her children, of which there were many. Rand was Billy's favorite. He was a lawyer in Washington, D.C., and had been involved in bringing the two families together. Besides, he was happily married which meant he had no interest in Eva. Billy was still learning the West Coast Coltons. He stuck to Eva's side, determined to get her back to the dance floor as soon as possible, where he could hold her in his arms again.

But he introduced her to his sister, Sky.

Eva immediately said, "You're the one who made Samantha's wonderful necklace."

"Yes, I did," Sky said proudly.

"Did you make the necklace you're wearing, too? You have such unique designs."

"Why, thank you," Sky said. "I modeled it after a piece worn by a Comanche bride I saw in an old photograph."

Billy enjoyed the praise Eva gave to Sky's work. She was a talented jeweler, specializing in Native American pieces and was beginning to make a name for herself.

When they moved away from Sky, Eva leaned

closer to say, "Now I really appreciate your compliments. Sky is beautiful."

"As are you, only in a different style," Billy assured her. But her appreciation of his sister pleased him.

Enough visiting. Time for more dancing. The soft lights from the crystal chandeliers and the gleaming wood floor always made him think of fairies and dreams. When Eva was added, he could believe anything was possible. He wrapped her in his arms. Feeling her against him was as if an essential part of his body had been restored. His cousins, Ashe and Logan, kept close to them, as if they were waiting their turn to dance with Eva. Billy had no intention of sharing what little time he had left with Eva with the vultures.

Since they were dancing near a side door, Billy edged her to the door and out into the hall.

"Where are we going?" she asked, as he grabbed her hand and with long strides turned a corner where they couldn't be seen.

"I'm not going to share you with all the competition. We'll go find our own place to dance."

"I wish I could, Billy, but I need to leave right away. I should have been at the other party an hour ago. If Papa checks on me, I'll be in real trouble."

He remembered the limo driver's reaction. "Real

trouble? Does he punish you with a whip? Or torture?''

She looked at him, startled. "Of course not! What ever gave you that idea?''

"Jerry seemed frightened of your father.''

"He is always frightened that the generous fees will disappear.''

Billy didn't quite buy her explanation of Jerry's fears, but he let it go. It probably didn't matter. "So he should be. He didn't protect you well at all tonight.''

"But that's your fault!''

"Right, but I have good intentions. He didn't know that.''

"But Billy—''

She stopped because he grabbed her hand again and drew her toward the staircase. He didn't stop until they reached the second floor. She stopped at the second closet where her coat and music box were.

"Thank you for your hospitality, Major,'' she began as if she were leaving. But Billy had no intention of letting her go so soon.

"You're not leaving yet.''

"Billy, I must. It's almost nine o'clock.''

"Even Cinderella didn't leave until midnight,'' he assured her. "Okay, I won't keep you that long, but I had to share you with too many people down below. I haven't even discovered where you live now." He tried to think of a room she would not object to. Then he saw in his mind's eye the moonlight shining into the attic. And knew she would be comfortable there. "Come upstairs with me for only a few moments, some peaceful conversation."

Her blue eyes softened. "Oh, I would love that. The attic is so—so fairy-tale-like in the moonlight."

He took her hand and started up the stairs, carefully closing the door behind them so no one would search them out.

At the top of the stairs, he slowly moved to the center of the room and slid his arm around her waist. "If we had a waltz, we could continue our dancing here."

She went willingly into his arms and they danced slowly through patches of moonlight and shadows. Afraid of where his hunger might lead him, he stepped back. "I can't have conversation when I'm holding you." He gathered some pillows stored across the room and piled them up on the floor. He bowed to her. "Your throne, princess."

With a smile she dropped down upon the pillows and motioned for him to join her. He couldn't resist doing so, even though he knew it wasn't wise.

She was struggling with the long split in her dress, trying not to show too much thigh. "I don't

think this dress was meant for attic-room chats,"
she said, a little embarrassed.

"Don't worry, princess." He reached for a
nearby coverlet and spread it over her legs.

"Oh, thank you. That was very gallant of you."

He smiled, then changed the subject. "So do you
visit your home often?"

"My home? You mean Chekagovia? Once a
year. I'm afraid it feels more like America is my
country. Though German is our language, of
course, and I'm fluent in it."

"And French?"

They both spoke French for several minutes, then
he slid back into German. They discussed their
childhoods. She told him how jealous she was of
his family. Without brothers and sisters, she was
lonely, having only her father's staff to spend time
with.

"Poor baby," he said with a teasing smile.

Eva's cheeks flushed. "I know I shouldn't com-
plain, but I was lonely. Nice things can't take away
loneliness."

He thought about that before he nodded in agree-
ment. "Very wise, princess. My children will not
be lonely. There'll be enough cousins for one thing.
Did you see all the pregnant women downstairs?
Rand's wife insisted on coming tonight even though
she's pregnant and due any moment."

Eva giggled, an enchanting sound in Billy's head. "Oh, my. That could cause complications."

"Yeah, but she said she was closer to the hospital here than at their home and she didn't want to miss all the fun. Rand agreed." He looked at Eva, a teasing grin on his face. "But then Rand always agrees with her."

"Are you telling me that Rand Colton, that strong, muscular man, is henpecked?"

Billy chuckled. He'd wondered the same thing when he'd first met the couple. Finally he'd gotten up enough nerve to ask Rand. Rand explained that he'd been wise enough to marry a smart woman. And he wanted her to be happy. "Now I understand what he was saying."

"You do? Why?"

He leaned over and cupped her cheek. "Because I'd want you to be happy...always."

In a bold move, Eva leaned forward to kiss him.

Chapter 6

Eva felt her cheeks grow hot. She wasn't surprised. She didn't usually initiate a kiss. But there was something about Billy. Was she the only one who felt something between them? He certainly seemed to like her, but she wanted more than liking, she finally admitted.

She was beginning to think that strange feeling this morning was love at first sight. She hadn't even really believed that such a thing existed, but what she felt for this man, and only this man, made her forwardness seem appropriate...and exciting.

Billy drew back from their embrace to catch his breath. He'd come too close to losing control.

"Cinderella, tell me where you live. I don't want to wait until midnight and have you run away." It amazed him how much he feared losing her. Women came and went in his life. But he couldn't imagine Eva doing that.

"Too bad the prince didn't have a telephone directory."

"You mean Cinderella was listed?"

"Why not? Do you think there are a lot of Ritkas in D.C.?" she asked, smiling.

"Maybe not, but telling me would be simpler."

"Yes. I live three blocks east from here. The redbrick with white trim on the southwest corner."

He stared at her. "I've passed that house a number of times. You really live there?" It seemed strange to him that he could have been so close to her and yet have no knowledge of her presence. Now he seemed so attuned to her presence.

"Yes. Papa didn't want to leave the area. That house is more modern and has more up-to-date security. Papa has been more concerned with security lately. There is a lot of unrest in Chekagovia."

Billy's antennae went up. He had read about Chekagovia's problems, but he hadn't paid that much attention. His normal pattern would be to ask questions about the country's problems, but he was more interested in Eva's personal problems at the moment. He murmured expressions of concern.

Then he lay back against a pillow and said softly, "Maybe they need an attic where they can feel safe, like you did as a child."

"You feel it, too, don't you? I used to pretend, when I was a little girl, that I was always safe here. My mother had recently died, and I felt so lonely." She changed the subject suddenly, as if she wanted to hide the emotion that brought tears to her beautiful eyes. "Your parents seem nice."

"Yes. We have a good family. We're all very close."

"Where are you from?"

"Oklahoma, but we traveled a bit. Dad was in the service."

"Papa has been a diplomat all my life. I have scarcely lived in Chekagovia."

"That must make it difficult."

"Yes. And I always wanted a big family, like yours."

"How about I share them with you? We've always got room for one more." Mental visions of a beautiful little blond girl, alone in the big attic, made him wish he'd been there for her. She was weaving a spell over him. He'd never felt like this before. He wrapped his arm around her pale shoulders and drew her close to comfort her.

Comfort? It was sexual desire, of course. He

wasn't a sentimental man. She laid her head on his shoulder.

"I wish I could be part of your family. But Papa needs me. I act as his hostess, you see. I have ever since I was sixteen."

"Didn't you ever have a childhood? Time to get in trouble? To play and be carefree?" Billy asked, thinking about his summer days with his brothers, when they played, made up stories and fought.

She shrugged her beautiful shoulders. "There wasn't time."

He bent his head and softly caressed her lips. "Poor baby," he said, sincerely this time.

She shoved against him. "I didn't suffer," she assured him staunchly, as if she didn't want his concern. "I had everything I wanted. I was lucky."

"Except a family."

"That wasn't my father's fault. He loved Mama. He cried when she died."

"Of course." He shifted and drew her more against him. He craved her warmth.

"It's true!"

"I believe you. But I feel badly that you were deprived of so much of your childhood."

"Well, I can speak five languages!"

"Good for you," he said tenderly.

"And what can you speak?" she asked eagerly.

"Russian, Portuguese, German, French, Italian, Spanish, oh, and Comanche."

"Wow! You must be very good at languages. You must be a genius."

"I don't think so, but they do come easily to me." Suddenly he burst into laughter.

"What is it?"

"What if we had a child? He'd definitely be able to learn languages, wouldn't he?"

She laughed, but then she turned serious. "How do you know it would be a boy? Maybe she'd be a girl?"

"Maybe, with my hair and your eyes. She'd be a beauty, like her mother. I'd have to work out to fight off the boys who'd chase her."

Eva reached up to touch his face. "And she'd have brothers and sisters. She wouldn't be alone."

"Of course not. Making babies would be one of our favorite activities." He stroked her arm. Just thinking about making love to Eva stirred him up. "Shall we build them an attic, too?"

"Our children wouldn't need an attic. They'd have lots of family. And a mama and papa who loved them, who'd cuddle them when they were scared or sad."

"Didn't your father do that?" he asked, frowning, his heart squeezing in pain at the thought of her all alone.

"He was very busy. I had a nanny who was kind to me."

"Oh, Eva," he said softly and drew her even closer, "I'm glad you had the attic." He kissed her gently on her soft lips.

"I've never told anyone—you mustn't say anything to anyone." She put her arms around his neck.

"No," he whispered, "your secrets are safe with me." He kissed her again and this time she kissed him back. Their kiss deepened. She began unbuttoning his uniform and he slipped the straps of her gown down her shoulders. They each wanted warm flesh to touch, to kiss.

Thought of stopping never occurred to Eva. It seemed so right, so perfect. While her father had trained Eva in correct behavior, he'd never taught her about matters of the heart. But the feelings Eva had for Billy were so strong, she couldn't resist inviting him closer. She didn't want to follow her father's directives. She wanted to give Billy full rein of her heart, body and soul. Her skin yearned for his touch.

Billy had never felt this way about a woman. As if Eva were a gift for him to protect and care for. As if she actually were the mother of his future children. Nothing seemed more right than to hold her against him, to become one with her.

He stroked her body as if it were a great work of art, a sacred treasure. She shivered and he drew her closer to him. "Are you okay?" he whispered. As difficult as it would be for him, if she wanted to stop, he would. But she sighed and nuzzled closer, letting her lips run down his neck.

"I'm perfect," she replied, and he couldn't agree more. When he felt he could wait no longer to enter her, he gently spread her legs and lay on her, bracing his weight with his strong arms. She ran her hands over his chest, then put them around his neck and tugged, as eager for him as he was for her.

When he entered her, he paused, afraid he would hurt her, but she urged him on. "Don't stop," she said, breathless, holding tight to his broad shoulders. He followed her command and plunged into her, stunned by his utter desire for her, the rightness of his holding her, becoming one with her. Then he began moving slowly, wanting the experience to be perfect for Eva, his love.

His earlier conversation with Jesse, over morning coffee, flashed through his mind. He owed his brother an apology. Now he knew what Jesse had meant. He knew what Rand meant when he said he did whatever it took to make his wife happy. Forever, he would put Eva first. She, in the flash of an eye, had become his partner, his better half, his forever woman. He stroked the supple body beneath him, growing more excited by the moment, leading Eva to delirious completion, as fulfilling as love between a man and his woman could be.

Later, he held her against him, not wanting to let her go, to end the heaven they'd shared. He was making plans in his head for their future. He whispered to Eva his plans, but he wasn't sure they made sense to her. She said nothing.

"You are safe in my arms," he whispered.

His fingers traced designs on her skin as he thought about the evening and her words about her life. "Your father didn't think the two of you were safe here in D.C.?"

"He didn't think the security in this house was good. He had concerns. He said the uneducated people of Chekagovia are impatient. They are not willing to wait to be taught wisdom. Terrorist groups have been formed."

"I have heard rumors. Your father is right about what he said, but I think more could be done."

"My father has done his best but some of the old rulers refuse to give up the power. But those against the government don't distinguish between those in power."

Billy's mind immediately snapped to. "Eva, did you tell Jerry why you were coming here?"

"I don't think so," she murmured, her lips inviting him to kiss her again. Then she opened her eyes wider. "I said I needed to pick up an important object. I remember thinking, for an instant, that he knew what I meant, but he said nothing."

"It's just that he looked frightened when I told him to leave," he said slowly, trying to figure everything out. "Maybe he's involved somehow with one of the terrorist groups."

"Jerry? Surely he wouldn't betray us!" Eva exclaimed.

"There are ways to make people do unspeakable things. Fear for their own lives…or for people they love. We'll find out. I'll talk to some people tomorrow."

She sank against him. "Hold me, Billy. I want to feel safe."

"You're safe, my love. I promise." Even as he held her, he sensed tension in the air.

Just then the night calm was disrupted by the sound of gunfire from below.

Alice and Thomas stood quietly drinking their last glass of champagne. "Did you see the way Billy looked at her?" Alice asked softly, finally discussing what they both were thinking.

"Of course I did. We all saw it. I hope she won't object to his Indian blood."

"That's ridiculous. Besides, if she does, Billy won't want her. Where did they go, anyway?"

Thomas rolled his eyes. "Some place private." They were chuckling again softly, when the ballroom doors were slung back against the walls and a spray of machine-gun fire was shot into the ceiling.

There were muted screams, but Thomas checked quickly to be sure everyone was safe and where his sons and nephews were.

Then, his shoulders squared, he stepped forward quickly, followed by Senator Joe Colton, his nephew Bram, a sheriff, and numerous of their young men. Good stock, he thought to himself. "Please don't hurt anyone. What is it that you want?"

The uncouth man who faced Thomas snarled at him. "Don't panic, and no one will be hurt. We want Miss Eva Ritka. Don't say she is not here, because we know she is."

Bram spoke to his uncle in Comanche. "We cannot give her away."

"We have no choice. Your aunt and our other ladies mustn't be hurt."

Jesse added, "Billy is with her." That was enough for all of them. They knew they could rely on Billy.

"Stop that. What are you saying!" the leader screamed at them, slamming a crystal vase he had grabbed off a table beside him onto the ground, shattering it into a million pieces.

"Easy!" Thomas said. "We do not know the exact location of Miss Ritka. We believe she might have left already." Thomas watched as the man turned back to talk to his band of thugs. They seemed unhappy with his answer. He turned back to Thomas.

The leader stated that he would take some of the men to search for Eva. One of Thomas's sons murmured a word he did not want to hear. "Rape." He knew, as well as his sons, that might happen if they left the ladies with these bullies.

"No. That is unacceptable. We will allow you one of our men per search group. The rest of the men stay here with our women."

The man gave Thomas an evil grin, acknowledging his fears, but he agreed. "We have more important things on our minds tonight than women." He divided his men into three groups, and left several of them to stay in the ballroom with him. The sons and nephews of Thomas and Joe stepped forward.

From the group, the leader chose three. Thomas offered three more, so his sons would not be alone with the terrorists. Again he showed his evil grin. "No. I do not trust your sudden cooperation." He turned to his men and warned them to be careful, keeping their eyes on the enemy, not realizing that several of the Colton men spoke German. Like Billy, many of them had a gift for language.

Chapter 7

As soon as Billy had heard the sound of bullets, he immediately began to dress.

"Billy? What was that noise?"

"That noise was gunshots and I think it may be the people you were talking about, the impatient ones. Get dressed quickly."

"But why would they come here?"

"Because I think Jerry told them where you are. I think he betrayed you."

Horror slowly took over Eva's beautiful face. "Oh, no! I am so sorry!" She began dressing. "I have to go talk to them. I've put your family in danger!"

Billy wondered if he had ever been so naive. He didn't think so. "Listen!" he called suddenly in urgent tones. Then he ran down the stairs to put his ear to the door.

Eva appeared to think he was leaving her, tumbling down beside him, only half-dressed. Billy heard his cousin Bram's warning in Comanche only a few doors away. He grabbed Eva by the arm and dragged her back into the attic. "Dress quickly. We must escape."

Her eyes widened in horror, but she did as he ordered. After signaling her to silence, he ran to the windows quickly looking for means of escape. Only the sixth window, with its hiding place, showed promise. There was a rain gutter that had brackets to hold it against the brick of the exterior. If he removed his shoes, he thought he could safely reach the roof without slipping. Could Eva? Possibly if he helped her, which, of course, he would.

He turned around to find her behind him, waiting. "Will you trust me?" he whispered.

She wasted no time on silliness. He received a smile and a quick nod. As he opened the window, however, she spoke. "But I can't go without the music box."

"We don't have time. Why does it matter so much?" Billy had his suspicions about the music box, but he wanted Eva to tell him the truth.

She shook her head, an anguished look on her face. "My grandfather told me the future of Chekagovia rested on the control of the music box. That's all I know. Papa thought if I hid it no one would find it."

She turned her back to him. "I must stay here to try to hide it again. You must escape while you can."

"These men are terrorists. They will kill you, sweetheart. I cannot leave you here. They will find the music box whether you die or not. It would be a worthless sacrifice." He grabbed her arm and pulled her after him to the sixth window. "We must climb to the roof, so they cannot find us. Remove your shoes. Give them to me and I'll put them in my pockets." He sat down on the windowsill and removed his own shoes, tying the shoelaces together and putting them around his neck, tucking his socks inside the shoes. He made a quick inventory of the objects in the attic. A short rope was an addition that encouraged him.

"Papa will never forgive me," she said as she handed him her heels.

Billy framed her sad face with his hands. "I cannot let you stay." He took her hand. "Can you fix your skirt so you can climb the wall? And remove your stockings."

She tried several ways hurriedly but nothing

modest could be achieved. "I can't—" She looked at him hopelessly.

"Don't worry about your modesty, Eva. Just pull it up so it won't trip you. You can be modest when we are safe. And hurry!"

She turned her face toward the door and Billy knew she too could hear the pounding boots. She grabbed her split skirt and tied it around her waist. Then she peeled off her panty hose and hung them around her neck. He rewarded her with a kiss. Then he signaled that she should wait there.

With a silent prayer for their safety, he leaped onto the windowsill. Grabbing hold of the drainage pipe as high as he could reach, he swung out and found one of the brackets with his toes. He only had a few feet to go. He reached the edge of the roof quickly and pulled himself up. He braced himself against a fake dormer on the almost flat roof and took the rope from around his neck.

After tying a knot in one end, he lowered it, whispering Eva's name. Her sweet face appeared as she leaned out of the window. He carefully gave her instructions, telling her to hold on to the rope. For a moment, he feared she wouldn't have the courage to follow him, but then he felt her weight as she used the brackets beneath her toes to climb up the side.

As she collapsed in his arms, he pulled her away

from the edge, whispering in her ear praise for her bravery. But he also heard Comanche. He listened as the voices of his relatives told him that, as he'd suspected, the invaders were terrorists, looking for Eva. He also heard the terrorists yelling at the men to stop talking.

He froze as he heard the door to the attic bust open and thundering boots come into the cavernous room. He didn't think they could be seen from below, even though the window was open.

He barely whispered to Eva not to move. That was the only way they could be discovered. The voices grew louder. Thankfully, he heard the man in charge order some of his men to go outside and search around the house.

He was glad he hadn't chosen the tree as their escape. They would have been caught in minutes.

For five minutes after they'd heard the boots tromp out of the attic, he waited, afraid they might have left something there. Finally, he stood up and pulled Eva to her feet. Then he carefully led her to a chimney and sat her down behind it.

Before he sat beside her, he took off his jacket and held it out for her to wear. She opened her mouth to protest, but he pressed a finger to her lips for silence. She slipped her arms into the sleeves and pulled it close to her. He sat down beside her, pulling her body against his.

"We must wait," he whispered, "for a while, to make sure all the terrorists are inside the house. Then we will find a way down and notify the police."

She nodded. Then she shifted and he wondered what she was doing. But she was pulling forward her small purse she'd carried all evening. He'd forgotten about it. She unzipped it and pulled out a very small cellular phone.

He hugged her, indicating his watch to tell her they had to wait a few minutes. Then he kissed her cheek.

Whispering always, he began telling her how much their lovemaking had meant to him. "I was surprised at how right it felt, my love. I've never felt this way before. I argued with my brother this morning. Jesse was telling me he fell in love with his wife at first sight. I told him I didn't believe in it. I'll admit to you, though I didn't tell him, that I felt something when I saw you this morning at the cleaners."

Eva beamed at him and whispered, "I felt the same thing." Billy kissed her and immediately felt warmer as his temperature rose. But he stopped kissing her because it made him want to make love to her and a roof was a precarious place to indulge his hormones especially in the midst of a terrorist plot, he thought grimly.

He changed the subject, telling her about the town house he purchased that morning. "It's a beautiful town house, Eva. And I saw you in every room. I had to buy it. I feel like it was made for the two of us. Will you go see it tomorrow?"

"I'd love to, Billy, but let's get out of this first. A-and it's Christmas tomorrow." Eva looked like she was shivering—more like trembling with fear.

"Yes, it is, my love, but I'm going to meet your father in the morning, when this is over." He pulled her closer and smiled tenderly. "I need to introduce myself, and tell him my intentions. You do want to marry me, don't you?"

"Yes" was her simple, perfect answer. Her trembling had stopped. There was no hesitation or lack of confidence in her answer. "We'll face my father together."

"We'll start our family right away, too." He cupped her face with his palm.

Her cheeks turned rosy, but she agreed.

He had a sudden urge to kiss her.

He quickly changed the subject again in an effort to stay focused on the danger at hand. "We'd better try calling the police now."

He took her phone and dialed the emergency number.

"What is your emergency?" a friendly voice asked. Billy wasn't sure he should start with a description of their situation. "Ma'am, this is Major William Colton, Pentagon. A band of Chekagovian rebels have invaded my family's home." He quickly gave his address. "They are holding hostages and they have guns."

"Please remain on the line so I can get additional information. You do know that giving false information is punishable, don't you, sir?"

His voice hard, Billy said, "Yes, I do."

"What's wrong?" Eva asked in a whisper, leaning against him, watching his every move.

"Ma'am, if you want confirmation, call General Whiteside at the Pentagon. And do it fast!"

"It's Christmas Eve, sir. I doubt that any *real* general will be there."

Frustrated, Billy said, "Just send some men, or you'll regret it." Before he could give his address again, the tiny phone slipped from his grasp and slid down the side of the roof. "Damn, damn, damn!" Billy muttered. "I sure as hell hope she believed me."

"I'm sure she did, Billy," Eva whispered.

"I'm sorry about the phone. I'll get you another one," Billy promised, hugging her tightly.

"I think I'd appreciate a blanket instead. It's a little c-cold tonight."

"I know, sweetheart. We'll find a way down as soon as our rescuers arrive. That's when we can be sure the terrorists will all be inside.'' He tried to pull her closer, hoping he could provide enough warmth, but he was getting cold himself.

They sat there, listening intently. ''What if they didn't believe you?'' Eva finally asked.

''Then we'll find a way down and go to a neighbor's house and call again.'' He said it more confidently than he felt. But he didn't want Eva to worry.

Suddenly, the night air was full of sirens. He gave a sigh of relief. He took Eva's hand and led her around to the northwest side of the house where he saw a huge oak tree.

He stood there, staring at the old oak tree, assessing the best way to get Eva down. The upper branches that reached the roof looked too small to hold their weight. Finally he decided to risk them. He turned to Eva.

''Honey, I'm going to start down the tree. I'll have to go down several limbs before I can get to one that will hold me. I'll stop there and wait for you. You come down, just like me, until we're together. Don't panic if you start falling. I'll catch you.'' He only hoped he was right. He needed to get Eva to safety and put himself in a position to help his family.

He looked at Eva, afraid he'd see fear. But she smiled at him, faith in her incredible blue eyes.

Billy surveyed the area below the tree, worrying they might have placed guards outside. However, he figured the arrival of the sirens would draw all the bad guys inside. He couldn't see anything, but there were a lot of shadows. Once they got in the tree, they could take their time going down, looking for any reaction below. He kissed Eva briefly, drew a deep breath and leaped for the closest branch. He stopped when he got to the third one. His shoulders were just below the top branch, which meant he could protect Eva.

"Come now, Eva," Billy said in a whisper.

With the faith Eva had shown, she did as he said immediately. His hands clasped her waist as she came down to him. Once he had her in his arms, the two of them moved down two more limbs. Then they paused.

"You know, Eva, I climbed trees a lot as a child, which explains my ability. But how do we explain yours?" He grinned at her, hoping to loosen any tension.

She smiled back. "I'm just following you, Billy."

He hugged her to him. "Well you're doing a damn fine job. Do you want to sit down, or just stand here? We're going to wait a few minutes to make sure there's no response to the noise we've made."

Eva looked around her. "I don't mind standing."

"Okay," Billy said. "But you'll have to promise me not to move."

"Why would I want to?" Eva asked, a teasing grin on her beautiful lips. "I'm in your arms."

"Even three stories in the air?" he asked.

She nodded, saying nothing else.

Such unconditional trust made him want to be stronger for Eva. He never wanted to fail her. When Billy saw a man move out of the shadows below hurrying toward a door to the house, he knew he'd been right to be cautious. He and Eva stood there without moving for another five minutes.

Then he whispered in her ear, "I'm going to the next limb. Follow me." He lowered himself down and then waited for her to do the same. It slowed their descent, but it kept Eva safer.

When they reached the bottom limb, they were still about eleven feet off the ground. "Looks like we have to jump from here, Eva. Let me go first and I'll do my best to catch you."

"No, Billy. I might injure you. I can jump by myself," she assured him.

"Just wait until I get down there," Billy asked.

He squatted on the branch and grabbed it with his hands. He thrust his feet down and swung on the branch leaving himself less than five feet to drop. His landing sent tremors through his body, but he was okay. He looked up to direct Eva, but she had already followed his efforts and landed two feet away from him.

"Eva!" he called hoarsely. He gathered her to him, but the pain on her face alerted him to an injury.

"What is it? What's wrong?"

"My—ankle!" she gasped.

He sat her down on the grass while looking to be sure no one had seen them. Then he discovered her left ankle already swelling.

"I—I'm sure it's only sprained," Eva said slowly, not sounding like herself.

"I hope so," Billy said, trying to keep the worry out of his voice. "You should have waited for me to catch you."

"I'm not a baby, Billy. I don't want to be a burden to you."

It worried him that she'd injured herself trying to be brave, which meant he would have to carry her. If they met up with any terrorists, his hands wouldn't be free for fighting. But he wasn't going to point that out to her.

"You're a brave woman, Eva."

"But, Billy, I don't think I can walk."

"I'm going to carry you, sweetheart."

He scooped her up into his arms and headed for the front of the house, staring at the shadows as they went. As he cautiously rounded the corner of the house he saw the police and emergency vehicles at the bottom of the driveway. With relief, he realized they'd made it. He'd save Eva and he'd be able to help save his family.

Knowing they would be surrounded by police almost at once he took the opportunity to kiss her and make a promise. "Sweetheart, I love you. As soon as everything's back to normal I'll talk to your father and we'll be married."

A beautiful smile added to the warmth of her words. "I love you, Billy. I can't wait."

The police surrounded them and paramedics questioned him about Eva's injury. He was reluctant to surrender her, but he needed to give proof of his identity. When this was all over he'd be able to return to Eva's side. Where he belonged. For always.

TAKE NO PRISONERS
Linda Turner

Chapter 1

It was Christmas Eve, and D.C. was lit up like a Christmas tree. Icicle lights hung from eaves all over the city, and all across town, families and friends were gathering to celebrate. Everyone, that was, except Julianna Stevens. All decked out in a sparkly red dress and matching heels, she'd just finished dressing for a Christmas Eve party she'd been looking forward to for weeks when her beeper went off. Just that easily, her plans for the evening changed.

"That's what you get for playing the good Samaritan and volunteering to be on call Christmas Eve," she muttered as she zipped around DuPont

Circle. But how could she have known she'd get a call? It was Christmas Eve, for heaven's sake! Who needed the services of a criminal psychologist and hostage negotiator tonight?

Like it or not, she was about to find out.

Racing through Georgetown, she took a turn on what she liked to call Embassy Row because so many ambassadors lived there, and slammed on the brakes. Twenty yards ahead of her, the police had erected a roadblock, and from the blur of flashing lights that lit up the night sky, it looked like every squad car, fire truck and ambulance in D.C. had converged there. And if that wasn't enough, camera crews from all the major network news stations had set up shop just beyond the police barrier. The place looked like a zoo.

It wasn't the cameras or reporters or even the FBI agents, however, that drew her eye. In the whirl of lights and government personnel scrambling to deal with the situation, Julianna saw only one thing— the dozen or more men walking around with SWAT spelled out on the back of their winter parkas. In the blink of an eye, her heart stopped cold in her breast.

Irritated that her eyes had immediately zeroed in on those four letters, she told herself there was no reason to panic. It wasn't as if she hadn't known the SWAT team would be on the scene—they always were in a hostage situation. That didn't mean Kurt would be on duty tonight. In all likelihood, he was spending the evening with Suzanne and her family. For all she knew, they could be celebrating their engagement.

"They deserve each other," she muttered, only to wince at the bitterness she heard in her voice. Why did she let him do this to her, damn it? She and Kurt Hoffman were history, kaput, divorced…and had been for three years. She hadn't seen him since the day they walked out of the courthouse, their twenty-month-old marriage over before it had hardly begun, and that was just the way she wanted it. He could be married again, engaged to Suzanne Garner, his ex-girlfriend and the secretary at his precinct who had known more about his whereabouts than his wife, or involved with somebody else. Either way, Julianna didn't care.

Confident she was well over him, she flashed her ID at the police officer who was manning the blockade of the street and quickly found a parking place once she was allowed inside the barricade. Now if she could just find the command center, she could go about the business of doing what she did best and use her training as a criminal psychologist to solve the hostage situation. Then she could forget Kurt Hoffman even existed.

But even as she made her way through the mad-

house of different agency personnel who had responded to the emergency call for help at the
Georgetown mansion down the street, she had a
sinking feeling that her luck had run out where Kurt
Hoffman was concerned. He was there somewhere
in the crowd…she could feel him.

The thought had barely registered when the sea
of policemen blocking her path suddenly parted,
and there, fifty yards in front of her, was the man
she had once sworn to love for the rest of her life.
One look was all it took for her heart to turn over
in her breast.

Dear Lord, he was a good-looking devil! He always had been. When they'd met six years ago,
she'd taken one look at him and fallen like a ton
of bricks. He'd only gotten better with age. At
thirty-three, he was lean and muscular, and he'd cut
his honey-brown hair short to discourage the curl.
The passage of time had sculpted his chiseled face
with a maturity that hadn't been there in the past,
and although he was no Cary Grant, he could certainly give Brad Pitt a run for his money. Especially
with those green eyes of his. He only had to smile
for his eyes to dance with a mischief that seemed
to call to her very soul.

He glanced up then and those wicked green eyes
met hers. For a moment, the past, all the angry
words and hurt feelings vanished as if they had

never been. She took a step toward him, then another, and suddenly, all she wanted to do was run into his arms.

Horrified, she froze. What in the world was wrong with her? This was Kurt, the man she'd given her heart to, the man who'd walked out on her without ever really giving their marriage a chance. Dear God, how he'd hurt her! And she wanted to run to him? Like hell! If she ran anywhere, it would be as far away from him as her legs would carry her.

Her heart slamming against her ribs, she hesitated, tempted. But even as her heart urged her to run for the hills, her head refused to let her turn tail like a coward. There were hostages in the mansion down the street, and they needed her help...and Kurt's. Like it or not, they had to deal with each other.

Stiffening her spine, she reminded herself she was a professional. As a hostage negotiator, she had to work with anyone and everyone who could help get the hostages released. Kurt was just one of the crowd. Satisfied she had him put firmly in his place, she lifted her chin and headed straight for him. If he thought she was childish enough to avoid him, he could think again.

At Kurt's side, a government bureaucrat worried about the delicacy of the situation and the possibility of an international incident developing if they weren't careful, but Kurt couldn't see anyone but Julianna. She was sure and confident and so damn beautiful, his heart slammed against his ribs just at the sight of her. Obviously on her way to a party when she'd gotten the call about the hostage situation, she wore an expensive black wool coat and red heels, and it didn't take an Einstein to figure out that she wore a red dress under the coat. She'd always loved red. His mouth watered just at the thought of her curvaceous figure decked out in something tastefully low and red. He didn't have to see it to know that whatever the dress looked like, she was a knockout in it.

Drinking in the sight of her ruby lips and the way her long brown hair caressed her back with every step, he wondered how he'd ever found the strength to let her go. There was a time when he loved her so fiercely that he couldn't bear to be apart from her except when he was working. Then it had all fallen apart. He'd learned to live without her, but not having her in his life still hurt. After three years, he had to believe it always would.

Still, asking her for a divorce was the one thing he didn't regret. It was the right thing to do. She was studying to get her Ph.D., and he was working double shifts at work. They had little time together, and more and more often, that was spent fighting. He took a lot of the blame for that. He'd been too damn possessive, wanting her with him every second that he had free, hating the time she took away from him for school. He realized now that his unreasonable need for closeness had led to the demise of their marriage, but unfortunately, he hadn't been able to see that at the time. He'd just wanted her with him. That—and his job—had cost him everything.

Regret knotted in his gut. She'd worried about him every time he'd left the apartment. She'd hated the danger—he'd understood that, and sympathized. But as much as he'd loved her, he hadn't been able to give up his work for her. Not that she asked him to, he silently acknowledged. She would have never done such a thing. But he knew how she worried. Fear ate at her every time he went to work, and nothing he could say reassured her. In the end, it just seemed better to end things before they lost all love and respect for each other.

His decision had been based solely on what he'd thought was best for her, but she'd hated him for it. From the moment their divorce was final, she'd gone out of her way to avoid him, and that was what hurt the most. He'd missed her, damn it!

He had, however, no intention of telling her that. He had his share of pride, just like any other man.

She didn't need to know that he still reached for her in the night…or that when the call had come in about the hostage situation, he'd hoped she'd be on call tonight. After all, it hadn't seemed like too much to ask. It *was* Christmas Eve…and he still believed in Santa.

And with good reason, he thought, fighting a grin as she drew closer. She had her chin in the air, just like she always did when her back was up about something, and a glint in her eye that warned him not to mess with her. Oh, sweetheart, he thought, if you knew just how much I wanted to mess with you, you'd turn around and take that sweet little body of yours somewhere else.

But even as images flashed in his head of holding her again, kissing her until they were both out of their head with need, he knew there was, unfortunately, no time for romance with his ex. The extended family of former Senator Joe Colton was in the mansion down the street and being held hostage by God knew who. Nothing else mattered.

It was his job, as point person for the SWAT team, to help get them released. Standing beside the hostage negotiator and disseminating information and orders as the situation progressed was not a role he usually liked. He much preferred to be in the thick of the action. Tonight, however, there was nowhere else he'd rather be.

Julianna was going to have a fit, he thought, and just barely managed to hold back a grin. Other than making love to her, there was nothing he liked more than pushing her buttons. He felt sorry for the Coltons, but for him, Christmas Eve wasn't going to be so bad, after all.

"Julianna," he said, greeting her with a nod. "Glad you could join us. I see you dressed for the occasion."

She gave him a withering look and never knew how she delighted him. "I was going to a party," she retorted curtly. "Who's the point man? Dispatch didn't give me the particulars."

A slow grin curled the corners of his mouth. "You're looking at him, sweetheart."

"Yeah, right," she sniffed. "And I'm Julia Roberts. Quit fooling around, Kurt. I'm serious."

"And I'm not?"

Of course he wasn't serious, she told herself. The powers that be knew she was his ex-wife, and there was no love lost between them. Considering that, no one in their right mind would expect them to work together.

But even as she tried to convince herself this was all just some kind of twisted joke, she saw the glint of humor shining in his green eyes, and her heart sank. Oh, God, he *was* serious! He'd always had an offbeat kind of humor—this was just the kind of perverse situation that he would find vastly entertaining.

Damn him, she wouldn't do it! She wouldn't work with him. She wouldn't subject herself to this kind of…torture. There had to be someone else available tonight who could take her place. So what if it was Christmas Eve? This was an emergency!

But even as she racked her brain for someone she could call, she knew there wasn't anyone. Earl Thompson, her immediate supervisor at the Bureau and the first in charge negotiator, was with his family in Aspen for the holidays. Like it or not, she was on her own, not only with the hostage-takers, but also with Kurt.

Panic seized her at the thought. *No! She couldn't do it!* she thought wildly, only to stiffen when she saw Kurt was watching her with a wide grin. Then it hit her. He was expecting her to panic, to throw a fit, to storm off rather than work with him. She'd always been the more emotional one, the one who lost her temper first and usually acted like a two-year-old. And he was just waiting for that.

Well, not tonight, she promised herself grimly. He'd pushed her buttons for the last time. She'd grown up in the last three years, and she wasn't about to let him or anyone else rattle her so easily ever again.

Holding on to her temper, however, wasn't as easy as she'd have liked. She drew in a steadying breath, but it was several long moments before she could say coolly, "Dispatch said a wedding party and all the guests were being held hostage at a Chekagovian diplomat's house. Do we have any reports of injuries? Who's the diplomat? Have we been able to establish contact with him? What about the terrorists? Who are they? Are they talking yet?"

All business, she threw questions at him like darts, and Kurt had to give her credit. She was as cool as a cucumber—at least on the surface. But oh, those eyes of hers! They were beautiful and turbulent with emotions that reminded him too much of the passion they'd always shared. With no effort whatsoever, he found himself remembering the last time they'd made love.

Abruptly realizing where his thoughts had wandered, he swore silently. *Oh, no, you don't! You're not going there—it'll only get you into trouble.* And trouble was the last thing he wanted with Julianna. He'd been there, done that, and in the end, it hadn't been any fun. Only a fool would make the same mistake twice, and he liked to think he was smarter than that.

So he followed her example and deliberately focused on the matter at hand. "There's some question as to who actually lives in the house,'' he said in a tone as cool as her own. ''The place was leased to the Chekagovian government, but Helmut Ritka, a Chekagovian diplomat who's been living there with his daughter, apparently moved out at the end of October.''

''Who's the new renter?'' she said with a frown. ''Or did the owner move back in? Who's throwing the wedding?''

''We believe the groom is the nephew of former Senator Joe Colton. The entire Colton family appears to be there.''

Shocked, Julianna paled. ''Including the senator?''

''Apparently so,'' he said flatly. ''We're still trying to get the guest list, but so far, we're not having much luck. We haven't been able to locate the catering company that's handling the reception. It's Christmas Eve,'' he said with a grimace. ''The only businesses still open are convenience stores and the police department.''

''What about the hostage-takers? Who are they and what do they want?''

''Right now, they're not talking, but we do know they're a band of Chekagovian rebels. One of the hostages, Major Billy Colton, was able to give us that much before his cell phone went dead. Needless to say, we're taking a close look at Helmut

Ritka and his role in the Chekagovian government.''

"He has a daughter, doesn't he? I seem to remember seeing her picture in the paper once—I believe she was attending a state dinner at the White House with her father.''

Already one step ahead of her, he nodded. "The FBI is already searching for her—as well as her father and his staff—but so far, we haven't been able to locate them. Like I said, it's Christmas Eve.''

He was nothing if not thorough, and like it or not, Julianna couldn't help but be impressed. She'd worked with point men who were totally useless to her, and that only made her job more difficult. The more she knew when she actually spoke with the hostage-takers, the better chance she had of resolving the situation peacefully. With Kurt's help, there was a good chance that Senator Joe Colton and his family would walk unharmed out of the mansion down the street.

She should have been grateful. She would have been—if he just hadn't irritated her so easily. Damn it, why couldn't someone else have been assigned to work with her?

Chapter 2

The FBI had evacuated a three-block area, then set up a command center down the street from the mansion and well out of range of any weapons the hostage-takers may have had. It was here that Kurt led Julianna. "You know Tom Foster, don't you?" he told her with a nod toward the big, redheaded agent who was on a walkie-talkie, checking in with the other agents in the field. "I believe you two have worked together before."

Surprised that he knew—had he been keeping tabs on her career?—Julianna shook the hand Tom held out to her and smiled. "Of course, I know Tom. We both got a call to the Washington Monument in the middle of a thunderstorm. Everything turned out okay, thank God, but for a while, we were afraid a park ranger was going to go postal on us. How are you, Tom? Any chance Santa'll be good to us and let us all go home early?''

"It doesn't look like it," he said regretfully. "Whoever organized this knew what they were doing. In ten minutes flat, they had control of the mansion and had rounded up all the hostages' cell phones—but not before Major Colton was able to report that a group of Chekagovian terrorists stormed the wedding reception.''

Julianna didn't like the sound of that. Glancing at the phone she knew the FBI had set up with a direct link to the mansion, she asked, ''Any word yet on what their agenda is?''

His expression somber, he shook his head. "Not yet, but it's still early. Right now, they're making us sweat.''

And they were doing a damn good job of it, Julianna thought privately. Tension—and tempers— was running high, and with good reason. Without a name to the terrorists who held the wedding guests at gunpoint, FBI agents, the D.C. police and SWAT team members had no leads to chase down, no clues as to who might be helping the hostage-takers on the outside. And that left not only the hostages, but everyone on the outside working for their release, wide-open to danger.

Tension eating at her own nerves, the one thing Julianna hated the most about her job was the waiting. Her natural instinct was to snatch up the phone and call the hostage-takers to negotiate a deal before anyone got hurt, but she'd learned the hard way that that only put her in a position of weakness when it came to negotiating. Hostage-takers always had a message they wanted to get out to the world. Sooner or later, they would call with their demands. The thought had hardly registered when the phone directly linked to the mansion suddenly rang. Everyone within hearing distance of it stiffened.

"I believe that's your call," Tom told her. "Good luck."

Kurt didn't say a word, but she saw the encouragement in his eyes, and for some reason, his confidence in her steadied her nerves as nothing else could. Later, she knew that was going to bother her, but for now, it was time to go to work. Drawing in a steadying breath, she reached for the phone.

"This is Julianna Stevens," she said easily. "I'm working with the FBI to negotiate the release of the hostages. And you are…?"

Ignoring her question, a heavily accented male voice growled, "The hostages aren't going anywhere until Helmut Ritka is handed over to us, along with a million dollars, a private plane with enough fuel to reach Chekagovia, and the music box. When you're ready to comply with our demands, then we'll talk.''

"What about the hostages? Are they…?" she began, but that was as far as she got. A split second later, the dial tone rang in her ears.

Far from discouraged, she glanced up to find Kurt and Tom watching her with matching frowns. "Well," she said, "now we know what they want at least." Reeling off the list of demands, she added with a frown, "And they want the music box."

Surprised, Tom looked at her blankly. "What music box?"

She shrugged. "Beats me. He didn't say. Obviously, that's something we need to ask Helmut Ritka about."

"Among other things," he said grimly. "It sounds like Mr. Ritka's made a few enemies back home."

"What about Colton?" Kurt asked Julianna as Tom hurried to join his fellow agents and relay the latest information. "Do you think the commandoes know they're holding a former U.S. senator?"

Her eyes somber, she couldn't give him the reassurance she knew he wanted. "I don't know. All he said was the hostages weren't going anywhere until Ritka was turned over. If he knew he had Col-

ton, surely he'd have demanded a trade right from
the beginning.''

Kurt had to agree with her. ''Then we need to
find Ritka and make some kind of deal with these
jerks before they realize just who they've got.''

On the surface, tracking down a foreign diplomat
in the Washington, D.C. area shouldn't have been
that difficult. Thanks to the help of the utility company, they learned that Ritka had moved out of the
mansion two months before, when he'd had the utilities turned off, but, strangely, there was no record
of him having utilities turned on at a new residence
anywhere in the area. ''Someone in his embassy
should know where he moved to or a number where
he can be reached,'' Kurt said. ''Surely he keeps in
touch with his own people.''

But when Kurt called the embassy himself from
the bank of phones at the command center, a bored
recorded voice said, ''The Chekagovian Embassy is
presently closed. We will reopen for business on
Thursday. Merry Christmas.''

Swearing under his breath, he muttered, ''Yeah,
merry Christmas to you, too.''

''Let me guess,'' Julianna said when he hung up
the phone with a scowl. ''The embassy's closed for
the holiday. So what about the staff? If they're all
from Chekagovia, doesn't the State Department
have a list of all employees and their addresses?''

''They should—but that doesn't mean Ritka reported his change of address.''

''Even if he didn't, check with his secretary. She'll know where he is even when his family doesn't.''

Even to her own ears, her words sounded bitter, but there was nothing Julianna could do about it. She *was* bitter. She and Kurt had only had one Christmas together during their marriage, and they'd spent it apart. Because of a secretary.

Suzanne. Pain unexpectedly squeezing her heart, Julianna didn't want to even think about Kurt's exgirlfriend and all the trouble she'd caused them, but she was fighting a losing battle. It was Christmas and the memory of that time was like a thorn in her side. Every time she saw a Christmas tree or heard a Christmas song on the radio, it throbbed.

Two days before Christmas, she and Kurt had had a fight. It seemed like they'd always fought on his day off because he'd wanted her to spend every waking—and sleeping—moment with him, but on that particular day, the fight they'd had escalated into a nasty argument. He resented the fact that she chose to spend her time studying on the first day he'd had off in two weeks, and she was hurt that he never seemed to understand or care how important it was to her to get her Ph.D. His work was all that mattered, and when he got a day off, she was supposed to drop everything and be at his beck and call. She couldn't do it anymore.

Words were exchanged, and they both said things they shouldn't have. She was bitchy—she freely admitted it—and she regretted it almost immediately, but the damage was done. Furious, Kurt stormed out before she could take back her angry words. Hurt, ashamed of herself, she told herself he'd be back when he cooled off. Then she'd apologize.

But even though he didn't have to work, he didn't come home that night...or the next. She'd had a sinking feeling he'd done something stupid, and it was all her fault. She knew how to push his buttons just as he did hers—if she hadn't let him goad her into snapping back, they might have been able to resolve the problem sensibly. But, no, she'd acted like a two-year-old, and so had he. And in the end, they'd both been hurt.

Still, she'd been willing to let bygones be bygones. It was Christmas Eve, and she'd wanted nothing more than to spend it with him. So she called the precinct to apologize, only to get Suzanne. Julianna's stomach still knotted at the memory. She didn't know how she'd done it, but Suzanne had always had a way of making her feel insecure. Maybe it was because she'd had an intimate relationship with Kurt before Julianna had even known him, or because the other woman had always seemed to know more about what was going on in her husband's life than she had, but Julianna had wanted nothing to do with her. Unfortunately, she was the precinct secretary, and all calls for the SWAT team went through her.

As much as it galled her, Julianna had had no choice but to leave her message for Kurt with her. The conversation should have been mercifully short—she'd just wanted Kurt to call her when he got a chance. The words were hardly out of her mouth, however, when Suzanne sweetly informed her that Kurt had volunteered to work a double shift so that some of the guys with families could be with their kids. That was such a wonderful thing for him to do, she'd purred, and so understanding of Julianna. If Suzanne had been in Julianna's shoes, she was sure she would have been quite upset at the idea of spending Christmas apart the first year of their marriage.

Numb, Julianna didn't remember if she'd even responded to Suzanne's comment. She'd just hung up. For hours afterward, she'd clung to the sure knowledge that she must have misunderstood. Regardless of how angry he was with her, he wouldn't have volunteered to work Christmas. Not this Christmas. It was their first as husband and wife, and nothing was more important than the two of them being together. Regardless of what Suzanne said, he'd find a way to be with her, even if he had volunteered to work.

But Christmas Eve night came and went, and there was no sign of Kurt. That's when she knew there was no mistake. Christmas Day was even worse. While all her friends were with their families, spending the holidays with people they loved, she was alone. And she didn't even know where her husband was.

But Suzanne did. And Kurt never called.

To this day, that still hurt. Oh, they made up when he finally came home the day after Christmas, but they never spoke about the argument…or the fact that they spent Christmas apart. Julianna couldn't bring herself to ask if he'd gotten the message she'd left for him—she didn't want to know. Because as long as she didn't know, she didn't have to wonder if he knew she wanted to speak to him and just didn't call or if Suzanne conveniently forgot to give him her message. And in the end, what did it matter? Either way, Suzanne still knew where he was when his wife didn't.

And that hurt. Still.

Horrified, she reminded herself that whatever happened that Christmas was ancient history. She'd put the past…and Kurt…behind her. He no longer had the power to hurt her.

So why did she suddenly feel like crying?

Kurt watched the painful emotions flicker in her brown eyes and knew exactly what she was thinking. *Don't!* he almost cried hoarsely. *Don't go there. You're beating yourself up over nothing!*

She'd always been so insecure where Suzanne was concerned, and he'd never understood why. *She* was the one he loved. *She* was the one he married, the one he'd wanted to spend the rest of his life with. Suzanne was just…Suzanne. Yes, they'd dated at one time before he met Julianna, but that was years ago, and he'd never come close to feeling for her what he did for Julianna. Suzanne was just a friend, nothing more. And when she'd needed a job, he hadn't thought twice about telling her there was an opening for a secretary at the precinct.

He'd have done the same thing for any friend, but when he'd casually told Julianna about it, she'd looked at him like she'd caught him in bed with the woman! Her eyes had held the same betrayal they held now, and then, as now, that had frustrated the hell out of him. He'd never once given her a reason not to trust him. Damn it, he'd loved her with all his heart! From the moment he'd first laid eyes on her, he knew she'd been the only one for him…but she hadn't believed it—she hadn't believed him. He'd thought there'd come a day when that wouldn't hurt. He'd been wrong.

Chapter 3

Caught up in the painful silence of the past, surrounded by the controlled chaos of the command center, they didn't see anyone but each other. Julianna would have sworn she couldn't hear anything but the pounding of her heart and words of accusation that she'd decided long ago had to remain unspoken. Then, suddenly, she thought she caught the sound of a muffled hum that was totally at odds with the tension of the night.

Surprised, she lifted her head like a deer scenting something totally unexpected, and listened. "What's that?"

A slow smile broke across Kurt's handsome face.

"If I'm not mistaken, the hostages are singing Christmas carols."

Julianna couldn't believe it, but there was no mistaking the sound of "Jingle Bells" on Christmas Eve. It floated on the cold night air like the promise of a single snowflake, lightening the spirits of the entire command center. All around them, stern FBI agents and D.C.'s finest broke into unexpected smiles. And for a little while, at least, it felt like Christmas.

Relief flooding her, Julianna didn't know if she wanted to laugh or cry. "They're okay," she said huskily, blinking back the tears that threatened to flood her eyes. "Thank God!"

"They're a gutsy group," Kurt said with a grin. "They can't carry a tune in a bucket, but that's the sweetest damn sound I've ever heard."

She had to agree. She couldn't imagine what it must be like for them to be cut off from the rest of the world and held against their will at gunpoint by a bunch of crazed commandoes who could decide to shoot them all at any moment. They had to be terrified. Still, they'd found a way to communicate when all hope had to seem lost to them.

Given the chance, she could have listened to them all night. They might have been slightly off-key, and there was no question that they were practically yelling in order to be heard, but they made beautiful music together. Still, everyone at the command center knew that the hostage-takers wouldn't appreciate their defiance. The repercussions could be deadly.

Standing at her side, listening as the merry refrain drifted down the cordoned-off street to the command center, Kurt came to the same conclusion. His smile fading, he swore softly. "They're taking their life in their hands. We've got to get them out of there before someone gets hurt."

As much as he would have liked to rush the mansion with guns blazing, however, he knew that would have only resulted in a bloodbath. For now, at least, the Chekagovian terrorists were calling the shots and there wasn't a damn thing they could do about it. "Where the hell is Ritka?" he growled, scowling. "Someone should have tracked him down by now."

Tom Foster joined them then, a pleased smile lighting his freckled face. "We've got good news, folks. State just called. They were able to come up with the home phone number of the secretary and gave her a call. She's calling Ritka even as we speak."

"Thank God!" Julianna breathed. "Did she know where he is? Did she give us a number where we can reach him?"

"He's spending the evening with friends in Alexandria," he replied. "She promised she would call him immediately, so we should be hearing from him any minute now."

"Why didn't she just give you his number and let us call him?" Kurt asked with a frown. "We could have sent someone to pick him up."

"Apparently, that's what she was afraid of," he said ruefully. "I assured her that Ritka wasn't in any trouble and there was no need to protect him since he hadn't done anything wrong, but she wasn't taking any chances. She insisted on calling him herself, so I agreed to give her five minutes. If we haven't heard from him by then, we're not only picking her up, we're going to turn Alexandria upside down looking for him. He's got diplomatic plates on his car. He shouldn't be that hard to find now that we have a general idea where he is."

Five minutes came and went, and the phone never rang. Swearing, Tom said tersely, "I was afraid of this. I should have never tried to deal with the secretary over the phone. It looks like we're going to have to pick her up, after all."

Excusing himself, he'd hardly stepped away to discuss the latest developments with his co-workers when the phone the diplomat was supposed to call on rang. "Take it," Kurt told Julianna. "You need to talk to him, anyway. I'll get Tom."

* * *

If Julianna had been the kind of insecure woman who was overly impressed with titles, she might have been flustered. But she wasn't concerned with the Chekagovian diplomat's position in life—only with what he knew about the terrorists that might get the hostages released.

So she introduced herself and said quietly, "Thank you for calling back so quickly, Mr. Ritka. Did your secretary explain what happened tonight at your former home in Georgetown?"

"Yes, she did," he replied grimly. "Were there any casualties?"

"We don't know at this point—the terrorists have refused to tell us anything until you turn yourself over to them. The man I spoke to also wanted a million dollars, a plane with enough fuel to reach Chekagovia and a music box. That one surprised me. It's an odd request, don't you think? Why would a bunch of terrorists want a music box?"

"They're terrorists, Ms. Stevens," he retorted. "Who knows what goes on in the heads of such people?"

"So you don't own a music box?"

"No."

His answer was short and firm, and Julianna had no choice but to accept it. She wasn't, however, quite sure she believed him, though she couldn't imagine why he would lie. Still puzzled, she switched gears. "What about the caller? He obviously has some issues with you. Do you have any idea who he is?"

"George Kartoff," he said in disgust. "He goes by many names—Gustov, Gunther, Gerhardt—but it matters not. He is the devil! Anyone in Chekagovia will tell you the same. He's the leader of a group called the Chekagovian Freedom Fighters. He and his followers claim they want to right decades of oppression and make my country a better place for all people, but they're really just a bunch of thieving malcontents who have spent the last nineteen months trying to destroy Chekagovia. All they're interested in is padding their own pockets, and they do that by terrorizing people into signing over their homes and businesses to them. Anyone who doesn't cooperate turns up dead within a matter of weeks. There's nothing they won't do to get what they want."

"So what do they hope to gain by taking over the mansion?" she asked. "They must know that the U.S. government isn't going to hand over you— or a million dollars—to them, regardless of how many people they take hostage. They have to be after something else."

"I don't know," he began, only to hesitate when another thought struck him. "My daughter?" he

asked suddenly, sharply. "Have her whereabouts
been accounted for? She said she was going to a
party, but she may have dropped by the mansion
first. She had to leave some things behind when we
moved, and just yesterday, she mentioned that she
wanted to go back for them. What if she was there
when the CFF seized the place?"

Julianna could hear the panic escalating in his
voice and quickly moved to reassure him. "I don't
think you need to worry about that, Mr. Ritka. The
Colton family was having a wedding reception
there. Surely your daughter wouldn't have tried to
retrieve her things at such a time. And even if she
had, I doubt that she would have been able to gain
entrance without an invitation."

"You don't know my Eva, Miss Stevens," he
countered in a voice that was full of pride and
worry. "She is a beautiful girl, and smart, as you
Americans say, as a whip. She is headstrong,
though, like her mother was, and when she makes
up her mind to do something, there's no stopping
her. If she decided to go after her things tonight,
then she was in the mansion when the CFF took it
over."

"*If,*" she stressed, "she went back for her things
tonight. Just because you don't know where she is
doesn't mean she's at the mansion. You said your-

self that she was going to a party. Are you sure she
didn't?''

"No," he admitted.

"There you go, then," she said easily. "Does
she have a cell phone? Why don't you call her?''

"That's a good idea. I'll do that right now and
call you back after I've spoken to her.''

He hung up, not giving her a chance to say a
word, only to call back less than a minute later.
"She doesn't answer.''

There was no mistaking that he was worried, and
Julianna couldn't blame him. If Eva Ritka was as
impulsive as her father claimed, then there was a
very good possibility that she really was in the mansion. Considering how ruthless the CFF was, Julianna didn't even want to think about what might
happen to the diplomat's daughter if her identity
was discovered.

"I'm headed for Georgetown," Helmut Ritka
told her abruptly, making a decision. "There's been
some kind of accident—the traffic is crawling. I'll
be there as soon as I can.''

He hung up, and when Julianna followed suit,
she glanced up to find Kurt scowling down at her.
He'd heard every word of her side of the conversation, and it was obvious he wasn't at all pleased.
"It might not be as bad as it sounds," she began.

That was as far as she got. "The hell it isn't,"

he growled. "Ritka's daughter's in there, isn't she? She went back for something she left behind, and now the hostage-takers have her. Damn it, what the hell is wrong with the woman? If she forgot something, why didn't she just have the Coltons send it to her? I'm sure they wouldn't have minded."

"We don't have any evidence yet that she's actually in the mansion," she reminded him, playing devil's advocate. "She was invited to a party—"

"But her father thinks she's there, and he knows her better than anyone. What did he say about the hostage-takers? Does he have any idea who they are?"

"Apparently, the country's been terrorized by a group of thugs who call themselves the Chekagovian Freedom Fighters," she replied. "Ritka seemed pretty certain that the contact I spoke to was the leader. His name's George Kartoff, but he apparently goes by a number of aliases. If he's as bad as he sounds, Eva Ritka better pray she doesn't fall into his hands."

Kurt swore softly. "It was bad enough when we thought we just had to worry about Senator Colton's identity being discovered. Now Ritka's daughter is added to the mix. I'm not even going to ask about who the rest of the guests are. Somebody better call the Kennedys, though, and make sure they're in

Hyannis Port. With the way things are going, one of them is probably the groom's godparent.''

Her lips twitching, Julianna bit back a smile. ''I think someone already checked that, but if you need Ted's number, I'm sure Tom can get it for you.''

Worried about just what kind of trouble Eva Ritka could be in, Kurt started to snap back that all members of Congress had already been accounted for, only to see the twinkle dancing in her eyes. It had been a long time since she'd looked at him that way, and for just a moment, the need to reach for her was almost more than he could bear. How could he have forgotten what her teasing did to him?

''Kurt? Hello? Hey, what'd I say? Are you okay?''

No! he almost blurted out. He'd spent the last three years of his life without her, and he was mad as hell at himself and her for that. They'd loved each other more than any other couple he knew. How the devil had they ended up divorced?

If they'd been anywhere else but there, he would have demanded answers not only of her, but of himself. But there was no time for that…not when people's lives were at stake. Reminding himself to focus on work, which was the only thing that had gotten him through the awful days and months after their divorce, he growled, ''Nothing. Not a damn thing. Tom needs to know about Ritka's daughter...and the CFF. I'd better go find him.'' And without giving her a chance to say so much as a word, he stalked off.

Chapter 4

Julianna glanced around the command center and frowned. Something was wrong. Outwardly, everything seemed perfectly normal, but there was an increased tension in the air, and she didn't have a clue why. Where were Kurt and Tom? They both should have been back by now. Any second now, Kartoff—or whatever his real name was—was going to call, wanting some answers about the CFF's demands, and she didn't have any. And that left her in a vulnerable position when it came to negotiating. How could she negotiate a deal when she didn't know what her options were?

Lost in her musings and scowling down at the

red phone that linked her to the house, she didn't see Tom and Kurt crossing the compound toward her until they were almost upon her. "Thank God!" she breathed. "Where have you two been? Kartoff's going to call any minute, and I don't know what to say to him."

"We've got another complication," Tom said gravely. "We've had reports that there are bombs on all the bridges leading into D.C. from Virginia. It's probably just a prank, but we have to take it seriously. We've got to shut down the bridges, Julianna."

"What? You can't! What if Ritka is still in Alexandria? It'll be hours before he'll be able to get here."

"It gets worse," Kurt said, his expression as grim as Tom's. "One of the Ritkas' former neighbors said they spoke to Eva before she went into the mansion right after the reception started. The elderly neighbor said Eva mentioned she was back to pick up something she'd left behind in the move. The neighbor never saw her leave."

Julianna paled. "There has to be some kind of mistake. If she arrived right after the reception started, she had plenty of time to collect her things before the terrorists broke up the wedding. What's she been doing all this time?"

"I'd like to know the answer to that, myself," Tom said.

Julianna knew as well as the two men did that there was a chance they'd never get to ask Eva Ritka that or any other question. The terrorists obviously wanted to get their hands on her father. If they discovered they had Ritka's daughter, Julianna didn't even want to think what they might do to her in revenge for whatever wrong they thought Ritka had done to them.

Suddenly, the phone linking the command center to the house rang. For a long moment, the three of them just stood there, knowing that Kartoff could be calling to inform them that the CFF no longer needed Ritka now that they had his daughter.

Her heart slamming hard against her ribs, Julianna still somehow managed to answer the phone with a voice that was as calm as a saint's. "This is Julianna Stevens. What can I do for you, Mr. Kartoff?"

If he was surprised that she'd figured out his name, he gave no sign of it. "Maybe I didn't make myself clear, Miss Stevens," he said in a tone that was as cold as hell. "We want Helmut Ritka, and you've had more than enough time to produce him. If he is not delivered here to the mansion within five minutes, along with the money and the music box, I will give the order for the hostages to be shot one by one, every five minutes, until our demands are met. The clock is ticking, Miss Stevens. Unless you want the deaths of innocent people on your head, I suggest you get busy.''

Horrified, Julianna told herself he was bluffing. Then she remembered Ritka had said Kartoff was ruthless and had killed his own people in Chekagovia. She had to believe him. ''Ritka's on his way,'' she said quickly. ''But all the bridges are shut down because of a bomb scare and he's stuck in traffic.''

''Then I guess one of the hostages should prepare to die,'' he retorted.

''No, wait! He's trying to meet your demands. He just needs a little more time. Please be patient. He's on his way.''

For an answer, Kartoff merely hung up.

''What is it?'' Kurt asked sharply when Julianna dropped the phone back onto its base and looked up at him with stricken eyes. ''What did he say?''

''He's going to start killing the hostages one by one if their demands aren't met in five minutes.''

She looked so horrified that Kurt instinctively started to reach for her, only to remind himself that he no longer had the right to touch her. ''Don't let him get to you,'' he growled. ''He's yanking your chain. The hostages are the only safety net he's got. He wouldn't dare kill them.''

''That's right,'' Tom added curtly, scowling down the street at the mansion. Surrounded on all sides by the floodlights the police had erected, the house sat as silent as a tomb, the Christmas lights in its windows still twinkling merrily. ''Kartoff's not an idiot. He knows the only reason we haven't stormed the building is because of the hostages. If he starts killing them off, he's signing his own death warrant.''

Julianna wanted to believe them, but she couldn't forget Kartoff's cold-blooded words. He'd already proven himself to be a man who was capable of anything. If he killed Chekagovians, the very people he claimed to want to help, why would he hesitate to put a bullet in the head of innocent Americans who were no longer useful to him? What, after all, did he have to lose? The authorities knew who he was. Whatever happened tonight, the situation was going to end badly for him.

Suddenly chilled to the bone, she pulled her coat closer around her, but the cold night air only snaked around her ankles and drifted up under the hem of her dress. She was dressed for a party, she thought numbly, and across the street, a party of terrified guests were waiting to be executed. When had the world become so crazy?

One by one, the minutes slipped away with agonizing slowness, and with each tick of the clock, the tension in her belly tightened until she felt like she would scream if something didn't happen soon. Five minutes wound down to three, then two, then finally one. And when minutes gave way to seconds, she held her breath and didn't even realize she was shaking her head. "No…no…no."

The night was as still and soundless as death. All around her, FBI agents, police and emergency medical personnel stood rooted to the ground, waiting, their collective gazes all fixed on the mansion. No one dared to move, let alone breathe. Then suddenly, with the last tick of the clock, a single gunshot exploded in the night.

"No!"

Later, Julianna never remembered crying out in horror. Time itself seemed to freeze. Just a moment before, the command center had been a beehive of activity as agents and police communicated on walkie-talkies and cell phones, coordinating positions and strategies. But with a single shot, the terrorists brought everyone within hearing distance to a dead stop.

How long they all stood there in shock, Julianna couldn't have said. She knew it had to only be minutes—it felt like an eternity. Then somewhere behind her, someone cursed. With nothing more than that, the spell that held everyone motionless was broken. Grim-faced SWAT team members and FBI agents swore roundly, but Julianna never heard them. With a choked cry, she turned into Kurt's arms.

As stunned as she was by the turn of events, Kurt folded his arms around her and pulled her tight against him. His eyes still trained in disbelief on the mansion down the street, he swore softly. "Son of a bitch! I can't believe the bastard actually did it."

"It's my fault," Julianna mumbled against his shoulder. "He didn't believe me when I told him Ritka was on his way. I should have called him back and made him understand that I don't play games. He had no way of knowing that—"

"What the hell are you talking about?" Kurt cut in, scowling as he grabbed her upper arms and held her back far enough so he could see her pale, stricken face. "You aren't to blame for this!"

"Of course I am. I was the only one he was in contact with. Something I said must have convinced him that talking wasn't going to get him anywhere, so he was forced to do something drastic."

"The man's a murderer, sweetheart. This wasn't an act of desperation—it was an act of terror. It's no different than what he's done to his own people in Chekagovia. He either gets his way or he kills people.''

"But it's my job to see that something like this doesn't happen. Someone's dead because of me.''

Tears pooled in those big, beautiful brown eyes of hers, and it was more than Kurt could stand. In the past, she'd ranted and raved and even thrown things occasionally, and he'd taken it all in stride. Her tears, however, had always been his undoing, though he'd never let her know that. There were some things a man was better off keeping to himself.

But it had been too long since he'd held her, and the sight of her tears tore him apart. Unable to stop himself, he pulled her back into his arms and didn't give a thought to the fact that they might be drawing the interested eyes of his co-workers. The only thing that mattered was comforting her.

"Hush,'' he scolded softly. "No one expects you to be able to reason with a madman. If someone's dead tonight, it's because of Kartoff's orders, not because you did anything wrong.''

She was determined to beat herself up—Kurt could almost feel another argument rising up in her—but before she could say another word, the faint sound of carolling drifted toward them on the cold night air. And with each passing second, the singing got louder.

"Listen!" he urged, drawing back to grin down at her. "The hostages are singing again, only this time, they're singing 'God Rest Ye, Merry Gentlemen.' Listen to the words of the song, sweetheart."

In the sudden hushed silence of Christmas Eve, the combined voices of the hostages sounded like a choir of angels singing from on high. *"God rest ye, merry gentlemen, let nothing you dismay..."* With the last phrase, their voices rose significantly. Their message couldn't have been any clearer if it had been spelled out in lights.

His green eyes alight with good humor, Kurt chuckled. "Kartoff must think he's been saddled with the hostages from hell. Everytime he thinks he's on the verge of intimidating us into doing what he wants, they ruin it for him."

Stunned, Julianna blinked. "He was bluffing?" Even as she asked the question, she felt like a fool for even voicing it. Of course, he was bluffing! Kurt and Tom had warned her that he wouldn't be stupid enough to risk the lives of his captives, and they were right. Only an idiot would kill the only bargaining tool he had, and Kartoff had already proven he was no idiot.

Just that quickly, she was furious. Steam all but spilling from her ears, she jerked free of Kurt's touch and grabbed the phone to the mansion. A split second later, Kartoff answered the phone, and she blasted him with a spate of angry words. "That was a stupid thing to do, Kartoff! In case you don't realize it, I'm the only friend you've got out here, and what you just did was despicable. You try pulling another stunt like that, and I'm turning you over to the SWAT team. Have I made myself clear?"

There was dead silence at the other end of the line, and too late, Julianna realized letting her temper get the best of her may have been a mistake. But damn it, the jackass deserved it!

Still furious, she listened to his nearly soundless breathing at the other end of the line and knew better than to rush in and break the silence. That would only put her in a position of weakness, and that was just what Kartoff wanted. She'd be damned if she'd give him the satisfaction.

So she stood there with the phone pressed tightly to her ear for what seemed like an eternity, praying she hadn't just put the hostages lives in more danger than they already were. Then, just when she was sure she couldn't stand the silence another second, Kartoff growled, "There'll be no more tricks...on one condition."

Relief almost buckled Julianna's knees. *Yes!* she wanted to shout, but she couldn't. Not yet. She was finally making some progress, but there would be no celebrating until the hostages were free—and they were still a long way from that.

Her voice cool and even, she said, "And that would be?"

"You come here—to the mansion—and meet with me."

Stunned, Julianna couldn't believe she'd heard him correctly. "I beg your pardon."

"My comrades and I want our story told to the world, and you are the person to do it. If you want to guarantee the safety of the hostages until Helmut Ritka is turned over to us, you will come here alone and listen to our grievances. Then you will go in front of the television cameras that have set up camp behind the police barriers and tell everyone why we despise Helmut Ritka."

"But—"

"If you care about the hostages as much as you claim you do, Miss Stevens, I don't think this is too much to ask," he said smoothly. "You have my word you won't be harmed, so why do you hesitate? Don't you believe I will protect you from my comrades?"

He was taunting her, playing with her emotions, blatantly manipulating her. Julianna had expected no less from a hostage-taker. After all, he was in a hell of a spot. He and his commandoes were surrounded by an army of law enforcement officials, and the longer the situation dragged out, the less chance they had of walking out of the mansion with Helmut Ritka and a million bucks. They'd be lucky if they made it out alive, and then they had nothing to look forward to except a long prison term…unless he could make points with the press and win sympathy for their cause. Considering the circumstances, that wasn't likely to happen, but he had to try. And she was his microphone.

And she was all right with that. Because she had an agenda of her own. The more she could keep him talking, the greater her chance of resolving the situation peacefully.

Making a snap decision, she said, "Actually, I do believe you. I'll be there in ten minutes."

Chapter 5

"If you agreed to what I think you just agreed to, you can forget it," Kurt said ominously the second she hung up. "You're not going anywhere."

"He wants to talk—"

"Then let him call Larry King," he growled. "You're not available."

"The hell I'm not," she snapped, irritation flashing in her dark eyes at his autocratic tone. "In case you've forgotten, I'm a hostage negotiator, Mister High and Mighty. I can't negotiate the release of the hostages if I can't talk to the man who's holding them captive."

"I didn't say you couldn't talk to him...just not

face-to-face on his own turf. It's too dangerous. If someone has to go in, it's going to be either me or Tom.''

Frustrated, Julianna wanted to shake him. ''Don't be ridiculous. You know he's not going to trust a man. I'm not a threat to him—''

''Which is exactly my point,'' he cut in. ''If he decided to add you to the hostage list, there wouldn't be a damn thing you could do about it. Forget it. You're not going.''

He had that look on his face, the one that said he'd made up his mind and nothing she could say was going to change it, and that infuriated Julianna. Who the devil did he think he was? She didn't answer to him. And she certainly didn't need his permission to do her job! Her brown eyes narrowing dangerously, she said coolly, ''Charlie might have something to say about that. Shall I call him and see?''

Standing toe-to-toe with her, Kurt ground his teeth on an oath. Little witch! So she was going to pull out the big guns, was she? Why wasn't he surprised? Charles Baker was the chief of police and thought there was nothing Julianna couldn't pull off when she set her mind to it. If she told him she needed to speak to Kartoff alone, there was no question that he'd approve the idea.

Just that easily, she won the argument, and she knew it. Triumph flashed in her eyes, and even though she didn't smile, Kurt knew she wanted to. And it was that, more than anything, that pushed him over the edge. "This isn't a game, damn it," he growled, and reached for her.

It happened so quickly, he didn't have time to question the wisdom of his actions. One second, he was furious with her, and the next, she was in his arms. He didn't remember reaching for her—hell, he didn't remember his own name when his mouth came down on hers. His brain shut down and all he could do was feel.

Too long, he thought with a groan, dragging her closer. It had been too long since he'd kissed her, too long since he'd held her and ached to lose himself in her. He'd forgotten how soft she was, how sweet, how perfectly she filled his arms and fit against him. Need swept over him in a hot wave of longing, and for the span of a heartbeat, all he wanted to do was sweep her up in his arms and carry her off into the dark, away from the floodlights that lit the entire block like a car lot, away from old hurts and bad memories.

Then from somewhere in the distance, church bells softly played "It Came Across a Midnight Clear." Brought back to the present with a jolt, he remembered everything…their divorce, the last three years of loneliness, the hostages. And just that quickly, it was time to go back to work.

One second Julianna was in his arms and loving it, and the next, she was put from him with an abruptness that left her blinking in surprise. Dazed, her heart pounding, she swayed toward him and only just then saw the hard expression on his face. That brought her crashing back to earth as nothing else could.

Mortified, she stiffened, hot color flooding her cheeks. She couldn't have done what she thought she just did! she thought wildly. She wouldn't kiss Kurt in the middle of a hostage situation. She wouldn't kiss him period! The stress was just getting to her and playing tricks with her mind. There was no other explanation.

But even as she tried to convince herself this was all a bad dream, she realized her pulse was thumping like crazy and the spicy scent of Kurt's cologne clung to her coat. Tom cleared his throat, reminding them both of his presence, and when her gaze met his, there was no mistaking the clear glint of understanding humor she saw there. Silently swallowing a moan, she wanted to die right there on the spot. Not only had she lost her mind and kissed Kurt like there was no tomorrow, she'd done it right in front of the FBI, District police and the cameras of every television station within a hundred-mile radius! She'd never be able to live this down.

Normally, she would have made some kind of excuse and made a hasty retreat, but she never got the chance. Suddenly, Tom's walkie-talkie sputtered to life and a gravelly voice growled, "Two hostages just escaped from the mansion. Paramedics are needed at the northwest quadrant."

For a split second, no one in the command center moved. Then a shout went up, and suddenly everyone was pressing toward the tall man in full military dress uniform and the delicate blonde he carried so gently in his arms.

"Careful," he said roughly as paramedics rushed forward to help. "She hurt her ankle—"

"It's just a sprain," the blonde said, only to wince as she was lowered to a stretcher.

Paramedics quickly began to examine the injured woman, but that didn't stop FBI agents and SWAT team members from surrounding them, all throwing questions at once. In a matter of seconds, everyone in the command center knew the hostages' names. Eva Ritka and Major Billy Colton.

Amazed, Julianna couldn't believe it. How in the world had Ritka's daughter managed to escape Kartoff and his men? Did Kartoff know who he'd let slip through his fingers? What did Eva know about the music box?

Before she could ask, one of the paramedics announced, "Her ankle appears to be broken. It's very serious. We need to get her to the hospital for X rays right away."

"I can answer any questions for Ms. Ritka," Major Colton said to the agent next to him. "And I want a police escort to accompany her to the hospital." Concerned, Major Colton, who hadn't left Eva's side, only had time for a private word of encouragement before the stretcher that carried her was loaded into the ambulance. The major stood there staring after her for a long quiet moment, before he turned to face the questions.

Introducing himself, Tom said, "It's nice to meet you, Major. Your call earlier helped." Shaking hands with him, he introduced Julianna and Kurt, then asked, "How'd you manage to escape? We thought Kartoff had everyone rounded up in the ballroom."

"We got lucky," he said. "We were in the attic when the rebels took the mansion. The men searched the house, but my cousin warned me in Comanche that the band of terrorists from Chekagovia were after Eva. We managed to escape onto the roof just in time. That's where we were when I called 911. Unfortunately, I dropped the phone during the call, and we've been trying to make our way down from the roof ever since. If it hadn't been for that old oak tree on the north side of the house, we'd still be up there."

"You climbed down a tree in full military dress?" Kurt asked, admiration glinting in is eyes. "And the lady had on heels and a party dress? It's a wonder the two of you didn't break your necks."

"Eva nearly did," he said grimly. "I never meant for her to get hurt."

"Can you tell us anything about a music box?" Julianna asked. "Kartoff—the rebel leader—is demanding it be turned over to him, but no one seems to know what he's talking about."

"All I know is that Eva's grandfather gave it to her after her mother died," he replied promptly. "He claimed it was a national treasure and the key to her country."

Surprised, Kurt frowned. "What the hell does that mean?"

"Your guess is as good as mine," the major replied. "Eva couldn't imagine what it meant, either, and her grandfather never explained it to her."

"Did she find the music box?"

He nodded. "I put it in her coat pocket—which is still hanging in the closet at the top of the stairs on the second floor."

"You mean, after everything she went through to get it, she had to leave it behind?" Tom asked incredulously.

For the first time, a hint of a smile curved the major's stern mouth. "Like I said, we were in the attic when the rebels forced their way into the house. We couldn't go back down to the second floor without getting caught."

"Wait a minute," Julianna said, confused. "You said your cousin warned you the rebels were after Eva. The Ritkas moved out of the house over two months ago. How did Kartoff know Eva was in the house? She's not friends with the Coltons, is she?"

"She met my brother, Jesse Colton who works for the National Security Agency, right after she and her father moved out, but I didn't get the impression that they were friends or anything."

"So how did Kartoff know where to find her? Did he have her followed?"

He shrugged. "That's a possibility, but if I were you, I'd take a good look at her limo driver. He was jumpy…nervous."

Surprised, Julianna arched a brow. "When did you meet her limo driver?"

"When I talked her into staying," he retorted promptly. "He was hanging around, waiting to drive her home, so I gave him some money and told him to take the rest of the night off. I'd see her home."

"So he left?"

"Not willingly, at least not at first, which made

no sense. It's Christmas Eve, for heaven's sake. Most people would jump at the chance to take the night off with extra cash in their pocket. But not this guy. He kept looking around, like he was waiting for something to happen, and coming up with excuses to stay.''

"Do you think he was involved with Kartoff?" Tom asked sharply.

"I do," he said angrily. "He was certainly suspicious. My hunch is that he informed the terrorists that Eva was at the mansion. Considering everything that's happened, I wouldn't rule him out as a suspect.''

"It won't hurt to bring him in for questioning," Tom replied. "Let's put an APB out on him and see what he has to say for himself. You didn't happen to get a look at his plates, did you?"

Grinning, the major promptly rattled them off. "He was driving a white limo, propably a 2000 model, though I'm not positive about that. His name's Jerry—I didn't catch his last name. He was wearing a white shirt, black bow tie and black slacks. He was about five-ten, and slender. He had a cap on, so I really didn't notice the color of his hair. I think it was dark. Helmut Ritka can probably give you more details. Apparently, he uses the limo on a regular basis.''

"Speaking of Ritka," Julianna said, "has anyone called to let him know his daughter is all right?"

"Someone from the hospital has probably called him."

"Maybe, but he was awfully worried about her," she replied. "I'll call and see what he knows about Jerry."

"I'd like to call the hospital," the major said, falling in step with her as she headed for the phone bank. "Just to see how Eva is doing."

His tone was serious, but Julianna wasn't fooled. She'd seen how protective he was of the diplomat's daughter—there were obvious romantic sparks between them. And she couldn't help but envy them that. If only she and Kurt—

Suddenly realizing where her thoughts had drifted, she stiffened. There would be no *if onlys,* she told herself sternly. She and Kurt were finished, and she couldn't, wouldn't, torture herself with wondering where they would be now if they hadn't divorced.

Clinging firm to that resolve, she quickly called Helmut Ritka. "Your daughter has been found, sir," she informed him the second he came on the line. "She *was* in the mansion, but she managed to escape with the help of Major Billy Colton."

"Thank God!" he breathed. "Is she all right?

Why didn't she answer her cell phone? I want to speak to her—''

"Her cell phone was lost in the escape," she explained. "And I'm afraid you can't speak to her just yet. She's at the emergency room at District Medical Center."

"What?"

"She's all right," she quickly assured him. "She injured her ankle during the escape and apparently broke it."

"I have to call the hospital," he said worriedly. "I'm sorry, Ms. Stevens. I know I promised to help you, and I will, but first I must talk to my daughter."

Not surprised, Julianna understood perfectly. He was a parent first, a diplomat second. She couldn't fault him for that. "Of course you need to talk to her. I did want to discuss a new development with you. What do you know about your daughter's limo driver?"

"Jerry?" he said in surprise. "He's always prompt and courteous. Why do you ask?"

"Because he was acting very nervous this evening. He didn't want to leave when your daughter was invited to stay for the wedding reception. When Kartoff and his men stormed the mansion, they were looking for the music box *and* your daughter.

Jerry was the only one who knew where she planned to be tonight.''

"You think he told Kartoff?''

"It's a reasonable deduction, but first we need to talk to him. What do you know about him?''

"Not much,'' he said regretfully. "His full name is Jerald Trolo. His parents are Chekagovian, but Jerry was born and raised in America. He's twenty-five, and lives in D.C. with his wife and child.''

"And you still don't know anything about the music box they were looking for?''

"No. As I told you before, I have no knowledge of this music box everyone is so obsessed with.''

He sounded irritated and defensive, and Julianna didn't believe him for a second. Every instinct she had told her he knew something he wasn't telling, but she could hardly grill him about it on the phone. Face-to-face, however, was another matter. "I hope we can still count on you for your help once you're sure your daughter is all right,'' she said easily. "Any help you can give us with Kartoff will be invaluable.''

"Of course,'' he said quickly. "Hopefully, I will be there within a half hour. The traffic is starting to move.''

Hanging up, Julianna quickly relayed the latest information to Tom and Kurt, who, in turn, made sure the police and agents in the field were updated.

"He still claims he doesn't know anything about the music box," she added. "I think it's time to see what Kartoff has to say about it. If he expects us to turn Ritka over to him along with a million dollars and the music box, the least he can do is explain the significance of it."

Kurt couldn't believe she was serious. "This is a joke, right? You're not still going, are you?"

"Of course I am. There are still a hundred and ninety-eight hostages who need rescuing. I'm not going to walk away from them just because two managed to escape." Turning to Tom, she said, "Now that Kartoff is finally willing to talk, we have to seize the opportunity and go with it. If he'd consider talking to you or Kurt, that'd be different, but he won't. He's not going to allow anyone else into the mansion but me. I have to go."

If he wanted to stop her, all he had to do was say no. He didn't, but there was no doubt that he had strong reservations. Frowning, he studied her critically through narrowed eyes that missed little. "Are you willing to wear a wire?" he asked finally.

"No!" Kurt exploded. "What are you trying to do? Get her killed?"

She started to snap back at him, only to remember the kiss he'd given her right before the major and Eva escaped. She didn't even want to think

about it. "No one's going to kill me," she said
coolly. "And yes, Tom, I will wear a wire. Kartoff's only stipulation was that I come alone."

"He knows you're with the Bureau," the agent
said, ignoring Kurt's glower. "I imagine he'll be
expecting it. You might as well wear a camera,
too."

Another man might have been intimidated by
Kurt's muttered expletive, but Tom merely lifted a
brow at him. "Was there something else you
wanted to say, Kurt?"

"Yes, damn it! You're going too far. She's not
an agent—"

"Or an idiot," Julianna added sweetly, too
sweetly. "I'll be careful."

"Careful may not be good enough," he retorted.
"This isn't your run-of-the-mill criminal you're
dealing with. He's a terrorist, for God's sake! He
doesn't need a reason to kill you."

"He won't."

"Oh, so now you're a psychic? You've never
even met the man. How can you possibly predict
what he's going to do?"

"You always said that the reason you'd never
gotten shot on the job was because you followed
your gut. Why can't I do the same thing? Aren't
my instincts as good as yours?"

Put that way, he was damned, regardless of how

he answered. Another man might have been able to look her in the eye and tell her her instincts stunk, but he wasn't that good a liar. One of the first things that had drawn him to her was the way she could talk to anyone. She was friendly and caring, and had a way of drawing information out of people that had always stunned him. But that didn't mean she had any business walking into the middle of a hostage situation!

"Of course they are, but—"

"Then what's the problem?"

Wasn't it obvious? he wanted to snap. *She* was the problem! She—his ex-wife, damn it! It'd been three years since they'd walked away from each other with divorce papers in their hands; he should have been over her. Like it or not, he wasn't. And it was all her fault. She was the one who'd come to a hostage standoff dressed for a party. How was a man supposed to ignore a beautiful ex-wife when she looked good enough to eat in her long red dress and high heels? And the way she'd kissed him back when he hadn't been able to stop himself from kissing her...how the hell was he supposed to forget that? Did she really think he could just stand by without saying a word and let her walk into danger when he was still reeling from her kiss?

"I don't care what assurances Kartoff gave

you," he said flatly, "the man's a murderer. I don't trust him."

He might as well have saved his breath. He never saw Tom make the call for technical assistance, but suddenly a middle-aged woman agent appeared at Julianna's side and told her, "We'll need to conceal the equipment under your dress in case you're asked to take off your coat. I know it's cold, dear, but I need to see what you're wearing."

Scowling, Kurt stepped forward. "This is ridiculous!"

That was as far as he got. Julianna slipped out of her coat, and his mouth went dry. The sparkling red dress that fell modestly to her ankles wasn't nearly as modest on top. Except for two skinny little straps, her shoulders were bare.

"No!" he said hoarsely. Where was her brain? She couldn't wear that to meet a terrorist! "Damn it, Tom," he growled, "put your eyes back in your head and tell her she can't do this!"

"Not wearing that dress," he agreed dryly. "Mary, what else have we got that she can wear?"

"We're about the same size," the other agent replied, eyeing Julianna critically. "I've got a suit from the dry cleaners in the back of my car that should fit her. She can change in the first aid tent."

"No!" Kurt cried in exasperation as the two women walked past him without stopping. Kurt turned to Tom. "What's wrong with everyone? It's not just the dress! She's not ready for this!"

His auburn brows knit in a frown, Tom said, "Don't you think you're being a tad overprotective? She's a criminal psychologist, Kurt. She's negotiated hostage releases before."

"But she's never been in the field!" He knew— just because they hadn't spoken in three years didn't mean he hadn't kept up with her career. "She's not an agent. She won't have a clue what to do if she gets into trouble."

Tom disagreed. "She's got a sharp head on her shoulders. And Mary will fix her up nicely. We'll know everything that's going on. If the situation turns ugly, we'll—"

"What?" Kurt taunted coldly. "Rush in with guns blazing? She'll be dead by then."

"It isn't going to come to that," the agent assured him. "The last thing Kartoff wants is a hostage who came in under a white flag. It won't look good on the evening news."

Kurt wanted to argue that Kartoff didn't care about image or he never would have terrorized his own people the way he had, but what was the point? Julianna was determined to go through with this madness, and it was obvious that Tom wasn't going to do anything to stop her. And there wasn't a damn thing Kurt could do about it.

Worry eating at him, he almost went looking for Julianna to try to talk some sense into her one last time, but it was already too late for that. Before he could even take a step toward the first aid tent, the two women were crossing the command center and heading straight for where he and Tom stood.

Mary matched her stride for stride, but the only one he saw was Julianna. A monk couldn't have objected to the black pant suit and white blouse she'd changed into, and if she wore a wire and camera, they were well concealed. She looked businesslike, professional...and scared.

Thank God! he sighed, noting the shadows in her eyes and the stiffness with which she carried herself. She'd had time to think about the risk she was about to take and finally come to her senses. It was about damn time!

Relieved, he started to congratulate her on her good sense when she and Mary joined them, but she never gave him the chance. "I'm ready," she told Tom before he could even open his mouth. "Wish me luck."

Stunned, Kurt growled, "You can't be serious! Damn it, Julianna, we all know you're scared—it's written all over your face. And that's okay. No one's going to think less of you if you change your mind."

Surprised that he thought she might think that, she said, "Good. But I haven't changed my mind. That doesn't mean I'm not scared—only an idiot wouldn't be—but I'm doing the right thing."

He was furious with her, but she didn't have time to argue with him. She'd told Kartoff she'd be there in ten minutes, and it was already well past that. Turning to Mary, she smiled tremulously. "I feel like a walking sound stage. Are all my bells and whistles activated?"

"They're recording even as we speak. Ready?"

Her heart picking up speed, Julianna nodded. It seemed like she'd been working toward this moment from her senior year in high school, when she'd first decided to study criminal psychology. She was more than ready to put her years of study and training to work. That didn't, however, mean that she didn't share Kurt's fears. She was walking into a den of unpredictable terrorists—anything could happen. She knew that and accepted it...and prayed that her guardian angels stayed close by her side.

It was time to go—Tom and Mary would go with her as far as the barriers the police had hastily erected, sealing off the mansion—but she couldn't leave, not yet. Not when Kurt looked so furious with her for deliberately placing herself in danger. She shouldn't have cared what he thought—just hours ago, she would have sworn that she didn't. But that was before she saw him again, kissed him again.

Everything had changed, yet nothing had. She didn't know what the future would bring for either one of them, but she did know that if something went wrong tonight, she was glad that she'd had this time with the only man she'd ever loved. Giving in to impulse, she reached for his hand and squeezed it tightly. A moment later, she turned and walked away.

Don't! he almost cried. Fear a sick feeling in his stomach, he wanted to grab her, to stop her, to pull her into his arms and hold her until this was all over. For the first time, he realized how she must have felt every time his job took him into danger. No wonder she hated his work so much! He'd never understood…until now, when he was the one left behind with all the worry.

Chapter 6

Overhead, the thunderous blades of a helicopter beat the cold night air, keeping perfect time to the beat of her heart as Julianna slowly started walking down the drive to the mansion. Too late, she wondered if she'd lost her mind. Kurt was right—this was crazy! What had ever possessed her to agree to this? If she wanted to kill herself, there were easier, faster ways—like jumping off a bridge. At least, then, there wouldn't be any torture involved. Or rape.

Her steps slow and steady, she faltered, her stomach turning over at the thought. She hadn't considered rape, hadn't even thought of it. Surely, the terrorists wouldn't...

Unable to finish the thought, horrifying images flashing before her widened eyes, she stopped in her tracks. She couldn't do this. It was too dangerous. Once she was inside the mansion, she would be at Kartoff's mercy, and she didn't think the man even knew the meaning of the word. If he wanted to talk to her, he could do it on the front lawn, in full view of the battalion of law enforcement agents who had the place surrounded. Then she would feel safe.

But as she started to turn back to the command center, she knew Kartoff would never agree to such a suggestion. And right now, there was nothing she or anyone else could do to force him to cooperate. He held all the cards, and he knew it. If she was going to have even a chance of negotiating the hostages' release, she had to do things his way.

She wanted—needed—to believe he wouldn't hurt her. After all, even though he'd made threats against the hostages, they were still singing Christmas songs whenever they got the chance. Surely, they wouldn't be doing that if Kartoff and his men had turned against the women.

Hanging on to that thought for dear life, she slowly continued her lonely walk toward the mansion. All around her, she could feel the eyes of the FBI and SWAT team members drilling into her, watching not only her, but the windows of the mansion, as well. She didn't doubt for a minute that if they saw something they didn't like, they'd stop her well before she reached the mansion and call her back to the command center.

As she approached the steps of the mansion, the silence that followed her was broken only by the thundering of her own heart. Then, before she knew it, she was knocking at the front door and there was no going back.

The door was jerked opened almost immediately, but before she could say a word, she was pulled inside and a blanket was thrown over her head. "Do as you're told," a thick, unfamiliar guttural voice growled when she gasped, "and you won't be harmed."

Blinded, fear spilling into her stomach like hot lava, all she could think of was that the tiny camera that was embedded in the top button of her suit jacket was covered up. Back at the command center, Kurt and Tom were as blinded as she. Panic tightened like a fist around her throat, choking her, and without thinking, she instinctively began to pull at the blanket. She had to get it off so they could see the terrorists and possibly identify them.

"No!" her companion said coldly, grabbing her hand. "You will leave it on until you are told you can take it off."

"I can't! I can't breathe—"

"Then you will be restrained," he retorted, and grabbed her hand.

Her heart suddenly stopping in midbeat, Julianna froze at the feel of his fingers slipping around her wrist. Was Kurt right, after all? she wondered wildly. Was all of Kartoff's talk about wanting to tell his story just a trick to get her in the building? "Please," she choked. "Kartoff promised—"

"That you wouldn't be harmed," another, more familiar, male voice said coolly. "We will talk in the kitchen, Miss Stevens. Do as you're told, and there will be no problem."

He didn't have to tell her twice. "I'll go peacefully," she said quietly. "I was just startled."

The men exchanged a few words in what Julianna recognized as German, and a few seconds later, she was led toward what she could only suppose was the back of the house. Engulfed in a dark, almost eery silence, it was impossible to tell if the hostages were anywhere nearby.

Concerned, not sure what to expect next when her guide abruptly came to a stop, she couldn't stop her knees from knocking. What if Kartoff and his men searched her? They would surely find the wire. Then what?

Before she could even guess the answer to that, the blanket was whipped off her head. Surprised, she blinked…and found herself standing directly in front of a heavyset man whom she supposed was Kartoff. Dressed all in black, he didn't have to worry if she had a camera concealed on her or not—he'd taken the precaution of wearing a black ski mask that concealed everything but his ice-blue eyes. His men, she saw as she quickly glanced around the large, commercial kitchen of the mansion, were dressed the same. She could have worn a dozen cameras and it would have done little good. There was no way she—or the FBI agents watching from the command center—were going to be able to identify any of them.

Disappointed, she reminded herself that she couldn't be concerned with that. She was there to negotiate the release of the hostages. Nothing else mattered. Facing Kartoff squarely, she said, "Are the hostages all right? I would like to see them."

"They are fine," he retorted, then motioned abruptly to the wooden work table in the middle of the room. "Sit. We will talk about Ritka."

Relieved—he hadn't said she *couldn't* see the hostages—she had no choice but to play out their meeting his way. Taking a seat at the table, she sat back in her chair and lifted a delicately arched brow. "What is it you would like the world to know about Helmut Ritka?"

"He is our country's number one enemy," he said coldly. "He's ruining the Chekagovian financial infrastructure by siding with Western economic policies.''

Surprised, Julianna said, ''But I thought he was quite popular in Chekagovia. Wasn't he directly responsible for the increase of the sale of your oil to the West? Thanks to him, your country has more money now than it's ever had.''

''No!'' he roared. ''That's nothing compared to what we could be making, and he knows it. But does he care? No! The bastard is draining our country of its natural resources for a pittance, just to make points with the West.''

Julianna wasn't an expert on foreign affairs, but she'd thought that conditions in Chekagovia had improved drastically since it had allied itself with the United States and other Western countries. ''According to news reports, Chekagovia's economy is the best it's been in decades,'' she said with a frown. ''Ritka is one of your president's economic advisors. Obviously, he must be pleased with the job he's doing or he would fire him.''

''Peschuski is an idiot,'' he sneered. ''He wouldn't know a balanced budget if he tripped over it. It's Ritka's job to find a way to stabilize the economy, and he's done that by siding with Western economic policies that do not work in Chekagovia. The bastard is destroying us, and he must pay for that.''

"So you want Ritka delivered to you because of his poor economic policies?"

"Exactly. He has to stand trial for his misdeeds."

"In Chekagovian courts?"

"Of course not!" he snapped. "He has too much influence there. No, *we,* the people he has hurt the most, will try him at our camp in the mountains near Chekov, after you arrange to have him turned over to us."

Julianna sincerely doubted that the U.S. government would ever hand over Helmut Ritka to the likes of a man like Kartoff, but that was something she intended to keep to herself. The man obviously had a quick temper and little patience. He'd given his word that he would see that she was allowed to leave after their meeting, but she suspected he'd only promised her that because he thought he could use her to get Ritka. Once he realized that wasn't going to happen, her only value to him was as another hostage.

Her expression carefully neutral, she said, "Arranging something like this takes time, but I will start on it as soon as I get back to the command center. It would help your cause, though, if I could assure my superiors that all of the hostages are all right. If I could just see them for a moment—"

"No!"

"But—"

"The hostages will remain in seclusion until our demands are met."

Julianna would have liked to argue further, but even though Kartoff's face was well concealed behind his ski mask, there was no mistaking the rigid, implacable set of his jaw. He wasn't going to bend on this. If she continued to push him, she could not only put the hostages' lives in jeopardy, but her own.

Giving in gracefully, she said, "I understand. Thank you for giving me this time. I will relay your story to the press—"

A sudden loud knock at the door cut through the rest of her words. Kartoff gave a sharp command, and with the entrance of another of the terrorist's men, the tension in the room tightened like a fist. Alarmed and not sure why, Julianna watched the newcomer stride over to Kartoff and speak to him in a low voice. In the time it took to blink, the terrorist leader's eyes flew to hers.

"Bitch!"

Startled, Julianna jumped, and just that quickly he was on her, his hands tight around her throat. "She escaped! Ritka's bitch of a daughter was here and she got away. Did she take the music box with her? Tell me, damn you! Where's the music box?"

Terrified, gasping for breath, Julianna grabbed at the fingers that bit into her throat, but she couldn't dent his steel grip. He was killing her! Blackness clouded her brain, sucking the air from her lungs. Shaken like a rag doll, all she could do was gasp, "Don't! Please! I don't know anything!"

Her words were little more than a hoarse whisper he couldn't have possibly heard. His fingers tightened, cutting off the last of her air. Then, just when she was sure she was dying, he swore in German and shoved her away from him. "Get her out of here!"

Collapsing in a heap, clutching her bruised throat and sucking in precious air, she never saw the commando who had escorted her to the kitchen reach for the blanket. A split second later, everything went black.

When he got his hands on the bastard, he was going to kill him!

Standing as rigid as a fence post, Kurt stared unblinkingly at the fully lit mansion and grew angrier with every passing second. Kartoff had touched her, hurt her. And he'd been helpless to stop him. He'd had to stand there at the command center and watch the scumbag put his hands on her throat and shake her like a rag doll and he could do nothing. Nothing, damn it! Oh, he'd started for the mansion, but Tom and the others had stopped him before he could do anything but swear.

Where the hell was she?

Kartoff had ordered one of his men to get her out of there five minutes ago, and there was still no sign of her. Worried sick, he told himself she was all right, just a little shaken up. So why was she still inside? What the hell was going on?

"Something's happened," he muttered. "We've got to go in."

Beside him, Tom said grimly, "Give it a few more minutes. We haven't got a picture yet, but we've still got audio. If she was in trouble, we'd know it."

"She should have been out of there by now. If that jackass touches her again, I'm taking him apart, Tom. Don't try to stop me this time."

"I'll help you do it," the other man assured him. "But first, we have to give her time to get out of there."

Their eyes trained on the mansion's front door, they counted each tick of the clock and felt the tension mount. Then, just when Kurt was sure he couldn't stand it another minute, his walkie-talkie crackled to life and one of his own SWAT team members growled, "She's out!"

Still staring at the front door, which hadn't budged, Kurt didn't believe it. Then he saw her coming around the rear of the house. Wearing her black dress coat over the suit she'd borrowed, she looked small and fragile in the night, and it was all he could do not to go to her.

"I never should have let her do this," he told Tom grimly.

"You couldn't have stopped her," the agent retorted, admiration glinting in his eyes. "She's a gutsy lady. I don't know many women who would have gone in there alone."

Watching her draw closer, a conflicting mix of emotions swirling inside him, Kurt didn't know if he wanted to hug her for being so brave, or give her a well-deserved tongue-lashing for stubbornly insisting on taking such a risk. The second she reached the command center, however, there was no question in his mind that he wanted, needed, to hold her. She was pale, her eyes wide with the terror she'd just been through. She needed to be de-wired, then give a full accounting of everything she'd seen inside the mansion that her hidden camera might not have picked up, but Kurt didn't care. Stepping toward her, he reached for her.

Shaking, her eyes welling with tears, she stepped into his arms like she was coming home, and it was only then that Kurt realized just how close he'd come to losing her. Later, that would throw him for a loop, but for now, all he could think of was that he didn't want to let her go.

"Why don't you take her over to one of the paramedics and let them check her over?'' Tom suggested, his brow knit in a frown of concern. ''She needs a break. We can talk later.''

Her face buried against Kurt's chest, Julianna said in a muffled voice, ''I'm all right.''

Kurt almost smiled at that, but he couldn't forget how close she'd come to getting killed. ''You need to let the paramedics check you out, sweetheart. It'll only take a moment, then I'm going to get you something to eat. You didn't have dinner, did you? I didn't think so. C'mon. We'll see what we can find....''

His arm around her shoulder, he murmured reassurances to her as he urged her to where the paramedics waited patiently for something to happen. Almost immediately, she was helped into a nearby ambulance, where she was offered a measure of privacy while an EMT who looked like she was hardly old enough to drive examined her throat.

''You're going to have some nasty bruises,'' the paramedic told her quietly as she inspected her reddened neck. ''But overall, you were very lucky. Why don't you lie down here for a while and rest for a few minutes? You look like you could use it.''

''Oh, no, I can't—''

''Yes, you can,'' Kurt said from the open rear door of the ambulance. ''Tom said to take a break and that's what you're going to do. Lie back and relax. I'm going to find you something to eat—''

''No! Don't leave me!''

At her panicked cry, Kurt stopped in his tracks. ''I wasn't going far, sweetheart. Don't you want something to eat?''

''No. Please...I just don't want to be alone.''

He couldn't have left her then for a million dollars. Glancing at the paramedic, he asked, ''Is it all right if I stay with her?''

''Of course,'' she said, stepping out of the ambulance.

His eyes on Julianna, so small and pale and scared, Kurt's heart broke for her. Kartoff could have killed her and there was nothing he could have done to stop him. Shaken by the thought, he stepped into the ambulance and reached for her. He needed to hold her again, just for a minute.

Chapter 7

She'd never been so scared in her life. She was still shaking and near tears, and all she wanted to do was disappear in Kurt's arms. She didn't understand what was wrong with her—they were divorced, for heaven's sake! But no one could make her feel safe like he could. Whimpering, she sat up on the stretcher and threw herself into his arms as he came down on his knees next to her in the ambulance.

"It's okay, honey," he murmured, holding her close, then closer still. "Everything's all right."

"I thought he was going to kill me!"

"So did I," he said roughly. "And he's going to

pay for that. The coward's going to have to come out of hiding eventually, and when he does, he's going to know what it feels like to have someone's hands around his throat. But don't think about it now, sweetheart. Just put it out of your head and rest.''

''I can't! I can still feel his fingers squeezing my throat.''

''Then I'll give you something else to feel,'' he said huskily, and gently pressed his lips to her bruised throat.

The caress was whisper-soft…and the sweetest kiss he'd ever given her. The tight band of fear that constricted her ribs suddenly eased, allowing her to draw in a fresh breath for what seemed like the first time in hours. With a quiet sigh, she melted against him…only to remember that she was wired for sound and pictures.

Alarmed, she pulled back. ''Kurt—the wire!''

He jerked like he'd been stung, his scowl fierce as he glared at the collar of her coat where the tiny camera and microphone were concealed. ''Whoever's running the audio truck better turn the damn thing off,'' he growled. ''Here, let me help you get out of that thing.''

She should have stopped him. It would have been the smart thing to do. But what could happen when dozens of policemen, agents and EMTs were within shouting distance? Suddenly smiling at the thought, she said, ''It hooks in the back.''

Flipping off the interior ambulance lights so anyone standing outside wouldn't be able to see inside, he unbuttoned her coat and the buttons of her blouse, then slid his hands behind her to unhook the wire. At the first touch of his fingers on her bare skin, the air seemed to back up in her lungs, just as it had in the mansion. Only this time, it wasn't with fear.

In the darkness, Kurt's eyes met hers. ''I always loved your skin,'' he murmured quietly. ''It's so soft. Let me touch you, honey.''

She couldn't have stopped him. Not when he sent pleasure rippling through her with a single stroke of his fingers. And not when he leaned over and kissed her with a tenderness that destroyed her. Emotion pulled at her, and suddenly tears welled in her eyes. How long had she wanted, needed, this without even knowing it? With a quiet murmur, she reached for him even when she knew she shouldn't.

They had to get back to work—

The thought registered…and was gone in an instant when his warm, sure, knowing hands slid around her rib cage to cup her breasts. Slowly, softly, he stroked her sensitive breasts, and just that easily drove her out of her mind. Moaning, her body humming, she wrapped her arms around him and pulled him close, her mouth hot and hungry under his.

"Kurt!"

His name was all she could manage, but there was no need to say more. She could hear the desperate need in her voice and knew he heard it, too. She felt his body tighten in response, then he was snatching her close, and his kiss, just for a moment, turned wild.

One word was all it would have taken from her, and he would have taken her right then and there, the rest of the world be damned. Her heart slamming against her ribs, she realized she wanted to make love to him at that moment more than she'd ever wanted anything in her life. But they couldn't. Not when there were still hostages down the street, not when her co-workers and his were just steps beyond the ambulance.

"Kurt." She said his name again, but this time, the need that had roughened her voice only moments before was twinged with regret. "We have to get back," she whispered as she gently captured his face in her hands when he would have kissed her again. "We've been gone too long."

Groaning, Kurt buried his face against her neck. Less then fifteen minutes had passed since Tom had instructed her to take some time for herself, but she was right, damn it. When he made love to her again—and he had to believe it would be soon—it wouldn't be on the job. "All right," he groaned, forcing himself to let her go. "If you insist. But don't expect me to be happy about it."

Her own emotions still in a whirl, Julianna would have given anything to be able to have a few minutes to collect herself before they went to work, but that wasn't possible. Once they'd both straightened their clothing and their hair and stepped out of the ambulance, they went right back to work.

In the middle of a hurried conversation with another agent, Tom looked up at their arrival and immediately noted that Julianna was more relaxed. "You look better," he said by way of a greeting. "Are you ready to talk about what happened or would you like more time?"

"If Kartoff thinks he can scare me into not doing my job, he can think again," she said coolly, once again in control. "I'm tougher than that." And to prove it, she gave him an accounting of the number of commandoes and weapons she'd seen in the kitchen before Kartoff had tried to choke her to death without batting an eye.

"Good work," he said with a nod. "While you were gone, we got word that the limo driver was picked up at his home. He's being brought in right now."

The words were hardly out of his mouth when

Jerry Trolo arrived in the custody of another agent. "He refuses to talk," the agent said in disgust.

"He will kill me if I say anything!" the limo driver cried.

"Who?" Tom asked with a frown.

"Kartoff! He and his men have been threatening me for weeks, watching every move I made and waiting for the day I drove Miss Eva again. I had to tell him she was going to the mansion to look for the old music box her grandfather gave her or he was going to kill my wife and baby. And he would have done it!" he said, his blue eyes huge in his pale face. "You don't know him. He's already killed my aunt and uncle in Chekagovia!"

"What was he really after?" Kurt asked. "Miss Eva or the music box?"

"Both," he replied. "Miss Eva was his ace in the hole. He laughed about how he was going to get anything out of Ritka he wanted once he had Miss Eva. But it was the music box he was obsessed with. He claimed he would own Chekagovia once he found it."

"Really?" Tom said dryly. "That must be some music box."

"Please, you must help me and my family," Jerry said desperately. "I have told you all I know. If Kartoff finds out—"

"He won't," Julianna assured him. "He has no way of knowing that you've spoken to us—"

"I was picked up at my apartment," he reminded her. "If he had my place watched, my wife and child are sitting ducks."

"The three of you will be taken to a safe house," Tom assured him. "We may need to talk to you again, but for now, you can join your family. Don't worry. Kartoff won't be able to hurt you."

He still looked doubtful, but he didn't protest when he was escorted to a nearby car. His expression grim, Kurt said, "I think it's time to talk to Ritka again. He's got a few questions to answer."

Chapter 8

Helmut Ritka was expected any moment, but five minutes passed, then ten, and there was still no sign of him. Glancing at her watch for the third time in twenty seconds, Julianna felt sick with guilt. Now that his daughter was safe, Ritka obviously felt no obligation to stand by his word and help her negotiate the release of the hostages. Maybe Kartoff hadn't lied about him, after all.

"He's coming here whether he likes it or not," Kurt said gruffly when the major and Tom excused themselves to talk strategy with other FBI agents. "The man just found out his daughter was almost in Kartoff's hands. She could have been killed. But he won't back out now."

Julianna sympathized with that, but nearly two hundred people were still in Kartoff's hands. Their families were worried about them, too. "Kartoff can't be pleased that his men let two hostages escape. He won't wait long before he makes a move."

No one wanted to contemplate what form his revenge might take, and thankfully, they didn't have to. Three minutes later, Ritka called Julianna. "I apologize for the delay, Ms. Stevens. The traffic has cleared and we are almost there."

"Please hurry, Mr. Ritka. Not knowing where your daughter was had to be quite terrifying for you. She was very lucky to escape. But there are a lot of innocent people still in danger."

"I know. My daughter was very fortunate. I must thank Major Colton when I see him. My daughter could do nothing but sing his praises. As to the other hostages, they, too, must still be rescued. I'm willing to do whatever I can to help. I understand you met with Kartoff."

"Yes, I did," she said grimly. "It was quite frightening." Quickly and concisely, she told him everything that the other man had said about him. "I don't have to tell you that those are some pretty serious accusations, Mr. Ritka. If there's any truth to any of this, I need to know now. I can't negotiate effectively if I don't have all the facts."

"I have never done anything that would put my country in jeopardy—you can check the public record. Chekagovia is in better condition financially than it's ever been. Your own Secretary of State has said as much numerous times. I don't know what Kartoff is talking about."

The FBI *had* checked the records, and they were clean. "I believe you, Mr. Ritka," she assured him. "Now that we have that settled, it's imperative that you tell me everything you know about the music box. And please don't insult my intelligence by claiming you don't know anything about it," she said quickly, before he could do just that. "Your daughter's limo driver reported that she went to the mansion tonight to find the music box. And Major Colton backed up his story. Your daughter told him your father-in-law gave her the music box when your wife died. She claims it's a national treasure and the key to your country, and that's why she went back to the mansion for it. She found it and put it in the pocket of her coat. Unfortunately, it was left behind when she escaped, but Kartoff still hasn't found it. You must know its significance, sir."

For a moment, she was afraid she'd overstepped her bounds and ruined everything by practically calling him a liar. Silence hummed on the line between them. Then, just when she was sure he was going to hang up on her, he said quietly, "I never told Eva the secret of the music box because I felt like what she didn't know wouldn't hurt her. Unfortunately, she isn't the one being hurt here. Just now, I told her why Kartoff was so frantic to get his hands on the music box, and she convinced me that I can no longer keep quiet about this. There are too many lives at stake."

Releasing the breath she hadn't even realized she was holding, Julianna sighed in relief. "She's right, Mr. Ritka. We have to know everything if we're going to be able to save the hostages. What does Kartoff know that we don't? Why does he want the music box so badly?"

"Because the key that opens the music box is also the key to a vault in Chekagovia that contains millions of dollars' worth of gold bars that belonged to my country before it became a communist state after World War II. But now that we are moving toward a democracy, there have been talks to use the gold bars for investment in our country and abroad to stimulate our economy."

Stunned, Julianna sank into the nearest chair. "No wonder Kartoff is so insistent on finding it."

"He will never release the hostages as long as he thinks he has a prayer of getting his hands on the treasure, Ms. Stevens," he warned. "You've met with him. You know how ruthless he can be."

Julianna did, indeed. The memory of that meeting would haunt her to her grave. "According to Major William Colton, Kartoff is holding nearly two hundred guests hostage, Mr. Ritka. I know the treasure is important to your country, but we can't allow the hostages to be sacrificed for it. Because he will kill them if he doesn't get the music box. You do know that, don't you?"

"Yes," he said grimly. "But he also has issues with me. Hasn't he said from the beginning that he wouldn't release the hostages until I was turned over to him? Tell him I will meet with him...*after* the hostages are released. You must make it clear to him that this is not negotiable. I won't talk to anyone who's holding innocent people at gunpoint."

"You would do that?"

"Only if the hostages are released."

If Julianna had had any lingering doubts about him, they all vanished with his offer. "I don't know if the FBI will actually let you do that—you'll have to discuss it with them when you get here—but I'm certainly going to run the idea past Kartoff. He's so determined to get his hands on you and the music box, that may be the carrot we need to dangle in front of him to convince him to release the hostages."

"Call him and see," he said. "I'll be there as quickly as I can."

"Well?" Kurt said as soon as she hung up. "What did he say? What's this carrot you're going to hold out to Kartoff?"

"The music box," she said, then quickly explained its significance and Ritka's offer to meet with Kartoff to discuss it. "Keep your fingers crossed," she told him as she picked up the phone and punched in the number to the mansion. "If Kartoff wants the treasure as badly as I think he does, this may actually work."

Answering on the third ring, Kartoff said coldly, "I hope you have good news for me, Ms. Stevens. My patience is growing thin. Where is Ritka?"

"On his way," she replied evenly, refusing to be intimidated. "He is willing to meet with you…on one condition. You must release the hostages. Your complaint is with him, not them."

For a moment, there was nothing but silence, then he snapped, "Ritka is in no position to dictate terms to me! No one is going anywhere until he turns himself over to me and my men!"

Not giving her time to say another word, he slammed the phone down, severing the connection. Far from discouraged, Julianna merely replaced the phone on the receiver and looked up at Kurt with a crooked smile. "Well, that went over well. Let's give him time to stew over it and see what happens.''

''If Kartoff really wants Ritka, he's not going to get a better offer. He'd be stupid not to take it.''

Julianna agreed, but hostage-takers weren't the brightest people in the world or they wouldn't take hostages in the first place. It was generally a no-win situation and all they achieved by their desperate actions was jail time. Still, she was, at heart, an optimist. Surely Kartoff would see that this was an offer he couldn't refuse.

Later, she couldn't have said how long she and Kurt stood there watching the mansion and waiting for the phone to ring. Tom rejoined them after a while, once again accompanied by Billy Colton, and she quickly informed them of the latest turn of events. ''Ritka is willing to meet with him once the hostages are released. Kartoff immediately rejected the idea, but I'm hoping he'll come around once he thinks about it.''

''If he doesn't,'' Tom said, ''we have to be prepared to take action. The major's offered us his expertise. He recently headed up a Russian/American boot camp in St. Petersburg.''

Impressed, Kurt didn't doubt that he would be an asset to their campaign. Six foot two, he was the picture of a lean, mean fighting machine. ''We can use all the help we can get,'' Kurt told him. ''Especially since you've already been inside. Thanks.''

''My pleasure,'' he said grimly. ''I want to get this bastard.''

Julianna only had to look at him to know that he was the kind of man who enjoyed a good fight. She appreciated his input, but she was still holding out hope that diplomacy would win the day. The clock continued to tick as tension tightened everyone's nerves. Still, the phone remained stubbornly silent.

''The man's a jackass,'' Kurt muttered, swearing. ''He's got to realize he can't win this.''

''Maybe we should consider going in the way the major helped get Ritka's daughter out—through the roof,'' Tom suggested, turning to Billy Colton. ''There's bound to be some bloodshed, but right now, there doesn't seem to be any other way to resolve this.''

''No, wait!'' Julianna cried. Her gaze still trained on the mansion, she couldn't believe her eyes. Someone had pulled the front door open, and suddenly a mad rush of wedding guests were spilling out onto the front lawn. ''Look! It worked. Kartoff is releasing the hostages!''

Chapter 9

Behind the yellow police tape that cordoned off the mansion and command center from the press and the curiosity seekers, pandemonium reigned as the released hostages ran to freedom. Pale and shaken and, in some instances, crying, the women practically fell into the waiting arms of the emergency medical staff that had been waiting for hours for their release. In the time it took to blink, it quickly became apparent that there were no men among them.

"Kartoff refused to allow them to leave. You have to get them out of there!"

"The man's crazy! He said he'd line them all up and shoot them if his demands weren't met."

All talking at once as blue Santas from the police department circulated among them, passing out blankets and hot chocolate, they huddled in the cold night air, retelling their story again and again.

"They wouldn't let us have anything to eat or drink or even go to the bathroom. They're monsters!"

"They tore the house apart looking for a stupid music box. We really thought they were going to shoot us. I'd never been so scared in my life!"

"It was crazy. Kartoff kept asking about Ritka and the music box. He kept insisting that someone had to know where it was. We didn't know what he was talking about."

As Tom and a dozen FBI agents took their statements and questioned them about the conditions in the house, a cry suddenly went up from the crowd of Colton women and someone yelled, "Oh, my God! Lucy's having her baby! We need help!"

Suddenly, everyone was talking at once. "Give her some space! Somebody call an ambulance! We've got to get her to a hospital."

"No! Not without Rand!" Her voice a cry of pain in the night, Lucy Colton pushed her way through the crowd with her hand cradled protectively over her swollen stomach. "Meredith, please, your son promised me he would be by my side when the baby came."

"But he's still in the mansion," Meredith Colton said worriedly. "You have to think of the baby, honey. Rand will join you as soon as he's freed."

"No! Someone has to go in there and get him out. I'm not going anywhere without him."

She had a desperate look on her face that warned Meredith and the rest of the clan not to argue with her. Turning to the EMTs, her mother-in-law sighed in relief when the ambulance crew didn't bat an eye at her stubbornness. The smallest EMT, a tiny fairy of a woman, clucked her tongue and soothed, "I know how you feel, dear. I felt the same way when my first one came. I didn't want my Johnny out of my sight. Of course, he was a basket case when we got down to the nitty-gritty—he passed out right there in the delivery room—and I had to do it all by myself anyway."

Helping her toward the stretcher, she patted her kindly. "You'll be fine, sweetie. How long have you been having contractions?"

For a moment, the younger woman didn't seem inclined to answer, then she admitted sheepishly, "Two hours."

"Good Lord, and you're just now saying something? Why didn't you speak up when you first started having pains?"

"Because I didn't want that pig anywhere near my baby!" Lucy said fiercely. "I thought if I could just hang on until we were released, the baby would be safe.''

Helping her down onto the stretcher, the EMT chuckled. ''You've got more guts than I do. You just take it easy and let us take care of you now. Have you decided on a name? I remember when Johnny and I were picking out names....''

Chattering on as if they were best friends, she quickly and efficiently strapped her onto the stretcher, then nodded for her two co-workers to wheel Lucy to the ambulance. She was still reminiscing about her Johnny when Meredith hurried forward to join them. ''I'm going, too.''

Only then did Lucy acknowledge that, like it or not, she was going to the hospital. Tears glistening in her eyes, she reached for her mother-in-law's hand. ''You can't go,'' she said huskily. ''You need to stay here for Joe and Rand.''

''The others will be here,'' Meredith assured her, her own eyes also bright with tears. ''I can't let you have my grandchild by yourself, dear. I'm coming with you.''

She could be just as stubborn as her daughter-in-law, and Lucy knew it. Her smile tremulous, she said, ''Thank you,'' just as another contraction hit her. Seeing the pain on her face, Meredith quickly climbed into the ambulance. A split second later, it pulled away from the curb.

The scream of the siren was still echoing on the night air when the bride, still wearing her wedding dress and looking more than a little frazzled, pushed through to the front of the crowd and grabbed Kurt by the arm. "Please…we need some help!" she cried. "My sister's missing!"

"We haven't been able to find her anywhere," an older woman said as she joined her. "I'm her mother, Ellen Cosgrove, and this is my daughter, Samantha. No one's seen Juliet since that monster Kartoff and his men forced themselves into the mansion."

Pulling out a small notebook, Kurt quickly began jotting down information. "Her name's Juliet Cosgrove?"

The bride nodded, blinking back tears. "She's five foot six, slender, with golden-brown hair."

"She was wearing a burgundy bridesmaid's dress," the older woman added as she slipped an arm around her daughter's shoulder. "I'm afraid something awful's happened to her."

"I understand, ma'am," Kurt said sympathetically. "We'll do everything we can to find her. When as the last time anyone saw her?"

A tall blonde standing in the middle of the crowd of women raised her hand and said, "She was talking to Ian Rafferty a few minutes before Kartoff's men forced their way through the front door."

Jotting the name down, Kurt glanced back up at the blonde. "What did she do when she realized that terrorists were taking over the house?"

"I don't know," she said regretfully. "When I turned to tell her to run, she was gone. It was like she just vanished."

"And Mr. Rafferty?" he asked, arching a brow at her and the other women. "Did anyone see what happened to him?"

"He was gone, too," the blonde replied. "No one has seen him or Juliet since."

"They must be hiding somewhere in the house," Samantha Cosgrove said, her blue eyes dark with worry. "You have to find them."

"We'll do what we can, ma'am," Kurt assured her. "The hostages' safety is always our first priority. If your sister has managed to stay hidden this long without being discovered, chances are, Kartoff and his men won't find her."

Sympathizing with them, Kurt wished there was something else he could say to reassure them, but he'd learned a long time ago that there was no way to predict how a hostage situation would turn out. And that was the one thing he hated about his job. All he could give worried friends and family members were words.

Tears welling in Samantha Cosgrove Colton's

eyes, she said huskily, "I guess all we can do now is wait and pray."

"Yes, ma'am," he replied roughly. "If we hear any news about her or Mr. Rafferty, I'll let you know."

Turning away, wishing he could do more, Kurt rejoined Julianna just as a black Mercedes was granted entrance to the cordoned-off area and parked in the spot where the ambulance had been only moments before. He took one look at the dignified gentleman who stepped from the car and said, "That must be Helmut Ritka."

"Thank God!" Julianna sighed in relief. "I'll get Tom. If Ritka's going to meet with Kartoff, we need to make some plans."

She didn't have to look far for Tom—he and Billy Colton had seen the Mercedes pull in and had realized, as they had, that Ritka had finally arrived. Stepping forward to greet the diplomat, Tom introduced himself, then Julianna and Kurt. When he came to Major Colton, he said, "And this is Major Colton. He escaped with your daughter."

Holding out his hand, Billy said, "It's a pleasure to meet you, sir."

The older man gave him a hard look, but he shook his hand graciously. "You rescued my daughter. I'm forever in your debt, Major."

"It was my pleasure, sir," he said gruffly. "Your daughter is quite a remarkable woman."

Ritka nodded, his hard expression softening to that of a proud father. "Yes, she is. I would like to meet with you later and talk, if possible."

"Of course," Billy said. "I look forward to it once this mess is settled."

Turning back to Tom, Ritka said, "As I have told Ms. Stevens, I will do whatever I can to help the situation, including meet with Kartoff. My daughter wants me to give up the music box...and the key to the vaults. She insists that no amount of money is as valuable as human life, and I am forced to agree with her. If Kartoff will release the hostages, the music box is his."

Tom exchanged a speaking glance with the others, and said, "It's funny you should mention that. We've been tossing around the idea of using the music box as a carrot—with your permission, of course. We want to offer Kartoff the music box in return for the release of the rest of the hostages."

"I have no problem with that," the older man replied, "but I seriously doubt that he'll agree to it. Once he takes a stand, he doesn't back down. What will you do if he says no? Or he agrees, and you tell him where the music box is, and then he refuses to release the hostages?"

"We are prepared to use force, if necessary," he said flatly. "This situation cannot continue."

Ritka, to his credit, didn't hesitate. "Make him whatever offer you need to."

"Thank you, sir," Tom said. "We'll put the wheels in motion."

"I'd like to speak to some of the women who were released," he said. "I feel responsible, though I had no way of knowing that Kartoff was planning such an outrageous raid. I would have warned the Coltons—and the police."

"Of course you would have. No one is blaming you, Mr. Ritka," Julianna assured him. "Whatever Kartoff thinks you may have done in Chekagovia, nothing justifies his actions tonight."

"I appreciate that," he said gruffly. "I still wish to speak to the women and apologize for the actions of my countrymen. If you need my help in any way, just let me know."

He left them with a nod and made his way to where the worried bride and her mother, along with the Colton women, were gathered near the first aid station. Sipping coffee and hot chocolate, they stood wrapped in blankets, watching the mansion down the street, waiting.

In the silence left behind by his leave-taking, Billy Colton said, "If anyone's interested in my opinion, I think he's right. Kartoff isn't going to release the hostages. He needs them to get out of there and back to Chekagovia.''

"So you don't think we should even try to negotiate with him?''

Tom asked with a frown.

The major didn't hesitate. "Oh, you can try. But you should also have a backup plan…just in case.''

"What would you recommend?'' Kurt asked.

"I'd go in at 0200,'' the major said promptly. "Kartoff's men have been on alert for hours. By 0200, they'll be tired, and I doubt that they'll be expecting a raid on our part.''

"Ready or not, they're not going to let you storm the mansion without putting up a fight,'' Julianna pointed out. "A lot of people will be killed.''

"Not necessarily,'' Billy argued. "I'm not talking about going in through the front door. That's why we'll need all the plans of the house that can be found, from the time it was built to the present. There may be an old entrance that no one knows about that we could use to gain admittance into the house.''

Impressed with the major's bold strategy, Kurt grinned. He knew there'd been something about Billy Colton he liked right from the beginning. He was a man who knew how to make things happen. "I like the way you think, Major.'' Glancing at

Tom, he arched a brow. "What do you say, Tom? Julianna's done a good job of negotiating so far, but I get the feeling Kartoff has only been playing with us. He's going to hold on to the men as long as he can. Before it's over with, we're going to have to go in."

Not as quick to make a decision as Billy Colton, Tom hesitated, and in that moment, his cell phone rang. Answering it, he listened a moment, then began to smile. "I'll tell him," he told the caller and hung up. When he glanced at the major, he grinned. "That was the hospital, Major. Apparently, Lucy Colton didn't quite make it to the hospital. She had a baby boy en route."

Relief flared in Billy's hazel eyes, then quickly hardened into determination. "That baby is not going to grow up without a father. And my father, brothers and cousins are still in there. I'm not going to stand by and let them die at the hands of a madman and not do anything."

Put that way, Tom had to concede he was right. Glancing at Kurt, he said, "See what house plans you can track down. If Kartoff doesn't cooperate, we'll go in at 0200, as the major suggested."

Kurt didn't have to be told twice. Turning to the phones, he quickly relayed the order to the police department.

* * *

When Julianna placed the call to Kartoff a few minutes later, her fingers were anything but steady as she punched in the number. So much was riding on this! All Kartoff had to do was to cooperate, and the situation could end peacefully, with no loss of life. The problem was, he didn't care who he had to kill as long as he got what he wanted.

"So, Ms. Stevens," he greeted her the second he answered the phone. "The women have been released. I expect something in return. Where are Ritka and the music box?"

"Actually, Mr. Ritka is here," she said smoothly. "As for the music box, I'll be happy to tell you where it is…on one condition."

"Which is?"

"You release the rest of the hostages."

"Of course I will release them," he said promptly, amused. "After I have the music box in my hands."

Julianna had Ritka's okay—all she had to do was tell Kartoff where the music box was and the hostages might be free in a matter of moments. Still, she cringed at the idea of giving the Chekagovian national treasure to a terrorist. Hesitating, she covered the mouthpiece of the phone with her hand and arched a brow at Helmut Ritka. "Are you sure this is what you want to do?" she asked quietly. "If you have any doubts at all, we'll find another way to negotiate the hostages' release. Just say the word."

"Thank you for the offer," he said graciously, "but it's the right thing to do."

Her heart pounding, Julianna turned her attention back to the phone and Kartoff. "All right," she told him. "I'll tell you where the music box is and you'll release the rest of the hostages. Agreed?"

"Agreed," he replied promptly. "Where is it?"

"In the pocket of Eva Ritka's black cashmere coat, which is hanging in a closet at the top of the stairs on the second floor."

"This had better not be a trick, Ms. Stevens," he warned. "I don't like tricks." And with no other warning than that, he hung up.

Sitting back, Julianna sighed. "It's done. Now we wait."

When they all assembled thirty minutes later, there was no sign of the hostages, and no one at the command center was surprised. Still, Julianna was outraged that Kartoff had lied so blatantly. "You gave your word!" she told him when she called him, demanding to know why he hadn't released the hostages.

"You haven't met all of my demands," he retorted. "If you'll remember, Ms. Stevens, I said I also wanted Ritka, a million dollars and a plane with enough fuel to take me and my commrades, along with Ritka, back to Chekagovia. Call me when everything's ready."

He hung up, obviously thinking he had the last word. He was wrong.

Resigned to the inevitable, she turned to Tom, who, along with the others, had blatantly eavesdropped on her entire conversation with Kartoff. "So much for negotiating," she said flatly. "Until all of his original demands are met, he's not releasing anyone."

"Then we'll go in and get them," Billy Colton retorted. With that announcement, he rolled out the house plans for the mansion on the folding table that had been set up in the command center.

Helmut Ritka had joined them not only to give them additional information about the mansion he had lived in for many years, but to also tell them everything he could about George Kartoff. He took one look at the plans and was as surprised as the rest of them when it was discovered that there was a secret underground entrance that connected the mansion with the house across the street.

"I had no idea," he said, shocked. "I had my security team go over the place from top to bottom before my daughter and I moved in, and I was assured that the house was as safe as your Fort Knox. How could my men have missed something so obvious? All they had to do was look at the house plans.''

Studying several of the plans that chronicled the additions to the mansion over the years, Tom frowned. ''Only one of the plans has any reference to it—the ones that were used to add a new kitchen onto the house during the Civil War. The owners must have felt like they needed an escape route in case Washington was ever invaded. The plans for a new wing twenty years later make no mention of a tunnel, which means it was probably boarded up.''

''How difficult will it be to uncover it?'' Julianna asked with a frown, glancing up from the plans. ''If Kartoff suspects what we're doing, there won't be any men left alive to rescue.''

''I've already got a team working on it,'' Tom assured her. ''They're trained for this type of thing—Kartoff won't hear a thing.''

''Good,'' Kurt said in satisfaction. ''The special forces and SWAT team can go in through the tunnel—''

''While Kartoff's escort to the airport arrives and distracts him and his men,'' Julianna said, already guessing where Kurt was going with the plan. ''We can even have Mr. Ritka in the car. As long as it's bulletproof, he'll be safe.''

''And Kartoff will think he's landed butter-side

up,'' Kurt continued. ''We'll let him think Ritka and a million bucks are waiting for him in the limo out front, and he and his men will never stop to think that the threat is coming from inside the mansion, not outside. By the time they realize their mistake, it'll be too late for them to fight back.''

Personally, Kurt thought he and Julianna had come up with a brilliant plan. Why couldn't they have done that when there were married? Instead, they'd continually argued over the smallest things and, consequently, never got around to even discussing the big things.

Impressed, Billy Colton studied the two of them. ''Have you two worked together before? You're damn good together.''

''You know what they say about great minds,'' Kurt retorted, avoiding the awkward subject. ''So what do you say?''

''It sounds good to me,'' Billy said. ''How about you, Mr. Ritka? Are you willing to play decoy? You'll be protected at all times.''

''I would do it even if you couldn't assure my safety,'' the older man said. ''Considering everything that's happened here tonight because of me, it's the least I can do.''

All eyes turned to Tom. This time, he didn't hesitate. ''O200 it is.''

Chapter 10

With the decision made to go in, the real work began. They all knew there would be no second chances, not when they were dealing with a man like Kartoff. If they weren't able to bring all the hostages out, there wasn't a doubt in anyone's mind that those left behind would be killed. They were determined that wasn't going to happen. So every segment of the raid had to be planned, right down to possible emergency contingencies. It was tedious—and nerve-racking. Julianna had to call Kartoff several times, pretending that she and the authorities were considering giving in to his demands. And all the while, she was terrified that she might inadvertently say something that might lead the terrorists to become suspicious. If she did, he gave no sign of it.

The planning of the raid wasn't any easier on the men. Each member of the SWAT team and the U.S. Special Forces that would be involved in the raid had to know not only their own moves, but those of the others. So time and again, they went over each other's roles, trying to plan for everything.

Then, all they had to do was wait, and it turned out that Billy Colton wasn't any better at that than Kurt. Prowling the command center like a big jungle cat who felt the walls closing in on him, the major finally growled, "I've got to get out of here for a few minutes. I'll be back in time for the raid."

He slipped away into the darkness with no other explanation than that, leaving Julianna blinking in surprise. "Well, that was unexpected. He didn't seem the nervous type. Where do you suppose he went?"

Kurt only shrugged, but he had a pretty good idea that the major had slipped away to have his talk with Helmut Ritka. He didn't know what had happened between the major and Eva when they'd found themselves trapped in the mansion's attic, but Kurt had only had to see the look that came across Billy Colton's face when he talked about Eva to know that he'd fallen hard for the diplomat's daughter. And he sympathized with him. Because he'd done the same with Julianna…again.

Another man might have been kicking himself for even thinking about starting over with her when nothing had really changed in their lives. They were both busy with their own jobs, and the danger that went hand in hand with his work would, no doubt, still worry Julianna. But he couldn't even begin to describe how much he loved her. He wanted her back, damn it! If he was lucky enough to win her back, he was confident they could make things work this time. They were both older and wiser. He'd learned the hard way that love could be strangled if it was held on to too tightly. That was a mistake he wouldn't make again. He couldn't change the danger associated with his job, but he was confident that despite how busy their lives were, they would always be there for each other…if she loved him as much as he loved her.

That was the sixty-four-thousand-dollar question. He wanted to ask her how she felt about him, but he couldn't. This wasn't the time or place. When he told her he loved her again, there wouldn't be any other people around and they certainly wouldn't be in the middle of a hostage situation. The two of them would be alone, with no distractions but each other.

In the meantime, he had to keep his mind on the

job at hand. Julianna didn't make it easy for him. Every time she moved, every time she smiled, he felt as if she reached out and touched him. Watching her, aching to touch her, to love her, he hardly heard Tom when he told him that he would be going in with the SWAT team.

Julianna heard, however, and her heart dropped to her knees in alarm. She didn't want him to go, didn't want him to risk going into a building where a madman and his followers were waiting to kill anyone who got in their way. But even as she waited for the old paralyzing fear to grip her, she couldn't help but notice the maturity and confidence with which Kurt consulted his fellow SWAT team members. In the past, he'd acted like a gun-toting cowboy ready to rush into battle, and that had always terrified her. She'd always been afraid he was going to get himself killed, but now she realized he would never take foolish chances. He was professional, coolheaded, in control of his own emotions and the situation.

Watching him, her heart expanding with love, she felt a huge load lift from her shoulders. She could trust him to take care of himself. There were no guarantees in life, but she knew it was safe to love him, to trust him with her heart. He would be careful and do everything he could to come back to her.

Tears gathered in her eyes at the thought, and at that moment, she knew she couldn't let him go into danger without telling him how she felt. He needed to know…and she needed to tell him. Impulsively, she stepped past Tom and quietly pushed her way past the other SWAT team members who had gathered at the command center to confer. "Excuse me, gentlemen," she said huskily, "but I need a moment with Kurt. There's something we need to discuss."

Surprised, Kurt let her pull him a few steps away. "What is it? Did we miss something—"

Without a word, she stepped close, looped her arms around his neck, and pulled him down for a long, slow kiss that told him everything that was in her heart. Still, she had to say the words, and she didn't care who was listening. Drawing back slightly, she smiled up at him through the tears that welled in her eyes. "I love you," she said huskily. "I wanted you to know that. I always worried about you when you're working, but I'm not going to fuss at you anymore to be careful. I know you will be."

If he hadn't already loved her, Kurt would have lost his heart to her at that moment. "Oh, honey, I love you, too. These last three years, I've been mis-

erable without you. I wanted to tell you, but..."
His smile rueful, he nodded toward Tom and the
group of SWAT team members who were trying
hard to give them a little privacy and failing mis-
erably. "These guys aren't exactly romantic, and I
wanted to be with you. Later, when this is all
over, we're going to talk. Okay?"

Wiping away the tears that spilled over her
lashes, she stepped close for a quick, fierce hug.
"Okay," she said thickly. "That's a date."

There was little time for any talking after that.
While they were telling each other how much they
loved each other, Billy Colton had returned and the
Special Forces and SWAT team had all donned bul-
letproof vests and strapped on extra ammunition.
The time to strike was now.

Kurt's eyes met Julianna's, his hands squeezed
hers, and it was time to go. Without a word, he
stepped away from her and joined his fellow SWAT
team members. Silently, soundlessly, they turned
and faded into the night as they made their way
toward the old house across the street, where they
would enter the secret tunnel that led to the mansion's basement.

A few seconds later, Julianna blinked, and just
that quickly, Kurt was gone. She didn't make a
sound, but beside her, Tom heard the worry she
wouldn't let herself voice. "He'll be fine," he said

gruffly. "You didn't find each other again, only to lose each other now. Hold on to your faith, Julianna. He'll come back to you."

If she hadn't believed that, she didn't know how she would have gotten through the next few minutes without falling apart. Watching the drama unfold across the street from the safety of the command center was one of the hardest things she'd ever done. She wanted to go after Kurt, to help him somehow, but all she could do was wait.

Down the street, the limo that held Helmut Ritka slowly started down the long drive to the mansion. To all appearances, the limo looked like any other limousine, but Tom had assured everyone that the government-owned vehicle was as safe as a tank. The windows were bulletproof, the doors and body of the car reinforced with steel. Nothing short of a bazooka was going to take it out, so even though Ritka was clearly visible through the untinted windows of the back seat, there was little Kartoff could do to hurt him.

The terrorist, however, didn't know that, and Julianna could just imagine the gleeful celebrating going on inside the mansion. At this point, Kartoff, no doubt, thought he had won and was already planning ways to spend the ransom money. What he didn't know was that the minute the limo started down the drive to the mansion, the SWAT and Special Service teams that had quietly slipped into the house across the street entered the tunnel linking it to the mansion.

Her heart pounding, Julianna prayed, but she couldn't say what she prayed. All she could think of was Kurt and how little time they'd had together. If she lost him now, after just now finding him again, she didn't think she could bear it.

Dear God, please keep him safe. Please, please, please...

Suddenly, angry shouting shattered the silence of the night. Hugging herself, Julianna stood still as stone, only to recoil at the rapid, repeated, hollow sound of gunfire that echoed down the deserted street. "Oh God, oh God," she murmured, horrified. "Please keep him safe. Keep them all safe."

The gunfire ended as quickly as it had begun, leaving behind a deadly silence that was far worse than the sound of gunfire to Julianna. Time jerked to an abrupt stop. Down the street, nothing moved. Her heart pounding painfully, Julianna waited...and prayed with increasing urgency.

A sob bubbling up in Julianna's throat and tears pooling in her eyes, she found herself holding her breath as the front door of the mansion was suddenly pulled open and Kurt and the SWAT team stepped outside with the terrorists held at gunpoint.

Behind them, the now free hostages stepped out into the dark, chilly night.

A cheer started to go up from the command center. Then everyone saw the hostage being carefully carried outside by the paramedics who had rushed inside just as soon as it was safe. At the wounded man's side, the groom held the wounded man's hand as he was carefully taken to a nearby ambulance.

From the crowd of women who strained to get past the barriers, whispers of concern traveled quickly. "Oh, my God!" she heard someone say. "That's Ian Rafferty!"

"It looks like he's been shot in the back!"

"Where's Juliet?"

No one had an answer for that.

Whatever triumph she felt evaporating, Julianna turned to Tom, who, like her, had had to stand on the sidelines and watch the drama unfold. Impulsively, she hugged him. "It's over, Tom," she said huskily. "Thank God, it's over!"

It was a Christmas Eve they would all remember the rest of their lives, but there was no time to discuss it. The Colton women, anxious to assure themselves that their men were all right, surged past the barriers and rushed down the street toward the mansion. As anxious as they to check her own man,

Julianna joined them and was quickly caught up in the desperate rush to find loved ones.

She had, however, lost sight of Kurt. In the past, she would have been frantic until she touched him again, kissed him, and she would have been hurt if he hadn't sought her out immediately. But she was no longer that insecure woman. She'd seen that he'd safely survived the raid, and she was confident he loved her. They would find each other eventually.

"Julianna!" Suddenly breaking through the crowd on the heels of her thought, Kurt reached for her, and in the next second, she was in his arms. She hadn't realized how much she needed the feel of his strong arms around her until she felt him hold her tight.

"Oh, Kurt, thank God you're all right!"

Pulling her closer, he would have liked nothing more than to just hold her until their hearts settled down to a slow, steady beat, but that wasn't possible. At least not now. "I'm fine, sweetheart. I wish I could stay and tell you all about the raid, but Kartoff managed to escape…with the music box, of course. We're searching for him now."

"Oh, no!"

"Don't worry," he said grimly, "there's no way in hell he's going to get away with this. But it could be a while before this is over. I just wanted you to know that I'm okay.''

The search for Kartoff was a frantic one, and Kurt needed to get back to it, but if there was one thing he'd learned over the last few hours, it was that Julianna's peace of mind was more important than his job. In the past, he would have sent one of his co-workers to tell her that he was all right, but not now. She wasn't in love with one of his co-workers—she loved him. And he loved her, more than he'd ever thought possible. He didn't fool himself into thinking they wouldn't argue in the future, but this time around, they knew how precious love was. They wouldn't chance losing each other again.

''I love you,'' he said huskily. ''Let's splurge and spend Christmas together at the Georgetown Inn. I'll meet you there as soon as I can and we'll make plans—if that's all right with you.''

With everything that was going on, they hadn't spoken of the future, and he suddenly wondered if he was taking it for granted that she wanted the same thing he did. But he needn't have worried. The smile that lit her face stole the breath right out of his lungs. ''One day, we'll tell our children about our first real Christmas together,'' she said softly. Rising up on her tiptoes, she kissed him tenderly. ''I'll be waiting for you,'' she promised. ''Hurry.''

She didn't have to tell him a second time. Giving

her one last quick kiss, he rushed back to work with a smile that lit up his entire face. Whatever happened with Kartoff, however long the search took, he knew she would be waiting for him when it was all over. Nothing else mattered.

Epilogue

The original black-and-white version of *It's a Wonderful Life* played on the TV, and in the fireplace, a fire crackled merrily. Still in bed at eleven o'clock in the morning, Julianna couldn't remember the last time she'd felt so content. Everything she wanted was right there at her fingertips.

Watching her dreamy smile as she slowly stroked her fingers up and down his arm, Kurt lifted an amused brow at her. "What are you thinking?"

"This is the best Christmas I ever had and I didn't get a single gift," she said with a grin. "Except you."

"So I'm the best Christmas you ever had?"

She didn't hesitate. "Absolutely. We were very lucky to find each other again."

Sobering, he agreed. "We weren't the only ones. Last night could have been a real tragedy for the Coltons. Their entire family could have been wiped out."

"But they weren't, and that's what's important."

"I don't know how Kartoff found a way to slip through our fingers," Kurt said in disgust. "He won't get very far—there's an APB out on him, and after all the news coverage of last night, he won't be able to show himself on the dark side of the moon without somebody recognizing him."

"Even if he does somehow manage to get to Chekagovia, he'll never get his hands on the treasure. Ritka will have it well guarded by now. But enough about that," she said, shaking off the somber mood. "It's Christmas and we have a lot to celebrate." Her brown eyes twinkling, she gave him a quick kiss and sat up in bed to grab the very expensive bottle of champagne they'd ordered from room service earlier.

Watching her, loving her, Kurt wanted to drag her back down to the bed and celebrate another way, but he grinned instead and told himself he could wait. "And just exactly what are we celebrating?"

Her dimples flashing as she poured them both

champagne, she said, "Well, for one thing, a new baby boy in the Colton family."

"Fair enough," he chuckled, clicking glasses with her. "What else?"

"We got everyone out alive."

"Thank God," he said, clicking glasses with her again. Taking another sip of champagne, he grinned. "And?"

"Us," she said proudly, raising her glass again in a toast. "Last night, I didn't think there was a chance in *H*-*E*-Double-*L* of the two of us ever speaking again, let alone getting back together. That just goes to show you what I know."

"Then Kartoff crashed a wedding and had the ill manners to hold everyone at gunpoint," he said with a rueful smile. "'Yes, Virginia, there is a Santa Claus.'"

"This time, we'll make it work," she vowed.

"Forever," he promised.

Their eyes shining with love, they solemnly clicked their glasses together, then leaned close to seal their vow with a kiss. Moaning softly, she pressed against him and felt like she'd stepped into a dream. Old hurts had been healed, the past had been forgotten. There was only today...and the future...and a love she never wanted to end.

Emotions rising in her, she didn't say a word as he set their champagne glasses aside, then traded kiss for kiss, but she didn't have to. They'd never had a problem communicating without words. Her mouth softened under his, her hands tenderly stroked his face, his chest, the back of his neck. It seemed like she had been waiting three years for this moment, and she hadn't even known it. She couldn't ask him if it had been the same for him, but she didn't need to. Leaning over her, stroking her hair back from her face, he said thickly, "Nothing has been the same without you. Let me love you, honey."

She couldn't have denied him any more than she could have denied herself. He kissed her with a gentle hunger that brought tears to her eyes and just that easily, he made her body hum and her senses blur. During the twenty months of their marriage, they'd made love too many times to count, but it had never been like this. Not slow and hesitant and infinitely sweet, but as if it had been the first time for either of them. Their fingers stumbled, brushed skin on skin, and their breaths caught in a soft hush that seemed to echo like a gasp.

And when he moved with her, filling her, stoking a fire that already burned too hot, her heart just seemed to expand.

She loved him so much more than before.

The truth was like a comet streaking through the

night, stunning her, filling her with a joy she had to share. "Kurt!"

"I know, sweetheart," he groaned, gathering her close against his pounding heart. "It's different, isn't it? Better?"

"Perfect," she said, tightening her arms around him. "I didn't think I could love anyone this much."

"Me, either," he said, kissing her again. "Somehow, we found our way back to each other. I don't know how, but I know we'll never lose our way again. You're mine."

"And you're mine," she echoed.

Smiling into each other's eyes, they once again reached for their champagne glasses and toasted their love. "Forever."

This time it really was forever.

JULIET OF THE NIGHT
Carolyn Zane

Chapter 1

Juliet Cosgrove jumped half out of her shoes and emitted the itsy-bitsyest, teeny-weeniest—well, okay, though she was loath to admit it, a very unladylike—shriek, and then looked around sheepishly when she realized that the sharp retort came from a champagne bottle and not a gun. How ridiculous. Who would be—she shot a quick glance at the ceiling—packing *heat* at her sister, Samantha's, wedding reception? Absurd. And here she was, shrieking like the starlet in a teen scream flick. Luckily, she was not the only jitterbug and everyone shared a good laugh at the expense of those who were easily startled.

A glance across the crowded ballroom at the Coltons' Washington, D.C., estate told Juliet once again, that *he* was watching.

Mr....Mystery.

She shivered. On and off, throughout the evening, she'd noticed him glancing in her direction, stony-faced, aloof, almost...as if he'd judged her on some nebulous criteria such as the style of her shoes and she'd come up somehow wanting.

Until she'd screamed.

Then, his granite jaw nearly cracked as his lips curled into a smirk, which, she supposed, was better than nothing, but still, he gave her the willies. Who was this grim reaper? And who'd invited him to Samantha and Jesse's wedding?

With a little shudder, she averted her eyes and, as she stepped away from the throng at the champagne fountain, nearly bowled over Liza Colton Hathaway, her new cousin-in-law, and an old friend.

"Hey, keep it down over here," Liza teased as she slid a sisterly arm around Juliet's waist.

"Sorry. I've always been a screamer. It's so embarrassing. Especially in church."

"You should have been the opera singer in the family. Your C above high C is window-shattering caliber."

"Thank you." Juliet giggled and dipped forward

to kiss Liza's cheek. "Merry Christmas Eve. We're family now!"

"I know. Isn't that cool? You look gorgeous tonight. I've never seen a more lovely maid of honor." They stood back and smiled the warm smile of old friendship. "Can you believe it? Your little sister and Jesse are married! Where did the year go?" Liza wondered aloud.

"I know. I don't think I've seen you since..."

"My wedding?"

"That long?" Juliet frowned. "That's terrible! Let's have lunch this week and dish about all that girlie stuff we've neglected. By the way, speaking of shattering windows, I caught your PBS music special. You're singing was brilliant, as usual."

"Oh, pish. You think? Well, okay, I have to agree." Liza laughed. "Except for that one camera angle, where you could see halfway down my throat."

"Yes, but you have a very attractive uvula."

They clutched each other and giggled like girls sharing a forbidden cigarette behind the woodshed. Again, Juliet glanced across the room and caught that man staring. Who the devil was he?

He was standing alone, which was a feat in itself, given the number of people crammed into the Georgetown mansion's ballroom. Over by the massive fireplace he stood, warming his hands behind him, and surveying the masses the way a king would survey a kingdom.

Pompous poop.

Determined not to let him cast a pall on her enjoyment, Juliet focused on Liza's warm conversation and enjoyed the virtual wonderland that was the Colton ballroom. A Christmas tree, twenty feet in height, had been transported from the great Northwest just for the occasion and was decorated with gold, burgundy and dark green ribbons and baubles. White lights twinkled in evergreen swags that were hung about the ceiling, stair banister and fireplace mantle and tied with huge velvet bows. A harpist plucked out Christmas carols, while the orchestra took a break and the champagne fountain in the middle of the floor gurgled richly.

A beautiful grandfather clock against one wall chimed its melodic tones, announcing the hour was now nine o'clock.

"So how is the world of publishing treating you?" Liza asked. "I saw two of your authors at the top of the bestseller list this week."

"It's going great. I've been telecommuting from here to New York and it's working out really well. Power lunches on Fridays in the Big Apple and I fly out to the West Coast quarterly for some sunshine. I'm keeping busy." She lifted and dropped a shoulder. "But enough about me. How's married life treating you?"

Liza beamed. "I've never been so happy. You should try it."

Juliet grimaced. "I don't think so. I'm off men, right now. Only just now recovering from a very nasty breakup with Parker last year. Remember him? Tall, dark and jerk?"

"Oh, dear. What happened?"

"I was from Venus. He was from hell."

"Ah." Liza's head bobbed in sympathy. "He run around?"

"Like a blasted triathlete. You name it, he pulled it. And I trusted him." Juliet expelled the air from her lungs. "I miss the companionship, but not enough to start looking for my Romeo any time soon. Lucky for me, Samantha has taken the pressure off me with her own wedding."

"They look so happy."

"Don't they?"

Again, Juliet's gaze snagged that of the Popsicle by the fireplace. Though she hated to, she had to admit he was sort of handsome in a James Bond kind of way and, under that Armani suit, there lurked some serious muscles. But he needed a crash course at charm school. He seemed vaguely bored. Brooding. Sulking. Humorless. And at a wedding? Please.

"Hey, Liza. Don't look over by the fire. No!" Juliet giggled and smacked her friend's arm. "I said *don't* look, you goose. Anyhow, in a minute, look ov—"

"Ian Rafferty."

Lips screwed into a lopsided purse, Juliet arched a brow at Liza. "Now, how did you know what I was going to ask?"

"I noticed that he's been glancing in this direction, and figured you'd noticed. Isn't he a dreamboat? His eyes are like sapphires, huh? And look at those lips. Begging to be kissed."

"Honestly, Liza, you're married."

"But not dead. I think he has a crush on you."

"Oh, gag. Don't be a loon."

"C'mon. I'll introduce you to him. He's an old family friend."

"No! Forget it. I'd rather neck with Dracula." Something about him reminded her of Parker, and she had to fight the urge to march over and sock him in the guts.

"Okay, later then."

Juliet sighed and looking askance she watched Bond, James Bond, make small talk with the odd person who dared to penetrate his wall, but it seemed clear that he'd rather be left alone. Fine with her.

When the clock chimed the half hour, Juliet decided to stay just a little longer, then wish her sister a happy honeymoon, kiss her parents and brother good-night and then go home and get some much-needed sleep.

"Ian! Thanks for coming, man." Jesse Colton grasped Ian's hand in a manly grip and clapped him on the back. "I'm so glad you could make it to my wedding."

"I wouldn't have missed it. It was a beautiful ceremony. You're a lucky man, Jesse."

"Got that right." A gentle grin graced his lips as Jesse sought out his bride across the room and shot her a wink that told her he was longing to get to the honeymoon. "So, when are you going to take the plunge?"

"Me?" Ian laughed. "Find me a woman who can tolerate my crazy hours and I'll get back to you." Against his will, his gaze strayed to Jesse's new sister-in-law.

She had been the maid of honor, this much he knew, and since she was maid and not matron, that made her single. She was beautiful in that deep burgundy gown and to Ian's way of thinking, overshadowed the bride. Disgusted with himself for this uncustomary lack of self-control, he had to battle his gaze away from the way the nearly backless dress hugged her hips. When she moved, the shimmering skirt swished against her shapely ankles in a most fascinating way. Somehow or another, defying the laws of gravity, the dress clung to her bustline, revealing her long, delicate neck.

It was hard to say how tall she was, as she had on very high heels. But, as far as he could tell from this angle, he figured she must be about medium height. Looked as if she led an active lifestyle, too, if her tan meant anything. Maybe she'd just returned from vacation. Some vacation where there were hot, sandy beaches. And bikinis. She'd look great in a bikini.

Really, it annoyed him, the way she had him staring, like some kind of gaping adolescent at a peep show. Never before had he been so captivated by a person's appearance.

Once again, she caught him staring and he grimaced, molars grinding. With a deep breath, he set his jaw and attempted to project a professional demeanor. Truth of the matter was, though he'd been invited as a friend, he was also here to work.

Unfortunately, Jesse had followed the line of his vision and spotted his interest in Juliet. "Yeah, she is something."

"Who?"

"Don't play dumb, man. I saw the gleam in your eye."

"Damn. And I've been working so hard to disguise it." Ian turned and shot a sheepish grin at the fire. "I didn't want her to think I came to the wedding to pick up women."

Finally, curiosity got the better of Juliet and she broke down and asked Liza to fill her in on Ian Rafferty.

"You've heard of IntraCom Security Systems?"

"Who hasn't?"

"He owns it. Built it from the ground up. Aside from the wedding, he's here to look the place over for a new security system, now that the newest Mr. and Mrs. Colton will be living here. After so many years as the Chekagovian embassy and then diplomatic residence for the former Chekagovian ambassador, Jesse and Samantha thought that security might be an issue. Who knows what enemies the people that have lived here have made, you know? Anyway, Ian Rafferty is rich, baby. Totally, stinking rich. Richer than your average Colton, and that's saying something."

Aahhh. Juliet nodded sagely. That explained the king-of-the-world attitude. Money. Big deal. She'd never been impressed by money. He was just another Parker. Cold, uncaring, arrogant, playboy. That much was apparent.

"But," Liza gushed on, "you'd never know it.

He never talks about himself. And the strange thing is, he is single.''

"I don't find that strange. He seems to have the personality of Hitler's Doberman.''

"Ian? You're kidding. He's a pussycat. Women all over the world have tried to snare him, but so far, no luck.''

"Maybe he's a gay pussycat.''

Head back, Liza hooted. "*Ian Rafferty?* No way. I didn't say he didn't enjoy *women,* he just hasn't let one catch him yet.''

"Why buy the cow and all that, huh?''

"No. Honestly, Juliet,'' Liza gripped her forearm and jostled her back and forth, "you are so cynical for such a sweet young woman.''

"That's what having a political lawyer for a father will do for you. Politics and law. That, and a lying, cheating, conniving ex-boyfriend do tend to make one a little jaded.''

Liza took Juliet's hand and tucked it into the crook of her arm. "Lucky you, Ian is neither a politician nor a lawyer. Come with me. I want you to meet him.''

"No, no, no, that's okay. I don't want to meet him. Really. I was just interested in who some of the guests are…in fact, see that woman in the bright red velvet and bead thing? Who is she?''

Unfortunately, Juliet's diversionary tactics did

not work. Liza was bent on introductions to this Ian character and that was that.

As she was tugged along, Juliet sighed and wondered why she'd asked the bubbly, social butterfly Liza about Ian. She should have known it would lead to uncomfortable introductions. Heavenly days, she'd rather sing karaoke naked right now, than have to make small talk with someone who reminded her so much of her arrogant ex.

"Liza—" Juliet tried to inject some carefree gaiety into her laughter as she trotted after Liza "—really, I must use the powder room. My nose is positively Rudolph. And I've had more than several cups of coffee. And champagne. My teeth are sort of floating... Just...uh..."

Liza ignored her limp excuses and proceeded to nudge Juliet toward Ian.

Cheeks stretched taut, Juliet pasted her smile firmly in place and battled her way through the clouds of perfume, screeching laughter, and haute couture. The air was becoming thick, down here in the people forest. Thick with heat. Thick with inebriation. It was definitely time to go home.

A waiter squeezed past with a tray of full champagne flutes and Juliet set down her empty and snagged a new one. Slowly, like a machete-wielding safari hunter, Liza small talked and chit-chatted her way through the mob and over to the

fireplace. A fire popped merrily inside the massive
rock structure as, hands behind his back, Ian
warmed himself.

"Ian!" Liza squealed and, towing a hapless Juliet in her wake, stopped short and thrust Juliet into
his frigid field of vision.

Up close, Juliet could see that his eyes were a
cool and steely blue. At complete odds with the
heat that belched from the fireplace.

"Liza."

"Ian Rafferty, I'd like you to meet the sister of
the bride, Juliet Cosgrove."

Ian held out his hand. "How do you do?"

"Fine," she lied, suffering from an unfortunate
case of déjà vu. She'd met Parker at a wedding. A
good friend had introduced them. The regrettable
similarities were astounding. Tall, dark, handsome,
and cool as a Christmas cucumber. At least he had
a halfway decent handshake. Probably paid some
image consultant to teach him how.

Liza beamed back and forth between the two, as
she blathered.

"Ian and his company, IntraCom Security de-
velop security systems for various businesses such
as jewelry franchises and also the government and
the private sector. I don't really understand all that
Ian does, but I find it fascinating to listen to him
tell how his work has foiled even the most brilliant

criminal minds when it comes to securing valuable points of interest in the D.C. area,'' Liza parroted from the commercial on TV. "Right, Ian?''

Ian smiled tolerantly. "Something like that, yes.''

Juliet pulled her curled lip between her teeth. Yes, sir. Parker would have smiled and answered with the same arrogant demeanor. She detested him already.

Liza seemed not to notice that he was such a social boob as she continued to natter like one of Cupid's salesclerks on commission. "Juliet grew up in Washington, D.C., and is used to being around politics. Her father practices law. Her mother is very active in charitable organizations and other social groups. Her younger brother is a college man…he's running around here somewhere… Anyway, Juliet is a literary agent extraordinaire. She represents some of the biggest fiction talent in the nation.''

Seemingly unimpressed, Ian lifted a brow and deigned to bestow her with his precious gaze. "Oh? And have I heard of your authors?''

"Probably not. I deal mainly in women's fiction.''

"Ah. Romance novels and How to Lose Weight, How to Build Self-Esteem, that kind of stuff?''

Juliet chafed at his attitude. Somehow, he had,

with only a few words, managed to affront every one of her sensibilities. "How-to books are *non-*fiction," she gritted out, then took a deep breath to calm herself and remember that he was, in his Cro-Magnon way, just trying to make conversation.

He raised a skeptical brow.

"I can tell by the dubious tone in your voice that you are not a fan of women's fiction," she added coolly.

"Hearts and flowers have never been my choice in entertainment." His tone was laced with sarcasm.

"Don't tell me," she eyed him speculatively, "you read Grisham and Clancy."

"I enjoy a good book, yes."

"And they are very good. But I believe it is possible to enjoy all kinds of fiction."

Ian shrugged. "Politics and murder and international espionage make for more interesting plot, than boy meets girl, girl is stupid enough to misunderstand everything the poor guy says, boy loses girl, and then boy is stupid enough to propose to irrational girl."

"This is beginning to sound like personal experience. Was someone stupid enough to misunderstand your irrational proposal?" she asked, blinking innocent eyes. Juliet could only imagine the poor girl who'd been foolish enough to imagine that there was a compassionate person under that facade. The man was as cuddly as concrete.

"No. It's just that Tom Clancy's work is actually more in line with my version of reality than the sexcapades of some silly boy and girl."

"You must lead a pretty adventurous, non-silly life, huh? That must explain your complete and total boredom with something as tame, and romantic as a wedding reception."

Over her shoulder, Liza spied a friend across the room and excused herself. "You two enjoy yourselves," she said, mistaking their biting conversation for witty repartee, and hustled off.

"My mind is on other things, yes." He said it with such an air of condescension it made Juliet want to scream.

"Matters of espionage and murder, no doubt," Juliet acknowledged as sweetly as she could muster, but ready to pounce.

"As a matter of fact, yes."

"Oh, do tell."

"No."

She grinned at his obstinance. "Has anyone ever told you, that for a supposed nice guy, with a lot of class, that you are neither?"

"Who said that?" The tiny lines forked at the corners of his eyes.

"What? That you are nice and classy?"

"Well, I assume it wasn't you."

"Liza."

"Ah, Liza has always been a romantic." The condescending attitude was back.

"Coming from you, a backhanded compliment." Take that, she thought.

"Your cousin is a lady."

Ouch, and she was not. Didn't take a phonics course to understand what he was trying to say. He found the fact that she was independent with strong opinions unladylike. Just like Parker had. Juliet fell silent.

The staff made the rounds with food and drink. They both loaded their napkins with gourmet finger fare and stood quietly. As they ate, they turned away from each other, as if they'd talk to other people, if only some other people would show up. But alas, no one did.

Juliet looked out the window.

Ian stared into the fire.

The orchestra returned from their break and struck up a rousing waltz. Thomas Colton, patriarch of the Oklahoma Colton clan, took his turn with the bride, whirling her around the dance floor like a seasoned veteran. Over by the champagne fountain, more corks popped, startling more people, and raucous laughter followed from a few who seemed to have imbibed a bit too much.

Ian knew he'd blown it with Juliet. He couldn't really say why he'd been so cool, except that he'd been trying to exude confidence all evening, and when Liza suddenly surprised him with introductions, he hadn't been able to change gears fast enough. And then she'd gone and gotten kind of huffy about her career and he hadn't known how to backpedal, and...*damn!*

He glanced sideways and noted that she didn't seem aware that he existed. A small grin tugged at his mouth. She was an opinionated little spitfire and about as cute as a cobra, but he was intrigued. He liked a woman who said what she meant and didn't mince words.

And, if her body language was any indication, she was trying to tell him to drop dead. Oh, well. He was here to work on a protection system for this family. He had to remember that. He forced himself to stare at the fire. Maybe sometime this week, he'd call her and apologize for being a boor.

No, that would never cut the mustard with a romantic like her. He sighed. The time to apologize was now. As he wracked his brain for the proper words, he allowed his gaze to trail a man in a dark trench coat across the room. He squinted as he attempted one more shot with Juliet.

"About your career. I didn't mean to cast aspersions on the type of fiction you represent. I mean,

I'm sure that there are redeeming reasons to read up on relationships, and self-improvement and love and all that stuff—''

By degrees, her head rotated and the heat in the room shifted from the fireplace to her narrowed gaze. ''You don't have a romantic bone in your body, do you?''

''I'm a realist.''

''You're a party pooper.''

Ian cocked his head and shot his brows as if her opinion mattered not one whit to him. ''Every party needs one.''

Slowly, he tore his gaze away from the man across the room and settled it on Juliet, feeling suddenly inspired. ''You see the mistletoe hanging over our heads on this mantle as something romantic. Perhaps a reason to share a kiss with a lover. Or even a stranger.''

A lazy step forward brought Ian's nose just inches from her own and suddenly Juliet's heart was chugging and her blood pumping. For a split second, she was convinced that he was going to lean in just a fraction and settle his mouth upon hers. And, oddly enough, she—for one harebrained moment of insanity—wanted to taste those chiseled, sarcastic lips. That is, until he said, ''I see it as fungus.''

She snorted. ''Amazing. That's how I see you.''

His laughter rang out as Juliet once again turned to the window near the fireplace. She liked his laugh. It was a heartfelt affair and her opinion of him moved up a notch. There was frost on the windowpanes and, from where she stood, she could see the snow was falling in great, huge tufts, and building on the ground. Under the streetlamp, it was a veritable fairyland.

She rubbed the gooseflesh on her arms. It was drafty over here by the window, where a long hall, just behind them, stretched from here, to the other end of the building.

Reflected in the window, Juliet watched Ian fish his cell phone out of his breast pocket and voice dial his company. "IntraCom Security," he said, and then listened for an answer.

The man was doing business. In the middle of a party. Her opinion dropped two notches.

"Hi, Rudy? Ian. Listen, I'm at the Colton mansion right now. I was wondering if you could check out a—" *Beep.* "No, don't worry about that. It's my battery. I forgot to charge it last night. Yeah." *Beep.* "Damn. Anyway, can you hear me?

"Okay, in a second, I'll try to get to another phone. But first, listen, I want you to check on something odd I noticed here, about the way the current security system—" *Beep.* He glanced up at a camera mounted in the far corner. "—seems to suddenly be malfunctioning. Did you get that? Rudy? Rudy? You there? Damn.'' Ian shoved his phone in his pocket.

A satisfied grin bloomed on Juliet's mouth. Since he'd made it clear he had others to talk to, she decided it was time to take her ego home and put it to bed before it took any more hits. ''Well, it's past my bedtime.'' She bared her teeth in a pseudo smile, and took a few steps back. ''I've gotta run. This has certainly been so…very…''

''Wait, and I'll help you with your coat.'' Ian grabbed Juliet by the arm and pulled her back near the closet in the hallway.

''You'll what?'' How caveman! She jerked her arm away. He may be rich, but money didn't buy everything. Nobody treated Juliet Cosgrove like some kind of helpless female who couldn't dress herself. ''My coat is lying on my sister's bed.''

He grunted, but didn't release her arm. She rolled her eyes as, like 007 on a wedding buffet reconnaissance mission, Ian's gaze darted nervously about the tables and out to the couples on the dance floor. In Juliet's humble opinion, he really took this security thing *waaaay* too seriously. She could tell he was buying time for some reason when he said, ''Look, your new uncle Joe is about to make a toast to the newlyweds. You don't want to miss that.''

"He's not my new uncle Joe. He's my sister's new uncle Joe."

"Whatever."

"Don't worry about me. I'll just enjoy it from the other side of the room."

She tried to enter the ballroom, but Ian took a step forward, his giant body blocking her escape. For pity's sake. She sagged against the wall behind him and decided that rather than making a scene at her sister's reception, she'd disappear as soon as the speech was finished. Even if she had to run down the hall and sneak out the back door.

Joe Colton tapped the microphone with his finger and the Christmas music and murmur of happy guests mingling, began to wane. Standing up on a small stage, Joe lifted a glass in one hand and a bottle in the other and gave a short, but poignant speech about love and fidelity, family and bonds, and community and country.

Soon, there wasn't a dry eye in the house and besides his voice the only sounds were the sentimental sniffles of the guests. Midspeech, Joe paused and glanced at his wife, Meredith, and then at Samantha and Jesse, and the tears welled in his own eyes.

"I've been very blessed in my life, materially speaking. But most important of all," Joe said, "is the blessing of love and family. No amount of money can ever equal the joy that finding one's soulmate can bring. To Samantha and Jesse. Here's to a future of passion and love.''

He held up a champagne bottle, peeled back the foil and popped the cork. Behind him, the wine stewards followed suit. More loud pops followed, amid much shouting and Juliet grinned broadly, really beginning to enjoy being a part of this big, rowdy family.

That is, until she realized that she'd just been tossed into a coat closet.

Chapter 2

"*Shhhh!*" Ian clapped a hand over the squealing Juliet's mouth. "Don't say a word."

Like a hyperactive squirrel, Juliet scrambled about in his arms, fists flying, feet flailing. *Man.* She was strong for such a slender thing, Ian had to give her that. The whirling dervish she'd become would put Jackie Chan to shame. It was pitch-black in the walk-in coat closet and Ian suspected that even when their eyes adjusted, it would be too dark to see much of anything.

Including the handbag that whapped him upside the head.

"Hey, hey, hey, chill out!" Ian grappled with her for the purse.

He was just a hair too late as she had already located her pepper spray and was preparing to blast him.

"No!" Ian grasped her wrist and peeled the spray out of her fingers. "Are you trying to get us killed?"

"Me?" She reared back and he could sense her jaw sagging. *"Me?"*

As his eyes adjusted, he could barely make out that she was fishing through her bag again, for heaven only knew...

"Ooowww!"

One hand flew to the sudden pain in his shoulder, the other to her wrist. Brass knuckles. Where on earth had she come up with brass knuckles? Holding his hands out in front of him, he took a step back, trying to defend himself from what seemed like an angry flock of chickens.

"Juliet! Stop! Before one of us really gets hurt."

"You don't scare me, you...you...*pervert!*"

"Shhhh!" He paused. "Pervert?"

"Yeah, I'm not just some easy bimbo, turned on by your money."

"We're not in here because I think you're easy. Woman," he rotated his throbbing shoulder, "you are anything but easy."

Arms in windmill formation, she ranted, "Okay, okay, Joe Colton's speech gave you ideas. You have a romantic side. I believe you now. You don't have to demonstrate. But let me set you straight right now, buster... I'm not just some *silly* girl looking for some *silly sexcapades* in the closet with you. Got that?''

"Juliet, listen—''

As she flailed, a coat sleeve landed in her mouth. *"Pppffffttt, pffffft! Blaaaaa pfft!* You have no right to uh, abscond with me this way, Mister...*Adventure!* Let go of me this instant!'' she demanded even as she found herself airborne and being propelled to the back of the closet.

"Oww!'' Ian muttered as he stumbled over a shoebox and impaled himself on an umbrella. "Would you please, please, be still?'' He grabbed the umbrella's handle and with a flapping whoosh, it inflated.

"Eeeeoooowww!'' Juliet shrieked and boxed the nylon webbing as they grappled.

"Would you shut up?'' Wrestling the umbrella from between them, he flung it over his shoulder.

"I most certainly will not. I can't *believe* Liza is so deluded that she actually thinks you are *normal!*''

Again, he clapped a hand over her mouth only to feel her teeth sink into the fleshy part of his palm. *"Okay!''* he huffed into her ear, "Okay, okay, *okay!* I won't do that again, but if you don't want

Juliet of the Night

to listen to me, just listen to what is going on, outside the closet door." Arms around her waist, he set her on her feet and attempted—unsuccessfully—to face her toward the door. "I'm not trying to hurt you!"

Together they fell and rolled among the coats, Juliet, still flapping like a Thanksgiving turkey under the ax.

"Listen!" Ian commanded. "You can hear for yourself. Someone has crashed this party and if I'm not mistaken, they are toting guns."

"You have read *far* too much Clancy—"

A series of shots, semi-automatic, judging by the number, suddenly fired from the ballroom. The music abruptly stopped. People were still screaming and the shouts of angry men followed, calling for silence, if their tone could be understood.

Juliet fell silent.

Men using a foreign tongue barked furious orders. One man with a heavy accent translated into English.

"Don't panic, and no one will be hurt."

The sounds of hurried footsteps and furniture scraping across the floor filtered through the closet as the crowd rushed to comply. Off at the other end of the room, a servant dropped a tray, and a man shouted in another language.

Fingers crushed to her lips, Juliet murmured,

"Oh no, oh no, oh no!" Heedless of the danger beyond, she staggered to the closet door but Ian was quick to haul her back. They fell back among the hanging coats and battled both the heavy garments and each other.

"You can't go out there! Are you crazy?"

"Ian, there are pregnant women out there!" She broke free and, crawling awkwardly over the length of her sparkly skirt, which was now caught on one of her super-high heels, she strained on her knees toward the door.

Ian beat her there and blocked her way. There was a low fury in his voice as he spoke. "They have husbands to care for them. You cannot help anyone at this point. You can, however, get yourself killed." Scooting up behind her, his fingers closed around her ankle and he tugged, dragging them both back from the door.

"But my sister! My little brother! My mother! Daddy!"

A glass shattered, followed by more foreign shouts. Several shots fired off, and people screamed.

Juliet threw it into reverse and crawled backward so fast, she landed in Ian's lap, and fairly wrapped herself around his head. Threading her fingers through his hair, she hung on for dear life and crushed her cheek to his.

"Okay," she whimpered, "maybe you're on to something…maybe, maybe, maybe…someone is here to shoot at Joe again. Maybe it's his sister-in-law, that Patsy Portman woman. I read about her in the paper. She's nuts. Or, or, or, or, or, maybe Joe's brother Graham showed up and finally went off the deep end. I've heard all about him, too. My dad warned my sister that this Colton clan was filled with more nuts than a can of Planters, but would she listen?" Juliet panted, "Oh, nooooooo—"

"Would you shut up?"

Juliet hyperventilated into her closed fists. "What," she whispered, barely audibly, "is going on out there?" Her heart was pounding like a pile driver on fast forward. Her hand shook as she raised it to brush her fallen hairstyle out of her face and, as she did so, her fingers came into contact with Ian's jaw.

He clutched her hand and laced his fingers with hers.

"I don't know yet. But it's big trouble," he muttered. "Sixty percent of all burglaries occur while a home is occupied. Thirty-eight percent of robberies are committed with firearms. In the United States alone, a burglar enters a home every fourteen seconds. And, they don't have a battery backup security system in this house. It's truly archaic. If they cut the lines, there is no override system. I had a feeling something was up when the cameras in the ballroom stopped scanning..."

"*Ohhh*—" Juliet pressed their locked hands to her mouth and moaned "—great. Just...great. I land in the closet with an infomercial for IntraCom Security."

"Sorry."

Booted feet stomped down the hall and harsh voices, speaking gibberish to Juliet's ear, filtered through the door.

"What did he just say?" Juliet demanded and clutched the placket of his suit jacket.

In a hurried whisper, Ian attempted to explain. "I don't know. I think they are speaking Cheka-govian, a dialect of German."

"*Chekagovian?* Never heard of it. You *speak* Chekagovian?"

"No. I speak some German, a little Russian. But I can catch a word or two here and there."

"Who the hell are you?" Suddenly he didn't remind her of Parker at all.

"Just your average, run-of-the-mill business guy." He began to search about behind him, exploring their surroundings. "Knowing a few languages comes in handy in my line of business."

"So, are you ever going to tell me what they said?"

"You are short on patience, aren't you?"

"Will you stop analyzing me and just *tell me what they said?*"

"Shhhh! They said they were terrorists—"

"*What?*"

"They said they were terrorists—"

"I heard that part! What else?"

"—and they wanted everyone to stay calm."

"Fat chance." Again, Juliet began to hyperventilate. "What else," she panted, "did they say? What...*huh, huh*...are they...*huh, huh*...saying right now?"

"Be quiet and I'll tell you."

There was more shouting.

"Sounds like they're planning on searching the house."

"The *whole* house?"

"Likely."

"Then, then, then, then, we're probably not safe in here, then, huh?"

"Uh...no. C'mon. Let's get as far back here, behind the coats as we can and pray that they don't think to look under the pile."

The walk-in closet was about twelve feet by fourteen feet and filled to the gills with storage cupboards for mittens and hats and scarves and other winter sundries. One wall was lined with shelving for boots and such and the other two walls had double rows of rods, currently packed with the coats of reception guests. There were furs and faux furs and wraps of all nature and size.

Together, Juliet and Ian frantically searched around, feeling the walls, patting the coats, and each other in their quest for the perfect place to hide. Every time Juliet knelt on her skirt and crawled forward, she could feel her bodice tug just a little lower.

Luckily it was dark.

She started as just outside the door a loud voice shouted in Chekagovian.

Ian gave a sketchy translation for Juliet's benefit. *"Soldiers! Come down here! Let a search begin in this hall also."*

"Just one moment."

More shouting, unintelligible now.

It sounded as if they'd opened the door into the room next door to them first. Muffled voices, furious cursing and the sound of ransacking were growing ever closer.

Juliet froze with panic. "Now what?" she squeaked.

"They're going to search one room at a time."

"Oh?"

"C'mon. According to my calculations, we're next. We've gotta hide."

"I can't see a thing."

"We can't turn on the light. Just keep feeling

your way.'' Arms outstretched, he patted his way over her backless gown to her sequined bottom.

"Sorry."

"S'alright."

Blindly, they crawled into the inky black shadows and behind the coats. Under a set of corner shelves, Ian found an area that just might work as a hideout, if they could quickly and silently unload some of the ski paraphernalia stored there.

Juliet grabbed a bag of miscellany on the floor and flung it over her shoulder, inadvertently hitting Ian in the head with a rubber boot.

"Hey, woman," Ian hissed, "we can't just throw stuff all over the place. We have to stack it neatly, or they'll know we're here."

Juliet muttered under her breath about how hard it was to find good help in the middle of a terrorist attack and falling in next to Ian, systematically worked, cleaning out an area that would accommodate the two of them.

Around her neck, Juliet's little gold party purse was beginning to cut off her air supply, and she was coming dangerously close to popping out of her dress's strapless bustline, but she figured there would be time for modesty and breathing later, when they were safe.

Feverishly they worked, a confusion of bodies

and breath and hair and muscles and hands. His hands landed in awkward spots. So did hers.

"Sorry," she mumbled as she accidentally crawled between his legs.

"No, I'm sorry," he admitted.

"You didn't know," she muttered, face flaming.

"Hey!" There was a spark of excitement in his stage whisper. "I think we might be in luck!"

"What?"

Ian inched on his belly and probing the wall with his fingers, found a vent that allowed air to circulate. Behind the grillwork, there was an opening that led to a crawl space under the massive stairs. He tore off the vent cover and rumbled with triumph.

Ian backed out, grabbed Juliet by the arm and before she knew what hit her, he was propelling her under the corner shelf and into the miniscule one-by-two-foot hole.

"Hurry, I found the perfect hiding place. You go in first and I'll bring up the rear."

Being that she was terrified of small, dark spaces, Juliet gratefully declined the nomination and chirped over her shoulder, "No, no, that's okay. You go in first."

"What? Don't be ridiculous! We don't have time!" On all fours behind her, he nudged at her bottom with the top of his head. "Get in there."

"No, it's too dark. I can't...see... You go first!"

"Get in there!"

"But I—"

"Damn it, woman, you are the most obnoxious thing I have ever had the dubious honor—"

His voice grew muffled as Juliet felt herself being jettisoned, face first through the opening. Frantically, she muscled her way up to her hips and stalled for a quick breather. As she rested, she wondered how a guy Ian's size would make it through this opening. Her heaving bosom caught her attention and she had to wonder how she'd ended up with her bare body in the crawl space and her dress...well, her dress had headed south for the winter and was now bunched around her waist and inside the closet. With Ian. The wadded fabric made getting through this particular rabbit hole just a smidgen more interesting.

More shots were fired and—dragging her purse—Juliet somersaulted into the mysterious space and cracked her head on a rafter in the process. Seeing stars, she paused to groan.

"You okay?"

"Mmfph." Just ducky considering all the king's horses would have a tough time putting her head back together anytime soon. That and the fact that she was sitting there, nude from the waist up. She

struggled to tug her dress back up under her arm-pits, where it belonged.

Once her eyes adjusted to the moonlight that fil-tered from a small vent near the ceiling, she could discern a few shadowy shapes. On the floor, there was a landing made of plywood, and then a catwalk of sorts, lying across evenly spaced floor joists that allowed access between the sprawling double stair-case. The walls were lath and plaster and pink fi-berglass insulation was stuffed between the studs. Between the joists, the floor was covered with some kind of cottony insulation that clung to, well, ev-erything, as she crawled down the four-foot wide boardwalk to make room for Ian.

Off in the dank, dark corners, Juliet could swear she heard the scratching of some kind of rodent. Rat? Mouse? Or worse... Bats? Lots of bats. Cer-tainly an area like this had to be bat heaven.

All possibilities had her shuddering. And there were spiders. Of that she became positive, as she spit a cobweb out of her mouth.

"Ewww."

Through the opening, Ian stuffed several fur coats and a sleeping bag he'd found in with the ski gear.

"Hurry," Juliet whispered. "Get in here." She forced herself not to give in to the sensations of panic that were washing over her. She had to keep a clear head. This was a matter of staying alive.

"I'm coming."

An avalanche of coats burst through the opening.

"We don't need all those coats. It's not like we'll freeze to death."

"Nag, nag, nag. Besides, famous last words. It's cold in here, baby. Too cold to hide for very long in that skimpy thing you're wearing."

He had a point. Juliet shivered. Man, she was scared. More scared than she'd ever been in her life. More scared than the time she'd stayed up late as a child with the neighbor girls and watched Alfred Hitchcock's *The Birds* and then had nightmares for months about birds nesting in her closet and under her bed and…in her hair.

She reached up and patted her head, just for good measure and found a clump of spider webbing. She shuddered.

"*Ufff.*" Ian's grunts drew Juliet from her anxious musings.

"What are you doing?"

"Oh, I thought I'd just lie here with my head under the stairs and let those idiots out there shoot at my butt. What are you doing?"

"Very funny." Juliet tossed the coats out of her way. Grabbing his arms, she braced her foot against a floor joist and tugged, trying to pull him through the hole. She grunted, and tugged some more. But nothing was happening. "If this is anything like childbirth," she panted, "you can count me out."

"Here," Ian huffed, "put your arms around my chest and on three, tug."

"On three?"

"As in 'one, two and…'?"

"I…uh…okay." Blast her stupid dress. Really inhibited crawling. Hiking her skirts up to her hips, she slithered up to the wall on her bottom and, bending low, snaked her arms around his great big, rock-hard chest. Then, she braced her feet and pulled for all she was worth.

"I…said…on…three," he bit out.

"Oh, right, right, right."

Together they counted. "One…two…*threeeee!*"

Nothing.

Outside, they heard more shouts from the terrorists.

"I have an idea," Juliet panted into Ian's ear.

"Spit it out."

"Exhale on three."

"Okay."

Again, they counted, again they strained through the hole and this time, they were met with success as Ian rocketed through the hole to land on top of her. They lay like that for a moment, nose to nose, breathing heavily, resting.

"Uuuuuh…" Ian groaned and rolled off Juliet and lay at her side. "Thanks. I feel like I should offer you a cigarette."

"I'd prefer a morphine drip. You're no featherweight. I feel like I've just slow danced with a speeding freight train."

Another loud yell, this time much closer, and they scurried to drag in the rest of the coats and to tug the vent back where it belonged. The louvers allowed some muffled noise to penetrate and they stacked some loose boards and bats of insulation against the sides of the opening, hoping to jam the vent into place and at the same time, confound the thugs.

Once they were settled into a nest of fur—Ian against the wall and Juliet fairly sitting in his lap—they listened.

Ian interpreted as much as he could understand for Juliet and the more she heard, the more she understood how grim the situation was becoming.

Ducking her head, Juliet suddenly emitted a muffled scream.

"What now?"

"A spider."

"So?"

"It's huge. Like a tarantula. All hairy and it has huge legs. Maybe…maybe it's a bat!" Juliet took a swat at the thing with her purse.

"Ouch! Those are not legs, they are fingers. Your spider-bat is my hand."

"Oh. Sorry. You need to shave your hands."

Ian snorted and tossed a fur glove at her.

"Here, shave this."

Dust flew when it landed in the cottony insulation. "Uh-oh…I'm going to sneeze."

"No," Ian commanded. "You're not."

"I can't heh…heh…heh…elp it."

"Ohhh, yes you can." With his fingertips, he groped her face, finding her lips and working his way north. He pinched her nose and hissed, "If you sneeze, they could find us. And kill us. Don't do it."

She nodded.

Slowly, he let go.

"Aaaacheeechhhieee," she squeaked.

Ian heaved a snort of disgust. "What the hell kind of a sneeze was that?"

"A perfectly legitimate one," she sniffed and geared up to sneeze again.

"Listen." He groped for her nose and pinched.

"Whaa's goink nn?"

Doors opened, doors slammed. The sounds ransacking the room across the hall had them both jumping as books and knickknacks crashed to the floor and glass shattered. Angry voices told Ian—

who whispered to Juliet—they hadn't found what they were looking for yet.

The voices became louder as their closet door was jerked open and the footsteps of more than one man clomped inside.

Juliet's eyes grew round. Her fingers bit into Ian's bicep. "They, they, they, they are inside our closet!" Raw terror closed off her throat.

Ian nodded and clapped his hand over her lips. "Don't bite."

"Mmm."

"And don't sneeze."

With a nod, Juliet burrowed back against his chest and was surprised at the fury with which his heart was beating. He circled her waist with his arms and their breathing became synchronized in its ragged labor. Cheek-to-cheek, they strained to see and hear through the pitch-blackness.

Through the vent, they could see the beam of a flashlight swing around. The beam landed on the vent and illuminated their feet.

They both froze.

Muffled foreign words were muttered just beyond the wall. Juliet stopped breathing and could sense Ian doing the same. Ever so slowly, the men backed out of the closet.

Ian and Juliet hovered for an eternity in silence

as thick as day-old pea soup, hearts thrumming, blood coursing, adrenaline flowing.

"What did they say?"

"I didn't get it. But they left and that's good. Maybe they're not in the mood to ski."

They both exhaled in huge relief, and then ventured some silent laughter. Still nestled in his lap, Juliet loosened her grip about his neck.

Whispering, Ian joked that in other circumstances, this would really be turning him on.

Juliet whispered back that in other circumstances, she would be slapping his face for the position of his hands.

"What do you think they are trying to find?" Juliet wondered.

"Could be anything."

"When do you think they'll leave?"

"Not until they find what they are looking for."

"Who are they?"

"I don't know, but I have a feeling it has something to do with the Ritkas. I seriously doubt that Jesse or your sister would have anything that a foreign rebel faction would find interesting."

"True. I wonder why would they pick Christmas Eve and a wedding of all times to do this?"

"Probably because they know that what they are after is here in the house today. Maybe they needed hostages. Maybe they needed publicity. They could be looking for a person. A guest at the wedding.''

''Who?''

''I don't know. Quiet. Here they come again.''

''*Here?* They are coming *back* here? To, to, to, to, to *this* closet? But they were just, just, just, just *here*—''

They both sucked in a deep breath and held it as the closet door was once again opened and heavy footfalls approached. Overhead, a light flashed on. The men muttered as they worked, ripping coats off the hangers and pulled boxes off the shelves over the hanger rod and onto the floor.

When everything lay in a heap, the men began to search the rubble. A flashlight beam flooded the areas beneath the lower shelves and circled the floorboards. The glow lit the knee wall through the metal vent.

Again, the light stopped and trained on the vent.

Juliet thrust her face into Ian's neck and stifled a scream as she wrapped his torso with her arms and legs. Ian held her tight and kissed her temple and whispered soothing words into her ear. The beam traveled on, and then back to the vent.

Chapter 3

The strange men conferred in low tones.

The light moved on.

Silently, absently, Ian stroked Juliet's hair and cheeks and, with the backs of his knuckles, he could feel her lips moving.

"What?" he asked.

"I'm praying."

"Oh." Why hadn't he thought of that? "Good."

"We're going to die," she whispered.

"No, no. We're not. Have faith."

"I'm scared."

"I know. Me, too."

"You don't seem scared. You seem all brave, like some guy out of a Tom Clancy book."

"Inside I'm some guy out of a Tom Jell-O book."

"What if they find the crawl space?"

"They won't."

"Why not? We did."

"They have no reason to believe we are in here. If we're still and quiet, they'll move away and search something else."

"But what if…"

Ian moved his mouth to her ear and murmured, "Juliet, you have to be quiet."

"But how do you…"

Stubborn woman! "Juliet, I'm not kidding. You *have* to be quiet. They are only a few feet away."

"But I'm scare…"

With an impatient sigh, Ian cupped her cheeks and pulled her mouth under his, to shut her up the only way he could think of at the moment. Juliet stopped struggling and froze. Only when she reflexively began to kiss him back, did he release her. They hovered nose-to-nose, lip-to-lip.

"Please?" Ian urged her silence.

Her forehead pressed to his, she nodded.

Eventually, the voices and the men moved out of the closet.

"They're gone."

Juliet exhaled and lay limply against Ian and knew that with that kiss, their relationship changed irrevocably. The difference now shimmered between them, like the electricity in the air just before a summer thunderstorm. And though this instant camaraderie was born of urgency and fear, it was no less real.

Juliet knew Ian felt it as keenly as she had.

Like a summer fog on a morning meadow, their animosity vanished and was replaced with trust.

Ian rested his cheek against her temple and thought aloud. "I have to come up with a way to get out of here and find help."

"No!" Juliet panicked and clutched his arms. "You can't go! I need you. Bold rescue moves like that only work in the books you read. Don't try to be some kind of hero. They'll just kill you. We can wait them out. Here. Together. Please, don't go. Please." She shuddered at the thought of being left alone.

"I promise I won't go until I figure out some kind of plan."

Somewhat mollified, Juliet fell silent for a moment before she asked, "So. What would Jack Ryan do in a situation like this?"

"Since we're not on a submarine, or in a tank, I'm at a total loss. You publish fantasy. Surely you've seen enough happily ever afters to know how this thing ends."

"Uhhh, no. One of my clients wrote a book

about two people stranded on an iceberg, but their biggest concern was making fire.''

''Do tell.'' Ian's tone was droll as he took off his suit jacket and loosened his tie.

''Yeah. I guess that wouldn't be much help now.'' Relishing the body warmth, Juliet picked up his jacket and pulled it over her legs with a groan of relief.

Ian's cell phone rang in her lap and they both scrambled through his pockets to find it.

Juliet won and quickly turned it off.

''Phewww,'' she whispered with a triumphant smile. ''That was close.''

''What the hell did you do that for?'' he snapped and snatched the phone from her hands in exasperation.

''Duh. It was *ringing?* Hello? You don't want them to find us, do you?'' she spit back furiously, hurt at his ungrateful attitude. Especially in light of the moment they'd just shared.

''If you'd answered it, we might have been able to get help.''

''Ohhh.'' Though she tried, Juliet couldn't keep the tears from her voice. ''I…didn't think of that.''

Ian groaned and she could fairly hear his eyes roll. ''Oh, now, don't go and start crying. I hate it when women cry.''

"Well. I wouldn't want to make you feel bad, now would I?"

A chuckle rumbled deep in his chest. "I'm sorry. I'm not exactly my jolly self today. Forgive me?"

"I guess." She sniffed.

"Thanks. Our first fight," he teased and gave her a playful nudge.

Over her shoulder, Juliet shot him a bemused look as he rubbed her arm and placed a quick peck on her temple. He really was quite sweet. When he wanted to be.

He held up the phone. "Maybe we have enough battery to get 911."

Juliet watched as he dialed. The light on the phone flickered.

Beeeeeeeep!

She winced. Bad sign.

"911 operator. Your emergency please."

"Police. Look, my phone is dying, so listen up. We are being held captive in—"

Beeeeeeeep!

"I need your name and location, sir."

"My name is Ian Rafferty and I'm at the Colton..." *Beeeeeep...*

"Sir...you are cutting..."

"Can you hear me?"

"Sir..."

"Hello? Hello?"

Nothing.

"Hopefully this will teach you not to check your voice mail in the middle of a party, in the future."

Ian exhaled without comment.

"Now what are we going to do?"

Ian rearranged Juliet on his lap. "For a such a sharp tongue, you have very soft curves."

"You're pretty witty yourself. Ever think about writing?"

He chuckled. "After this? I may."

She settled back against his chest, content to be nestled between his legs, his arms resting in her lap.

"Are you hungry?" she asked.

"No. Are you?"

"I always eat when I'm terrified."

"Sorry, I have nothing to offer you."

Juliet grabbed her purse. "Tic-Tac? They have one whole calorie per serving, or something."

"Do I need one?"

"No." She snorted. "You have really good breath." Embarrassed at her admission, she ducked her head and continued to rummage through her tiny, gold lamé clutch.

"You don't happen to have a flashlight in that pathetic excuse for a purse, do you?"

"Uh… Yeah, come to think of it, I have a little one on my key chain."

"Good. Give it to me."

She rummaged some more. "Here."

Ian nudged her off his lap and scooted to the edge of the plywood landing. Lying on his side, he flashed the small light under the eaves.

Juliet leaned toward him and whispered. "I hope everyone is okay out there. My...my whole family—" The emotions swelled, closing off her throat.

"I think they're probably all right." He sounded confident. But then, he always sounded confident, as far as Juliet could tell.

She sniffed and swiped at her eyes with her wrists. "How do you know?"

"I think the shots that have been fired were for shock value. The one guy did say that if they cooperated, no one would get hurt."

"That's true." She raked a hand through her hair. That morning, it had been so chic. Now, it felt like freshly thrashed hay. Again, she was glad for the darkness. "I feel so sorry for Samantha and Jesse."

"They'll never forget their wedding day, that's for sure."

"If they live long enough to remember it."

"I don't think these guys are after the bride and groom."

"How do you know? Jesse is with the National Security Agency."

Chin to shoulder, Ian glanced back at Juliet. "Hunch."

"The West Coast Coltons have enemies."

"Not this kind."

With aid of the tiny beam, they could now see that they were sitting in a little alcove, behind a closet and under the stairs. However, around the corner, there was a corridor of sorts that it seemed just may lead somewhere. Ian ventured off the platform and several yards down the catwalk.

"Where are you going?" Juliet cried, sotto voce. He was leaving? Now?

"Sit tight. I'm just going to crawl along this ledge here under the stairs. We may find an escape route, or a better vantage point to figure out what is going on and maybe even fight back."

"No! Don't."

Ian groaned. "Why not?"

"Because they might see you. Or hear you. Or you could fall, or something."

"Give me a real reason."

Struggling to her knees, Juliet battled her way out of the pile of coats and, crawling up behind him, put her arms around his neck. "Because I'm scared." Voice small and quaking with terror, she hated that she sounded almost childlike in her plea. "You are only one guy. There are a whole bunch of them."

Ian's shoulders flagged and she could tell she'd won this round.

"Okay. For now," he capitulated. "But, when things settle down out there, we'll need to go for help."

"Fine."

He followed her back to the pile of coats. Once there, he wrapped a fur around her shoulders and, sitting down beside her, lifted her into his lap. The insulation's paper backing crackled as he settled against the wall and surrounded her with his arms.

A heartfelt sigh of relief escaped her lips as she rolled onto one hip and snuggled against his chest.

Seconds passed.

Then minutes.

Beyond the closet, chaos. In here, safety.

Juliet listened to Ian's steady heartbeat and was comforted. The paper rustled as he dipped his head and nudged her face up with his nose. They peered through the darkness, trying to judge one another's intent. They lingered like this, transfixed.

"What if we die in here?" she whispered, her breath feathering his lips.

"Don't even think like that."

"I can't help it. I'm a realist."

"No you're not. You're an idealist. I'm the realist, and I say we're going to make it out of here alive."

"I'm glad you're here," she whispered.

"Ditto."

They fell silent, breathing each other's breath.

He'd kissed her once already. But that had been somehow different. He'd kissed her in order to silence her. Now, she was silent.

There was no real need now, other than comfort.

And want.

Her breathing quickened.

So did his.

Her heart thundered.

His did, too.

Again, his nose touched hers and gripping his shirt, she angled back into the crook of his shoulder and offered him her mouth.

Slowly, ever so slowly, Ian's lips found hers and Juliet had never felt so safe. She drooped against him like a snow-laden tree bough and relished the security of something as normal and wonderful as Ian's embrace.

This climate of danger yielded heightened senses, which in turn gave way to a poignant yearning and a need so powerful that Juliet would never be able to describe with mere words.

Juliet felt Ian's hands cupping the side of her face. He rested his thumbs in the dimples at the corners of her mouth and stroked her cheeks and explored the union of their lips. As his mouth moved over hers, their lungs labored and they clutched each other as if their lives depended on it.

Or, even worse, as if they had little life left to live.

And the kiss quickly ripened with impatience. Impatience to know each other, impatience to fast-forward their brief relationship into one of a lasting bond. Of implicit trust. Of mutual understanding.

She curled into his lap, her arms rising to rest at his shoulders, her hands splayed at the back of his head. His hair was so silky to the touch and smelled of manly shampoo. At his jaw, there was a trace of stubble as the hour grew late, and it abraded her cheeks most pleasantly. Heat rushed from Juliet's toes to the top of her head and its impact nearly left her faint.

He nipped at her mouth, and tugged her lower lip between his teeth. Against her smile, his bloomed.

But their moment of escape was brief. The sudden sounds of floorboards creaking overhead pulled them from their reverie, and with great reluctance, Ian broke their kiss and tilted his head to the rafters. "They've gone upstairs."

Quaking, Juliet nodded.

"Don't be scared."

"I can't help it."

"You have to be strong. Think of all the people out there, who are going to need our help."

"I know."

He kissed her gently on her mouth, her cheeks, her jaw and her nose.

"I really have to go. Soon. Waiting could mean people die."

"Going could mean *you* die."

"No."

"Then I'm going with you."

"No, you're not. You're staying right here, tucked under one of these furs. You'll wait until I come back for you. Is that clear?"

"Crystal." Her mouth twisted in frustration but he kissed it away.

"Good. I'll…be back."

Juliet sighed. "Roger, Arnold."

Ian patted her leg and, flashlight leading the way, began his precarious journey under the trailing stairs. After about twenty feet, he sat up, looked over his shoulder and exhaled with impatience. "What are you doing?"

"Coming with you."

"I thought I told you to stay put."

"You did."

"Then why aren't you put?"

"Because I want to come with you."

"Woman, you are the most pigheaded—"

"Yeah, yeah, yeah. Look, my knees are bruised, my stockings are ruined and my girdle is killing me and my strapless dress is no longer modest. Can we move it along?''

''Taking the dress thing into consideration, I could be persuaded to stay…''

''Move it,'' she commanded.

With a grin, Ian began to crawl, muttering all the while about stubborn women. Jerkily, Juliet teetered along on her hands and knees behind him until they reached the end of the corridor. There, they found another, identical alcove with a vent leading to another room.

''Where does this vent go?''

''Into the ballroom.''

''What do you see?''

''Nothing.''

''Nothing?''

''No one.''

''No one?''

''Empty.''

''…empty?''

Ian turned to stare at her.

''Would you stop?''

''Oh. Sure. Sorry.''

''As far as I can tell, people have left the ballroom. I can only guess that they have been moved to some other quadrant of the house.''

''It's really quiet.''

"Yeah. Let's keep moving. Maybe there is something around the corner."

Juliet fell in behind him until Ian abruptly stopped and bent back to peer into her face.

"What's wrong? Why did you stop? Bats? Please, tell me, it's not bats."

"No. My shoelace. You are on my shoelace. Would you—"

"Get off your shoelace?"

"No."

"No?"

"That's not what I was going to say."

"Oh."

Ian leaned ever closer and his breath stirred the hair at the side of her face. "Would you go out to dinner with me when this is all over? To, you know, celebrate being alive and everything."

"If we're still alive, sure." She could sense his grin.

"How do you feel about Florence?"

"Italy?"

"I'm partial to Italian food."

"Then I'll make us a lasagna. Costco. Ten bucks. They're really good. You don't have to fly me around, and spend a bunch of money to impress me."

"Why not?"

"Because I'm already impressed."

"Me, too," he whispered. "Me, too."

Chapter 4

"Listen," Ian said.

From rooms beyond the ballroom, they could hear the workings of the Chekagovians tearing the place apart and herding people into smaller rooms. Muffled conversation between at least a half-dozen men rose and fell.

"I think they have stationed guards at all the entrances to the ballroom."

"I'm so glad you didn't go out there. At least not now."

"Me, too."

Juliet rested her chin on his shoulder as she peered through the vent. "We don't have a phone and there are guards at the doors. Any ideas?"

Ian bunched his shoulders. "I'm stumped." The flashlight's beam illuminated the crawl space's walls and ceiling. The plywood catwalk did not continue on around the corner. "We seem to have reached the end of the road here."

"Mmm. What should we do now?"

"Wait until they move away from the doors, I guess. Then maybe I can sneak out unobserved. I don't know just yet. I have to think. Let's go." He gestured for her to return to the coats.

Juliet groaned as she wobbled about-face and led the way back. "I sure hope this mess doesn't take too much longer. I was on my way to the bathroom when Liza dragged me over to meet you."

"Possibly saved your life," he said. "You gonna be okay?"

"Just trying not to think about waterfalls. And oceans. And rain showers. And," she battled back her emotions, "you know, my little sister. This is the first day of the rest of her life, and now this. Some wedding night, huh?"

"Not the kind I have planned for when I get married, I'll tell you that," Ian said as they crawled into their places among the coats. As if it were the most natural thing in the world, Juliet settled into his lap and after he draped them in several coats, he circled her waist with his arms.

"What do you have planned?" she murmured.

"Well, I haven't actually *planned* it yet, but I can tell you it would be just me. And my wife. And a bed. That's about it. Location wouldn't really matter."

"Ah." She sniffed and dabbed at her eyes, cheering some at this interesting thought. "Sounds like fun."

"That, I could guarantee."

Juliet let loose with a little snort of laughter.

"What?"

"You are just so cocky."

"Not cocky. Confident."

"Whatever."

She snuggled more firmly against him, already familiar with his scent. And his feel. And the steady, comforting beat of his heart. They fit together very nicely, dovetailing plane to curve as if they had been created just for the purpose of holding each other.

"What do you have in your purse?"

"Why?"

"Just wondered if you had anything besides pepper spray or brass knuckles as weapons. I don't suppose you're toting a machine gun?"

"Sorry. Not at this reception."

"How about a fresh phone battery?"

"Nope."

"A steak dinner?"

"Noooo, but...let me see." Juliet found her purse against the wall and sitting up, emptied its contents into her lap.

Ian pointed the flashlight's beam as they explored. Lipstick, comb, compact, a mangled chocolate protein bar, wallet, keys, identification. Ian held up her driver's license.

"Hmm...let's see."

She tried to grab it back. "Gimme that! You're not supposed to look at personal stuff like that until I've known you for at least two more hours!"

"Why not? Says here that you are five foot six. Is that true? You look taller."

"Heels."

"Oh. How about this one-hundred-and-twenty-five-pound part here?" He was clearly skeptical.

"So, I lied. All women do." She huffed at his audacity.

"Why would you want people to think you weigh more than you do?"

She swallowed. "...More?"

"You couldn't be more than a hundred pounds, soaking wet."

"Are you trying to get on my good side?"

"Is it working?"

"Maybe."

"You're prettier in real life." He squinted at the

license, and then at her. Your birthday is in January? The eleventh, I see.''

"Yes.''

"We'll have to celebrate when we get out of here.''

"Oh, we'll celebrate all right.''

"We've been in here for over an hour.''

"Seems like a lifetime,'' Ian announced in a hushed voice. "I still can't believe we heard singing Christmas carols. I wonder if they were trying to send a message to the police.''

"I just hope they don't get themselves in trouble. But it hasn't been that bad being stuck in here with you, all things considered. Could be worse.''

"Oh, yeah. Other than the circumstances, it's been a swell first date.'' She could make out his grin in the dim glow of the flashlight.

"So, all together there are five in your family?''

"Mm-hum.'' Juliet nodded. "How many in yours?''

"Only four. My sister and me, and my mom and dad.''

"Everyone still alive?''

"So far.''

Juliet sighed heavily. "Yeah.''

* * *

"You're the old maid," Juliet gloated. They'd found a small deck of playing cards in a pocket of one of the coats they'd grabbed.

"I beg your pardon? I'm the old bachelor."

"Why does that sound so much more glamorous than old maid?"

"Being an old bachelor is not all sunglasses and autographs. Sometimes I'm actually bored. And lonely."

"Oh, poor baby."

"You say that like you don't believe me."

"A handsome guy like you? I'd think you had women all over you, all the time."

"*You* certainly didn't seem all that impressed when we first met."

"I said you were handsome. I didn't say personable."

"Ouch."

"Oh, come on. Admit it, you came across like a mackerel on ice."

"Keep sweet-talking me like that and I'll ravage you here and now."

Juliet giggled. "Holy mackerel."

Ian chuckled, then whispered, "I came across that way because I didn't want you to know that I found you attractive."

Juliet poked his ribs with her elbow.

"It's true. You must have noticed I couldn't stop staring."

"I thought it was because I had toilet paper clinging to my shoe, or something stuck in my teeth."

Ian laughed.

"So. Fess up. Do you have women all over the place?"

"No."

"Why not?"

"Because I've been too busy building my business to concentrate on building relationships. My sister is always harping on me to get married and settle down. Have a few kids. Never really seemed that important to me, until...now."

"Now?" Juliet touched her tongue to her lips. "Uh, why now?"

"I don't know." Ian rocked her a bit, then rested his chin at the top of her head and attempted a bit of levity. "Life and death situations always put me in a reflective frame of mind. This makes me realize that my priorities might not be in the right order."

"Yeah." Deep in thought, Juliet tore open the wrapper on the diet bar from her purse and offered Ian a bite.

"No thanks. I'll just wait for *them* to kill me, thank you anyway."

"What are you talking about? These are good.

Chocolate and soy protein powder. Delicious *and* good for you.''

''Gack.''

Juliet shrugged and bit the end off her bar. ''Anyway, I know what you mean about reexamining your life. For years now, my career has been everything to me. But ever since Samantha began talking about her own wedding, I've had an…I don't know…a yearning, for lack of a better word…it's silly.''

''No it's not. I know what you mean, though I'd never have admitted that until just now.''

''You ever come close to getting married before?''

''Twice.''

''What happened?''

''Well, the first time, I was seven. I fell madly in love with Alexa 'Hotlips' Madison in the first grade. She used to chase me around the playground, and when she caught me, she'd pick me up and shake me till my teeth rattled and then kiss me senseless. What a woman. She was about a head taller than I was and we were inseparable. We lost our teeth together, scraped our knees together, traded lunches and played house. I called her toots, which she loved, and she called me honey. We pinkie swore we would marry when we were grown up or in the sixth grade.''

"What happened?"

"She moved. I was heartbroken. Took me a week to get over her."

"A whole week?"

"I've matured."

"So, tell me about your second time."

"I was in college. This time, I knew it was for real. For life. Her name was Liv." Ian paused, then continued, "which was ironic, as she contracted leukemia right after college and died three days before we were supposed to be married."

"How awful!"

"Yeah."

They didn't speak for a reflective moment.

"What about you?" he finally asked.

"Me? Well, yes, I was in love several times. At one time or another, I was in love with all The New Kids on the Block."

"You come from a big neighborhood?"

Juliet laughed in spite of the dire situation going on somewhere beyond the walls. "No, silly, that old band, not the neighbors. Surely you heard of the New Kids?"

"Uh, I was more into grunge as a kid. Although, you could take the fact that I just bought another Sinatra CD as a sign that I'm getting old."

"I love Sinatra. And Tony Bennett."

"Mmm. Back then, they knew how to sing."

"Yeah."

"Anyway, that was a very evasive answer, Miss Cosgrove. Who were you really in love with?"

"Well, if we're going back to first grade, then it had to be Johnny Loika. Second grade was Jeff Roth. Third grade was Brett Canova. Fourth grade was Deuce Marion. Fifth grade was Marty Oui, ooo, that man could allemande left in square dance class. In sixth grade, it was Phillip Leopold…"

"You were kind of fickle, huh?"

"Yeah, but I've matured."

"Ever been engaged?"

"Yes."

"Married?"

"Other than to my work, no."

"What happened to the fiancé?"

"Hmm. How can I put this without seeming like a bitter harridan? He was a cheating, lying, thieving jerk, and those were his good qualities."

"I'm sorry."

"Don't be. You're not him. At first I thought you were, but you're not. Parker would have used me as a shield, when the shooting started."

"You ever think you'll get married?"

"You know, even though I sound like…"

"A bitter harridan?"

"Shut up." She reached up and gave his cheek a playful smack. "Anyway, it's funny, but earlier, when I was watching Samantha take her vows with Jesse, I knew that they had the kind of love that would sustain them through anything. It's a really pure, perfect love. I envy them that. I think if I ever found my soulmate, I'd want to hang on to that. So, yes. My answer is yes. What about you?"

"Same."

"I wonder what's taking the cops so long to bust in here?" Ian was growing impatient.

Juliet shrugged. "We could probably hear a lot more if this place wasn't so well insulated."

"No doubt. So." Ian shifted his position so that he could better see into Juliet's face. "How many kids do you want?"

"Hmmm... Three, I think. One of each."

"Ha, ha. What will you name them?"

"Well, if it's a girl, Beulah-Frenealla. And if it's a boy, Boceefus-Bob."

"Over my dead body."

"Oh? What say would *you* have in the matter?"

"I could not, in good conscience, let you scar your children for life."

"And what do you suggest?"

"William, after my grandfather. And, Liv."

"So, I'm naming my kids after your grandfather and an old girlfriend? I don't think so."

* * *

"Yeah, but can you sing the theme song at the *end* of the show?"

"Wasn't it the same thing?"

"Sheyeah—" Juliet snorted "—not."

"Okay, Miss know-it-all thang, you sing it."

"'No phones, no lights, no motorcars, not a single luxury, like Robinson Crusoe, it's primitive as can be.'"

"Kind of like this place."

"Yeah. Where's the Professor when you need him?"

Silence reigned as they resurfaced to reality.

They'd been here for ages, and still the confusion raged off in the distance.

Juliet's tongue clicked as she expelled a nervous sigh.

Ian drummed his fingers.

The walls seemed to close in. Suddenly, it seemed stuffy. As if there wasn't enough air.

Ian couldn't stand the waiting any longer. "I think it might be time to go check on our party crashers."

"What do you mean, 'go check'? You're not leaving?"

"I can't stay in here forever."

"Why not?"

"If I can escape, I could get the police access to the cameras positioned throughout the house."

"No! That's stupid. Stay here with me. We still haven't sung the theme to *Mister Ed* yet."

Gently, Ian stroked her arms. "I know. But there will be plenty of time to do that later. Right now, there are people in this house waiting for help. And frankly, none seems to be coming. I have an idea, but you'll need to stay here and wait for me."

"And what if I don't want to."

Ian raked his hands through his hair. "Woman, really, you vex me."

"Sorry."

"It's okay. Somehow, coming from you, I don't mind. Listen. I don't want to leave either. But someone has to do something. It may as well be me. At least I have some training in security measures and—"

"Jesse works for the NSA, let him do it! He's the expert!"

"He's also most likely a hostage, which is why we need to make a move. Soon. Before too much more time passes. Before the eye of the storm blows over."

"But I haven't told you what kind of house I want, yet. And about the station wagon, and the carpooling and the after-school sports. I have a lot of priorities that still need sorting. Why don't you stay and help me do that, before you go out there." She circled his biceps with her arms and pressed her cheek to the strength she felt there.

Ian kissed the top of her head. "You want a Federal-style minimansion in Virginia. To go with your minimansion, you need a minivan. Seven passenger. For all the kids, dogs and groceries. I'll help you with the car-pooling and coaching the after-school sports."

"You will, why?"

"Because it will be my responsibility, as their father."

"Is this a proposal?"

"Why not? We'll have the wedding here, hopefully sans party crashers."

"When?"

"Well, since I've turned gray in the past several hours and neither of us is getting any younger, I vote for next Christmas. That should give us plenty of time to convince everyone that you're not pregnant, throw a wedding together and pick names for our first two offspring."

"Okay. It's a date. So, in order to do this, you can't go out there and get yourself killed."

"I promise. I promise you, and I promise our children." He nuzzled her neck and growled like Arnold, "I'll be back."

Unable to stand the tension, Juliet broke down and cried.

Ian kissed her cheeks, tasting the salty tracks of her tears. "Do you believe in love at first sight?" he whispered.

"No." She wiped her face on his shirt. "But I do believe in loathe at first sight, but they say those emotions are very closely related."

"Did you loathe me at first sight?" Ian was wounded.

"Yes. I thought you were a boob."

"And now?"

"I think I love you, you boob. You know," she hiccupped, "as much as I can love you, given we've known each other for only a night."

"Yes, but what a night. More emotion-packed than some folk's lifetime. So…you love me."

"What's not to love?"

He gave his shoulders an I-dunno.

They both laughed to belie the seriousness of the situation. And the conversation.

"Are you sure I can't go with you? I think I'll go crazy, sitting in here by myself."

"I'm sure."

"You'll be careful?"

"If I can get into the kitchen, I think I can get out the back door and to the patio unnoticed, if I time it right. The door is only about ten yards from that vent. This time, you are not to follow me. Understand?"

Juliet didn't answer.

"Juliet, if you do, you could get us both killed."

"Okay," she murmured brokenly. Her lower lip quivered and she clung to Ian, even as she gave him permission to go.

With a groan, Ian gathered her into his arms and they shared one last kiss.

Juliet ran her fingers along the stubble of his jaw. "Do you believe in heaven?"

"Yes."

"They say it's like falling in love, only a zillion times better. And without the anxiety."

"Wow. It sounds wonderful. But, you know, don't go there. Not just yet, I mean. Wait for me. When we're old. Reeeeeeallly old. Let's do it then. After Boceefus has made us great-grandparents."

"You got a date."

He kissed the tip of her nose. "But if something does happen, I'll meet you just outside the pearly gates, and we'll go in together."

"Okay." Juliet whispered.

"Later."

And he was gone.

The waiting was killing Juliet. She'd only been alone for about five minutes at the most, but it was truly the longest five minutes of her life. She crouched at the vent, snuggled in Ian's jacket, breathing in his scent and straining to hear.

Nothing.

Where in the world was he?

She should go after him.

What if he needed help?

At least he had the brass knuckles and the pepper spray. That was something. But would it be enough?

She pressed her ear to the vent and listened to the silence, until a shot had her muffling a scream into the sleeve of a mink coat. This was no champagne cork.

Unfortunately, she knew the difference.

Chapter 5

It was just after 2:00 a.m. on Christmas day.

Just after Ian left, there had been gunfire and a lot of shouting but surprisingly enough—given that she was a screamer—Juliet had managed to stay remarkably calm.

She knew in her heart that Ian had escaped.

He'd promised he would. He'd promised on their children's future, which in other circumstances, would have seemed absurd, but not now.

Not on Christmas day.

From the relative safety of her nest, Juliet squinted at shadows in the rafters that she was sure must be hanging bats. Or perhaps they were simply roofing trusses, but it was hard to tell in this light. No matter. Very soon, help would be on the way. She had every reason to believe. And the shots? Simply a warning, she'd deduced. No doubt, when those gun-wielding blowhards had discovered he'd gotten away they'd fired off some shots to scare him, but then—a slow grin crept across her lips— they didn't know what they were dealing with in Ian Rafferty. Ian didn't scare easily, Juliet thought as she remembered the granite set of his jaw.

He was tough. Resourceful. Strong. If anyone could get away, Ian could.

Right now, she pictured him discussing everything that had happened with the authorities. Any minute now, this rebel faction would be taken into custody and all of the hostages, herself included, would be set free.

It would simply be a matter of moments. Perhaps…longer.

She glanced at her watch.

Time was sure dragging. There had to be something wrong with her watch. Holding her wrist to her ear, she listened to the steady ticking. But the hands didn't seem to be moving. Odd. She sighed. Maybe the battery was dying. Hours ago, she'd polished off the last of the protein bar and her stomach growled. She should have eaten more at the reception. But she was trying to trim off a few pounds,

as usual, and had passed up a delicious prime rib
buffet in favor of a blasted veggie plate.

Her mouth watered and she could fairly smell the
prime rib. She wondered what the Chekagovian
men had done with that because it was better than
thinking about the bathroom. Oh, the bathroom.

The bathroom.

The bathroom.

Cinched tightly at her waist, her girdle wasn't
helping matters, but she was afraid to remove it, for
fear the bad guys would discover her. A girdle
around the ankles would make it impossible to run.
She burrowed farther into the nest of coats and
again, silently thanked Ian for thinking to make this
place comfortable. At least under this downy pile
she could hide from the bats that she was sure were
eyeballing her neck.

A wide, shuddering yawn racked her body.

She was tired. It had been a long day. And last
night, she'd stayed up till all hours gabbing with
Samantha about the wedding. And marriage. And
love.

She wished she'd known then what she knew
now. That conversation would have been a lot more
meaningful. At least for her.

Juliet jolted awake. Fumbling under the coats she
found her watch and illuminated its dial. 2:45 a.m.

How on earth had she let herself fall asleep? She berated herself even as she stretched and tried to recall the fleeting remnants of a most wonderful, sexy dream of Ian.

What had she missed while she was asleep? she wondered and gave her face a vigorous rub with her palms. Was it over? Could she leave now? Hunger rumbled in her stomach and her bladder had been pushed to the limits of the Dutch Boy's dike. Maybe she should just crawl out of the crawl space and into the closet. She could listen very carefully before she slipped into the bathroom…on the other hand, being shot at by foreign rebels while perched on the potty was low on her list of glamorous demises. Even if it was for her country.

She picked at a hangnail till it bled, then stuck her finger in her mouth. Surely, she'd slept through the rescue and it was time to go.

Then again, Ian told her to stay put until he came to get her. He had been very serious about that. Pushing the furs and coats aside, Juliet crawled to the vent and pressed her ear against the louvered metal. It was eerily quiet. Off, beyond the ballroom, there was the low rumble of men's voices. But whose?

Since she couldn't be sure, she decided it best to wait for Ian. He wouldn't forget her. Of that, she was certain.

Back to the coats she crawled and sat, legs crossed.

Under her breath, she hummed the theme to *Mister Ed.*

He wouldn't forget.

Unless he got really busy saving people's lives.

Of course, of course.

Maybe he was comforting people. That would take time.

She rummaged around for the Old Maid cards and dealt them out in the dim light of her key ring's flashlight. She'd play for Ian, as he was certainly out there, helping to arrest the bad guys. There was a lot to do that would keep a guy busy.

After she'd tied Ian, two games-all, another glance at her watch told Juliet that only ten lousy minutes had passed.

Where *was* he?

Soon, the sun would rise in the east and it would be morning. For pity's sake, Santa could have arrived and rescued her by now.

The early mornings of Christmas past played in her mind. There, she could see herself and Samantha and her baby brother, Max, as children, all getting up before dawn—about this time in fact—and tearing into the presents. Then, they'd have their traditional Christmas brunch, honey-cured ham, cranberry sauce, and freshly baked sourdough bread with tons of creamy butter, fresh fruit and coffee. Hot, steaming coffee. Umm.

Man, she was really hungry.

Plumping a coat, she fashioned a pillow and lay back down. Perhaps sleep would help pass the time. That way, she could dream. Of Ian. Of her childhood.

Of her and Ian's children.

Little Willie and what'shername.

Really—Juliet tugged a fluffy hood up over her head and tied the strings under her chin—it was so cold without Ian's body warmth. So scary, without his confident strength. So lonely without his distracting conversation. It was quite amazing how much she missed him and how she'd never formed so many deep emotions toward a person in such a short time.

Drifting off on the sea of her confusion, she slept fitfully until some noises inside her closet had her wide-awake, heart pounding and wondering if the terrorists were back. She peered through the blackness.

Ian. Ian. Ian. Where was Ian?

It was just after 3:00 a.m.

Frozen, she sat burrowed under the coats and listened.

Men were speaking just outside the vent.

In English!

Like a butterfly emerging from the cocoon, she threw back the coats, tugged her dress up under her armpits and smoothed back the static in her hair. She knew she must look a fright and hated that Ian would see her this way. But surely it was nothing that a few moments in the powder room couldn't restore to rights.

"She's somewhere in here, back behind a vent in the corner." Juliet heard someone say.

"Yes, yes, here I am." Bursting with joy, she scrambled to the vent and began tearing away the bats of insulation and chunks of wood they'd used to seal the area off. "In here," she cried.

Out in the closet, the light flipped on and there were sounds of men clearing the rubble to make a path.

When the vent finally popped open, Juliet blinked into the brightness, her smile a mile wide. Ian was back, just as he'd promised.

"Juliet?"

"Yes," she breathed, as the silhouette against the bright light came into focus.

"Are you all right?" the voice asked. A deep male voice that—oddly enough—did not belong to Ian.

Juliet blinked, trying to reconcile this new turn of events. "Uh, yes?" She poked her head out of the vent and her heart skipped a beat as the realization finally dawned that the man standing before her was not Ian, but instead, a man whose name was embroidered on his SWAT team jacket.

Kurt Hoffman.

Not Ian Rafferty.

"Where's Ian?" she asked Kurt as she eased her body out of the vent hole while at the same time trying to maintain her dignity. "Is Ian here?"

"Here, let me assist you," Kurt murmured and averted his eyes as he bent to give her a hand.

"Thank you."

That he wouldn't meet her eyes, as he led her out of the closet was Juliet's first clue that something—other than the fact that she was having trouble keeping her top up—was amiss. The moisture suddenly evaporated from her mouth, leaving her tongue stiff and unable to form words. Her heart swelled to twice its size, crowding her stomach and throat, and the backs of her eyes stung with tears.

Where was Ian?

Why wasn't anyone saying anything?

As Kurt Hoffman led her from the closet, around the corner and into the ballroom proper, Juliet was amazed at the transformation that had taken place. The room, just hours ago teeming with celebrating humanity, was now eerily void of humanity. Broken glass and party debris littered the floor and the beautiful decor had fallen victim to vandals. Areas had been cordoned off with yellow *DO NOT CROSS* and *CRIME SCENE* police tape, and the forensics team and a photographer gathered evidence.

Juliet stopped dead in her tracks as she spied a puddle of blood and instinctively knew that it was Ian's.

"No," she whispered, then pressed her palm over her mouth as a keening wail built in her gut. *"Noooo!"* she howled and crumpled into Kurt's waiting arms.

As Kurt rocked Juliet, he did his best to reassure her with the sketchy knowledge he'd been given.

"It's true. Ian's been shot. We don't know how bad it is, yet. He's at the District Medical Center headed for surgery. But Juliet, you must know that it was because of his heroic effort several of the SWAT men were able to finally enter the house. And just now, before the anesthesiologist put him under, he regained consciousness and told us where you were. That's why it's taken so long to come for you. I'm sorry."

Blurry-eyed, Juliet stared up at him, and then blinked around the room, trying to digest what she'd just been told.

Ian was alive. That was all that mattered.

Kurt fished a handkerchief from his pocket and, as he led Juliet out of the house, her mother spied her from across the front walk and squealed with relief. Both of her parents, her sister Samantha, still in her wedding gown, and her brother, Max, rushed across the sprawling lawn and enfolded her in a family hug.

"Oh, my darling, sweetheart!" Ellen Cosgrove cried and sniffed as she attempted to run her fingers through Juliet's tangled hair. "We were so terrified for you. We had no idea where you were..." She crushed Juliet to her ample bosom and blubbered. "Tell her, Walter."

Her father, never one much for emotion, swiped at an errant tear. "I hear you were held captive behind the staircase?"

"I hid there, yes. With a security man. Ian Rafferty. He's the one who was shot."

"How are you, honey?" Samantha asked, and plucked some of the larger cobwebs and dust bunnies from her sister's hair.

"Fine." Though it was what her family needed to hear, it was the furthest thing from the truth. In reality, she was dying. She couldn't believe that Ian may have been snatched away from her just as she'd found him.

Ellen dabbed at the brackish makeup that flowed from her eyes with a tattered tissue and, as Juliet looked into her mother's fear-ravaged face, she could commiserate. There was nothing more terrifying than wondering and worrying about someone that you cared for. Juliet was learning that firsthand right this very minute.

Awkwardly, her father wrested her away from her mother's clutches and into his own embrace. "I love you, honey."

"Oh, Daddy," Juliet cried into the ruffles of his tuxedo shirt. "I love you, too. All of you."

"I think we all need some rest," her mother prescribed.

Taking charge seemed to make her feel a little calmer. "Come with us, darling. Walt, find her wrap. Max, pull the car around. Samantha, darling, you and Jesse get to the hotel. This nightmare is over."

Seeing how upset Juliet was, Samantha intervened. "Mom, if it's okay with you, I'd like Juliet to stay with me. Jesse has wisely decided to postpone our honeymoon until this mess is sorted out. And since Jesse still has business here to attend and, since it's almost morning anyway, I can take her to the hospital."

"The hospital?" Ellen gasped. "Whatever for?"

"Mom, one of Jesse's oldest and closest friends, Ian Rafferty, and the man who saved Juliet's life— not to mention the rest of us—is in surgery right now. I'm sure Juliet would like to check in on him."

Juliet sent her sister a grateful glance, amazed at the fine, sensitive woman she'd become.

"Oh. Well. Of course." Ellen nodded, though clearly befuddled by her grown daughters and their plans. "Well, at least come over for Christmas dinner tonight since you and Jesse are postponing your honeymoon."

"We'll keep you posted, Mom."

They bid their goodbyes and again rejoiced that the whole family was intact.

Once they'd arrived at the hospital, Samantha led Juliet, still dazed and confused, to a lobby bath and closed the door behind her, for privacy. Having finally, and blessedly, done her business, Juliet moved to the sink and let her tears flow down the drain with the water. After a good hard cry, she propped her hands on the porcelain and lifted her gaze to the mirror.

There, she stared at her reflection and was amazed to discover that she'd aged at least ten years overnight. Her face was drawn and haggard and there were dark circles under her puffy eyes. The hairdo she'd spent a fortune on arranging was covered with debris. And, it seemed fairly certain that she would be retiring the torn and stained bridesmaid dress for good after today. She dampened a paper towel with icy water and, squeezing it out, pressed it to her face.

When she'd sufficiently regained her faculties, she joined her sister in the lobby. Samantha, who had located Ian's room led her to the elevator. As the doors hushed closed, Juliet fell against her sister's shoulder and sobbed, while Samantha, usually the flighty younger sister, stroked her hair and murmured reassurances.

"Ian was shot, wasn't he?"

Samantha gave her an imperceptible nod, her face filled with tenderness and sorrow.

"Is he—" Juliet couldn't bring herself to utter the unthinkable.

Samantha lifted and dropped a hand. "We don't know yet, honey. We only know, it was…bad. We were told to stay in the waiting room on his floor until the surgeon could see us."

Juliet's lower lip trembled so that she couldn't speak.

"Oh, sweetheart. Don't cry."

"He saved my life, Sam."

"I know. His gesture was heroic and smart. Without his wits about him, and his bravery, a lot of people might have died. Because he distracted the guards, the SWAT team, who had slipped in through a basement passageway, was able to overtake them."

Juliet sobbed and great patches of wet slowly

grew on Samantha's already soiled wedding dress. "He read a lot of Tom Clancy."

"Mmm." If Samantha didn't understand the reference, she didn't let on, but, instead, rocked her sister and held her close.

"Oh, Sam. I'm so sorry about your wedding."

"Don't be. Jesse and I are fine. Thankfully, everyone is fine. There was only one injury, and that was…"

"Ian."

"Ian. Yes."

The elevator doors opened and the two sisters stepped out.

By 9:00 a.m. that morning, Juliet was still at the hospital, still in her maid-of-honor gown, still wearing Ian's tuxedo jacket. Though Samantha had encouraged her to run home for a quick, bracing shower and a change of clothes, Juliet had been too anxious to check on Ian's condition to waste the time. But she made Samantha go home to spend time with her new husband.

Liza had also arrived at the hospital, despite the veritable blizzard conditions that raged outside. Together, they'd settled in a hallway just off the nurse's station in hard metal chairs with pea-green Naugahyde pads and pretended to look at magazines while they waited for a report on how the surgery had gone.

Though it was early Christmas morning, no one seemed to notice. The Intensive Care Unit was a unique blend of bustling sobriety. Nurses rushed past in squeaking shoes, doctors carried clipboards and candy stripers wore smiles. The P.A. system paged in dulcet tones when a doctor was needed and elevator bells signaled the arrival and departure of visitors conversing in low murmurs. Gurneys, medical trays and wheelchairs were being wheeled in a constant traffic pattern down the black-and-white-checked linoleum floor.

But Juliet barely noticed.

Behind her, in the waiting room, Christmas music was piped in through round speakers in the ceiling panels. A group of men snoozed in front of a television as a ball game blared on ESPN. In a corner a mother and her two children opened a few Christmas gifts.

There was room in there for her to wait, but Juliet preferred to sit in the hallway. That way, she wouldn't chance missing Ian's surgeon pass by.

Since being transported to the hospital, Ian had been in surgery for five hours, then moved to recovery. They'd removed a bullet from the base of his spine, but that's all anyone knew, or was willing to tell her, at this juncture.

It was so frustrating.

The redheaded nurse at the information desk was kind, but clearly tired of dispensing the same prognosis over and over again. Even if Juliet had claimed to be his fiancée, in order to gain a little more news.

Operating on only a few hours of fitful sleep, Juliet was nevertheless wired. Numb. Feeling almost as if she was watching a movie. Tears welled as she remembered the feel of Ian's lips on her temple. Soothing, soft, sweet. She wanted to do the same for him now.

Liza reached out and patted her leg. "How you holding up, honey?"

Juliet glanced up and down the hall. Anywhere but into Liza's compassionate eyes. That would be her undoing. "I'm okay."

Liza, seated in a chair on her left, gave her tongue a skeptical click, but didn't dispute. "You hungry?"

"No. Not now."

"When you are, just let me know."

"Okay."

To distract, Liza said, "Jesse called Ian's sister and let her know that he was here."

Interest piqued, Juliet sat up a tad straighter. "Penelope? Doesn't she live in Canada?"

"Yes." Liza nodded. "Just up in Toronto. She's

making arrangements to fly down with her husband as soon as she can rustle up someone to take care of her children.''

Juliet dared a glance at Liza. ''Did Penelope call their parents?''

''They are at their place on the French Riviera for the holidays, and so they won't be able to make it back here as soon as Penelope will, but they are also on their way. Jesse arranged accommodations for them at the Marriott when they arrive. Maybe you should go home to freshen up a bit and get out of that dress. It can't be comfortable.''

Juliet was suddenly reticent. ''I don't know if I can leave—''

Just then, a short, well-built balding man in his mid-thirties, wearing surgeon's scrubs strode past them and into the waiting room. ''Is there a Ms. Cosgrove here? Ian Rafferty's fiancée?''

Liza turned to stare at Juliet who stood and rushed the few steps into the waiting room from the hall.

Juliet glanced at the redheaded nurse. ''I'm his fiancée, yes.''

''Ah, good. Let's have a seat, please.'' The surgeon led them to a grouping of club chairs in a quiet corner near the window. Elbows to knees, he let a clipboard dangle in one hand as he leaned forward and looked earnestly at Juliet who'd perched in the chair opposite. ''He came through the surgery about half an hour ago, and it will be some time before we know for sure, but the prognosis is not good.''

Chapter 6

Juliet's knees wobbled as she stood beside Ian's hospital bed and stroked his hair. According to the surgeon, "not good" meant near death. Possibly paralyzed.

Juliet could scarcely believe it.

Ian. So robust. Full of life. Even as he lay unconscious, he was a paragon of strength to her eyes. She drank in every detail now that they were in the bright hospital light. She could see the stubble at his chin, the strength of his jaw, and the heavy fringe of lashes that rested against his cheeks. His broad chest rose and fell with every breath.

If she hadn't known better, she would have

thought he looked just great. Ready to spring out of bed and begin the day. The steady beep of the heart monitor contradicted the seriousness of the situation.

With her fingertips, she smoothed the errant locks of hair that fell across his forehead. A lone tear slipped down her cheek and splashed onto Ian's. They'd told her she couldn't stay long. That he needed rest and quiet. She only had a moment or two left to tell him a lifetime's worth of aspirations. Intentions. Aversions.

He knew so little about her, and she needed him to know.

"Blue," she murmured. "That's my favorite color. And I hate turnips. But I love canned peas. I don't know anything about sports, but I love to go to basketball games and scream until I'm hoarse. I'm very uncoordinated. I was a horrible cheerleader. I had to take my driver's test four times. I love to sing, but I mangle all the words to most songs. You should also know that I'm a dog person. But cats are cool, too. When I was really little I had a guinea pig. Tiger Lilly. And I killed her. By accident. I left her cage in the…" Juliet's lip trembled "…sun.

"Good grief. What a boob. Why am I telling you that? That's a horrible thing to tell a man in your condition. Not that your condition isn't good," she backpedaled, just in case he could hear her. "I know you are a fighter. Fight, Ian. Fight. Go. Fight. Win. That's—" she pressed her fingers to her lips "—from my rather ignominious stint at cheerleading."

Ian didn't answer. Didn't flinch. Didn't bat an eyelash.

His doctor had said that even if Ian did pull through the next two days, there was a pretty good chance that he might never walk again.

Ian's plans for a long, busy life flashed through her mind and it struck her how one minute, a man could be standing in a ballroom, enjoying—okay, make that tolerating—a wedding reception and the next, fighting for his life in a hospital bed. How had this happened? Her eyes burned and her throat grew thick.

Just when she'd found her other half.

This.

Brokenly, she murmured to him, hoping to garner some kind of response.

"Ian, you big lug, you have to get better. I wasn't kidding when I told you that, you know, that I love you. I know—" she sniffed and hiccupped a little laughter for his benefit "—it seems a little premature to make a declaration like that, but it's true. I love you better than canned peas. Better than dogs. Better than…blue.

"You're my knight in shining armor. Just like that Asian fairy tale, you saved my life and so now you own me. Or, uh, I own you. Or something. I'll have to look that up, but anyway, you can't bail out on me now. I mean, I've heard of all kinds of excuses for not having a relationship, but this? Don't you think this is a bit extreme? You haven't even given us a chance. Do that please. Give us a chance."

With the backs of her fingers, she stroked his stubbled cheeks and babbled and blubbered, her resolve to remain strong crumbling with exhaustion and fear.

"We still have to have little William Boceefus and *what'shername* Beulah. And you..." she pleaded. Eyes, nose and mouth all running simultaneously had her wiping her face with his bedsheet. "Well, you have to coach all the sports...and drive the car pool... Oh, Ian. Ian. Please, please don't die...."

The nurse's gentle hand on her shoulder let her know it was time to go home and get some muchneeded sleep.

Juliet went home in a fog. She tossed the cabbie the contents of her wallet and bid him to keep the change, whatever that was. Leaving a string of footprints in the snow, she traversed her way to her door, fumbled with her key and made it to her couch where she flopped like a wet mop.

From where she sat, she could see the message light flashing on her answering machine and her desk, littered with books and manuscripts to read. All so very normal.

And all so very unimportant in the scheme of things.

Slowly, her eyes swept the wall, artfully arranged with framed awards for herself and her authors, newspaper articles regaling her successes, bestseller lists and other celebratory miscellany. Her career had afforded her a luxurious condominium in a trendy D.C. neighborhood. But her beautiful home was as sterile as an issue of *House Beautiful*. Completely void of the family clutter. Of love.

In a robotic fashion, Juliet hoisted herself off her couch and slogged to her bathroom where she removed her maid of honor dress and tossed it into the wastebasket. After checking the temperature of the shower, she slipped into the alcove and stood under the spray, willing it to wash away the horror of the last twenty-four hours.

But, of course, it didn't.

Slowly sinking to the tiled floor, she sat and cried, her body heaving with heavy sobs.

Paralyzed.

A bout of sympathetic hypochondria assailed her

and she tried to lift her own arms but couldn't. Guilt filled her belly, nauseating her, making her head swirl. She should have been at his side. Maybe then, the bullet wouldn't have hit him in the back. Maybe they'd have missed him altogether. If she'd been with him.

Going through the motions on autopilot, Juliet lathered her hair and rinsed away the crawl space grime from her body. After her shower, she dressed in a flannel nightie and fell into bed, where she lay, plagued by the sleeplessness that comes from overexhaustion.

Burrowed deep under her covers, she imagined Ian's arms around her middle and absently wondered what the world record for falling in love was. And, if these feelings were reciprocated. Her mind strayed to Ian, lying there so helplessly, and wondered—if he lived—how he'd deal with his paralysis.

No matter. She was going to help him.

Together, they could get through anything. They'd proved that, tonight.

It was dark when Juliet woke that Christmas evening. Disoriented and headachy, she flipped on her bedside lamp and phoned the hospital.

No change in Ian's condition. The nurse advised

her that since he was unconscious, spending Christmas with her family would be advisable.

Juliet disagreed but, since she knew her mother was expecting her, she grabbed a cab and headed to her parents' D.C. house. They actually resided in Connecticut most of the time and were planning on selling this house now that Samantha had moved out.

She could hardly enjoy the sumptuous fare. A somber pall had descended over the holiday this year and the topic of conversation at the dinner table revolved around the bizarre terrorist incident all evening, completely overshadowing the joyous union of Samantha and Jesse the day before.

And though the newlyweds were still starry-eyed over each other, there were new lines furrowed into their young brows. All evening, everyone merely picked at their food and the gifts under the tree lay forgotten. Various friends and relatives, here in Washington D.C. for Samantha's wedding, stopped by from time to time and there was much conversation and speculation on yesterday's incident. Everyone seemed to have a different idea, a different account of what was going on and why.

In the background, the television was tuned to CNN and every time the subject fell upon the recent events, Juliet's father would aim the remote like a seasoned gunslinger and the anchor's voice would fairly rattle the windows.

"—Colton wedding reception and reports that George Kartoff, leader of the Chekagovian Freedom Fighters is still missing. Kartoff, the rebel mastermind who escaped with a priceless music box is considered armed and dangerous and most likely still in the United States.

"Kartoff is now on the FBI's most wanted list in connection with this and other terrorist acts in Chekagovia. Apparently the key to the music box, which bears a wooden carving of the Christmas nativity, is also the key to a secret vault in Chekagovia that contains millions of dollars' worth of gold bars.

"Helmut Ritka, a Chekagovian diplomat, was targeted by the terrorists—who claimed that Ritka has been ruining the Chekagovian financial infrastructure by siding with Western economic policies. The Chekagovian Freedom Fighters had demanded Ritka as their hostage, along with one million dollars, a private plane and an escort before they would release the wedding party and its guests. Now with his family at an undisclosed location, Ritka is resting comfortably, obviously relieved that the ordeal is over.

"In a related story, Ian Rafferty, millionaire, entrepreneur and well-known philanthropist, was shot in the back during the hostage situation early this morning.''

A picture of Ian flashed on the screen, and Juliet felt her heart stop as the anchor provided an update.

''Preliminary reports from District Medical Center state that Rafferty is in critical condition and facing possible paralysis. Rafferty, a wedding guest of Jesse and Samantha Colton, managed to distract the gunman, allowing entrance for a SWAT team and possibly saving lives.

''In other news, President—''

Walter Cosgrove snapped off the television. ''Rafferty is a brave man. Anyone know how he's really doing?''

Juliet was unable to completely keep the anguish from her response. ''No change.''

Everyone exchanged curious looks over her emotional response, but no one said a word.

When family and friends had finally exhausted the topic, it was after midnight and that year's holiday was now Christmas past. Though it had ended on a far different note than everyone had expected, there was a lot to be thankful for and the family spent a great deal of time counting their blessings.

Samantha and Jesse took Juliet by her condo, and then headed on home to the mansion, where they'd decided to stay with a rather large contingent of the DCPD and members of the FBI.

Juliet again pulled on her flannel nightie and crawled into her bed. She lay there and listened to the silence, accentuated by the snowfall outside and suddenly realized that she lived alone.

Completely alone.

Samantha had Jesse to turn to tonight. Her parents had each other.

Liza had Nick.

And she…had no one.

Not even a cat to greet her and make her feel missed.

All of a sudden, Juliet was lonelier than she'd ever been in her life. She flopped onto her side and stared out the window at the poetic "crest of the moon on the new-fallen snow." She should have taken her parents up on their offer to spend the night at their house. She lay there for close to an hour when she finally forced herself to realize that sleep would not come softly this night. Reaching into her nightstand, she grabbed the remote and turned on CNN, glad for the company and hoping to catch Ian's smiling face before she drifted off to sleep.

When she spotted him, she was once again riveted by the story of his heroism. Still, they had no news of his condition, other than the fact that he was in the hospital, recovering from surgery for the removal of a bullet near his spine.

His spine. How awful.

Closing her eyes, Juliet sent up a prayer for his recovery and for the doctors and nurses that were caring for him at this very minute.

What if he died?

What would she do then? He was the one. Of that, she was amazingly sure. How she knew was a mystery, but she knew. Deep in her heart, she felt their connection. It transcended anything logical. It transcended time.

She'd just found him.

And now, she faced losing him.

Juliet lay back on her pillows and pulled her comforter under her chin. As the anchors droned on about the terrorists, Juliet drifted off and finally slept the sleep of the dead.

Later that morning, when the sun streamed through holes in the snow clouds and caused the icicles to *drip, drip, drip,* and the street to become a slick sheet of danger, Juliet woke, turned off the TV and automatically reached for the phone.

"He's regained consciousness, but he's groggy and disoriented. The doctor is cautiously pleased with his progress."

Somewhat relieved, Juliet got up, got dressed and

decided she was going to the hospital to comfort Ian despite the icy conditions on the street. If she had to, she'd find a pickax and cleats and claw her way there.

However, before she could locate her boots, Liza dropped by and shoved a box from the bakery into her hands.

"*Whoohoo,* it's not fit for man nor beastie out there!" Shrugging out of her heavy winter coat, Liza grinned and tamped her feet on the mat and clapped her hands together. She draped the dripping garment over a hook by the door and cupping her hands, blew. "Coffee," she ordered, shivering.

"Coming up." Juliet moved to the kitchen and Liza followed.

"You weren't planning on going out in this weather, were you?" Liza demanded.

"You did."

"Yes, but I'm nuts. You're the sane one."

Juliet sighed. "Not anymore."

Outside the sound of an ambulance rushing to the scene of an accident filtered up from the street. The coffeepot began to perk, sending the aroma of fresh java throughout her home. Juliet opened the warm box and the scent of warm cinnamon rolls greeted her nose.

Making herself at home, Liza rummaged through

Juliet's cupboards for plates and forks and mugs and insisted that Juliet sit down and eat.

"You need to keep up your strength if you are going to be any good for Ian."

Eager to get to the hospital, Juliet shot a longing look out the window.

"So, you want to tell me what exactly happened in that closet yesterday?"

Juliet turned to face Liza and looked her directly in the eye. "Liza, when did you know you were in love with Nick?"

"In love?" Liza pulled her chin into her neck and stared, openmouthed. "Ohhhh, my!"

"Yeah."

"Well now..." Liza's expression grew dreamy. "You know, Nick was my hero. He, in a way, saved my life, too. Or at least my career. He was the only doctor who could treat me and help me sing again. And not just sing, but really...*sing,* you know? So, I think that even though I didn't want to admit it, I was in love with him from the very beginning. I think it's a common occurrence for patients to fall for their physicians, though."

"I'm glad Ian's doctor is a short, balding man."

Liza laughed. "Ahh, humor. That's a good sign. So. While you were in the closet, you fell in love with our Ian? Tell Aunt Liza everything."

"Stop." Juliet laughed at her friend's comical

expression. "You know, it's the most amazing thing. When I first met Ian, I thought he was a creep."

"Really? But you two seemed to hit it off right away."

"Liza, we were fighting like hissing cats."

"I know. That's how I knew you liked him."

"You did?" Juliet scratched her head.

"Elementary, my dear. As in grade school. Tell me what happened. Start from the beginning."

Juliet touched her fork to the frosting on her roll, then touched it to her tongue. "I think he noticed a breach in the security system and was suspicious of some men who arrived late and were acting oddly during the party. I didn't notice any of those men, until he did. But I just thought he was using his work as an excuse to bail out on our conversation."

With a clatter, Juliet dropped her fork to her plate since she wasn't using it anyway and added a spoonful of sugar to her coffee.

"But, when the shooting started, he must have anticipated trouble, because he shoved me into a nearby closet. We found a vent in the back that led to a crawl space, and we hid in there for several hours. Liza, it was the longest night of my life. And that was all it took to lose my heart."

Her eyes misted over and Liza reached out to pat her hand. "Mmm."

"You know, I thought I knew what love was because of Parker, but I didn't know diddly."

"I had a feeling you two would hit it off. I just didn't know you'd spend a night in the closet together. At least," Liza joked, "not under these circumstances."

Juliet's smile was tremulous. "I'm so scared I'm going to lose him. Just when I found him."

"I take it he feels the same way about you?"

"I think so. We're going to have two children. A boy and a girl. He's going to coach and drive car pool part of the time. We are going to buy a house in the country and I'm still going to work part-time."

"Oh, my. You two have it bad." Liza's smile was wide with happiness and hope. "With those plans under his belt, I don't see how he can fail to get well."

"From your mouth to God's ear."

"Find your snowshoes and let's get you to the hospital, to visit the father of your two children."

Chapter 7

In the cab on the way to the hospital, Liza told Juliet, "Ian's sister, Penelope, and her husband, Terry, are coming in late tonight and will be staying in a suite at the Marriott since that's where Nick and I will be all this week and next anyway. You'll really like his sister. She's a kick. Spunky. Full of life."

"Mm. Good. That's exactly what we need." Restlessly, Juliet twisted her gloved fingers together. She could get out and walk faster than this stupid cab was creeping down the street. "What about his parents?"

"They're on their way, too. Their names are

Donald and Barbara. Rafferty, of course. You'll
love them. Over the years, our families would vacation together up in Martha's Vineyard from time
to time. Anyway, they'll be here first thing in the
morning on December 27th, which is, uh, let's see,
tomorrow—'' Liza glanced at her watch ''—yeah,
tomorrow, and they'll check into the hotel, too. You
want to come with me to meet them when they get
here?''

''If it's okay, yes.'' Juliet pressed the sleeve of
her coat to the car's window and rubbed a little hole
in the fog. ''They'll probably want to hear firsthand,
about how heroic Ian was during the attack,'' she
murmured.

''No doubt. Are you sure you're up for talking
about it?''

''Um-hum. I want to help out any way I can.
Especially with his family. I feel as if I know all
about them already.''

Her grin lopsided with curiosity, Liza turned in
her seat and stared at Juliet. ''You guys did some
pretty intense communicating there in the old
closet.''

''Crawl space.''

''Whatever.''

''Yes.'' Juliet smiled at Liza. ''We…communi-
cated.''

Liza held up her gloved fingers and ticked off

items as she spoke. "Family history, future dreams, a house in the country, carpooling, two kids, a dog...so you must have discussed a wedding. When's the date?"

"Actually we were thinking—"

Liza stared, agog. "*I was kidding!* You actually have a *date?*"

Juliet felt the heat stain her cheeks. "Ian mentioned next Christmas day. We're not getting any younger."

Liza slapped her thighs so hard, Juliet feared she'd left handprints. Slumping on her side, Liza shook with infectious, joyful laughter.

"What?"

"How idiotically Type-A. You guys are so totally perfect for each other. While terrorists hold you hostage, you mastermind a plan to save the day and at the same time manage to fall in love, and settle on a wedding date." Liza's head lolled back and she hooted at the dingy ceiling of the cab, her glee causing the driver to laugh, though Juliet doubted he spoke enough English to understand what he was laughing at.

"Shut!" A giggling Juliet whapped Liza in the arm. "Up!"

Liza insisted that Juliet go on ahead, while she took care of the cabbie. She wanted to go to the maternity ward to check on Lucy and Rand's baby, who had decided to come in the middle of the hostage crisis. Liza would meet Juliet in the cafeteria at noon for a little lunch and from there, they'd head to the hotel to pick up Liza's SUV—which Nick was having fitted with snow tires that very morning—and from there, off to the airport to pick up Penelope and Terry.

Juliet nodded over her shoulder and slipped through the glass doors that opened at her approach. As she entered the hospital and got into a blessedly empty elevator, she tried to still her racing pulse. In the small mirror in her purse, she checked her reflection and was surprised to see that she looked a lot calmer than she felt. How was he? Was he better? Worse? Would he be glad to see her? She hoped so, as she couldn't wait to see him.

A gentle chime signaled the arrival at Ian's floor, and she took a tentative step out of the elevator.

The antiseptic smell of the halls sent a wave of panic rushing to her head. She'd always hated hospitals. Ever since she lost her grandparents, these smells signaled death, rather than healing. She battled back the panic that bid her to run screaming and forced herself on wobbly legs, to the nurses' station in the ICU.

A cheery nurse looked up and smiled her greeting.

"Hello, I'm… I'm… I'm here to visit Ian Rafferty?"

"Are you related?"

"Why?" She'd told the nurse and the surgeon yesterday that she was the fiancée because she'd panicked.

The nurse tapped Ian's name into the computer. "Rafferty. On doctor's orders, only family can visit in short spans at this point. Infection. Big risk."

"I'm his…his…his…"

The nurse frowned.

"His fiancée," Juliet finally managed, figuring that life was too short to quibble about titles. She'd made a rare connection with Ian last night. But if "rare connection" didn't qualify as family member, then "fiancée" it was.

Brow curved, the nurse glanced at her bare ring finger.

"We just became engaged the other night. Only moments before he was…shot."

"Oh, dear, how sad. And may I offer my congratulations along with my sympathies."

"Sympathies?" Juliet's heart took a nosedive. What sympathies?

"For the proposal, honey, that's all. Nothing like a bullet to ruin the mood, right?"

"Oh, right." Juliet brightened. "I'd like to visit him now, if that's okay."

"For a few minutes, sure. He's been moved out of recovery and into his own room." The nurse gave her directions and pointed down the hall.

As Juliet padded down the broad corridor, her gaze—against her better judgment—strayed with morbid fascination inside the rooms she passed. People were groaning, taking meds, limply watching TV and visiting with loved ones. Some were healing, some crying, some…dying. Feeling the tears prick the backs of her eyes, Juliet forced her gaze straight ahead and trotted the rest of the way to Ian's room.

When she arrived at his door, she clutched the doorframe and hesitated, peering around the curtain, taking in this experience a bit at a time. Slowly, she inched inside his private room, and making her way to the edge of his hospital bed, she could see that he was still hooked to all manner of solutions and monitors, all quietly beeping and flashing with the rhythms of his life. A rolling breakfast tray sat at his bedside containing an untouched water bottle with a bent straw. Off in the distance, a siren sounded, growing higher in pitch as it approached.

Clutching the bedside rails, Juliet leaned close and studied his face. His eyes were closed and his pallor was ghostly in the early morning light. But he was breathing. That was all that mattered.

Since she knew he needed every bit of rest, she took a seat in a comfortable, reclining chair by the window and, covering herself with an extra blanket, watched Ian until her eyes grew heavy. She'd had such a rough day yesterday. She'd just rest here, till Ian woke.

"Your fiancée has been here for over an hour now," the nurse who was dressing Ian's wounds told him as he slowly surfaced to consciousness from the dark abyss in which he'd been floating.

Parched as a stale cracker, he touched his dry and swollen tongue to the roof of his mouth. "My…fiancée?"

With a gentle smile, the nurse pointed to the woman, curled into a ball over in a chair in the corner. "We didn't have the heart to kick her out," she whispered, "even though she's not supposed to be here."

Ian focused on the golden-brown head, peeping out from under the blanket, her face so sweet in repose. Juliet. The woman who'd filled his dreams since he'd come to this hellhole.

"Do you remember the surgeon talking with you this morning?" the nursed asked.

Fear clutched Ian's heart. Yes. He remembered hearing in Technicolor detail why he couldn't feel anything from the waist down. With great effort he swallowed and managed to croak, "Paralysis."

"Mmm." The nurse nodded. "But nothing is certain yet. Give the swelling some time to go down. Sometimes, these things reverse themselves. Try to keep your spirits up. Attitude is half the battle."

Ian grunted. A bullet in the spine gave him a piss-poor attitude.

A half hour later, Ian's eyes fluttered open from a pain-filled catnap. His agony was only intensified when he glimpsed Juliet hovering at the edge of his bed. The pity radiated from her gaze, and Ian struggled with the fact that he might be seeing a lot of that in the future.

Ian was not one to tolerate sympathy.

He'd always prided himself on being in charge of his destiny. In control. Not needing to depend on another human being for help of any kind.

It could never be. Not now. Not the way he was.

Now, he was useless.

Feeling incredibly sorry for himself, Ian set his mouth in a hard line, tasting the bitter bile of misery as he did so. She was probably here to kiss him off. To thank him for saving her hide and cutting her losses while she still could. He couldn't blame her.

In fact, he'd give her an out. Cut her loose before things got any stickier between them.

"Hi," Juliet murmured, her voice soft and breathy like heaven's spring breezes.

He steeled himself against the yearning he felt to have her come and climb into this bed and lie beside him and distract him from the fear that clawed at his heart.

Without answering, he turned his face to the window and watched the snowfall.

She seemed not to notice and moved to the edge of his bed.

"How are you?"

Now there was a question. How the hell was he? Ian took a deep breath, wondering what to say. When he finally spoke, the words came out far more caustically than he'd intended and he hated the wounded look that flashed in her eyes.

"How am I? I'm great, considering I'm half a man."

She grasped the stainless steel rails till her knuckles whitened, and whispered, "Ian, you could never be half a man."

His eyes slid closed as her whispered words brought back so many feelings from the other night.

"Right," he sighed. "Everything from the belt up works just fine."

"And soon, the rest of you will, too. You have to have hope."

"Juliet, you don't know what you're saying."

"Yes, I do. Sometimes those things change. And even if they—" she swallowed and Ian could sense her struggling with the idea of being chained to a cripple "—even if they don't, it wouldn't matter. I care about you. Not about things beyond our control."

"You say that now, but what about your future? I'm paralyzed from the waist down! There will be no son. No daughter. No honeymoon. No coaching, no carpool—"

"You don't know that—"

"—ing, so get that through your head. Now. The sooner, the better for us all."

"No. Your future is what you make of it."

"You learn that in cheerleading school?"

"Ian, I'm here for you. Don't drive me away. Yesterday, we learned that life is precarious at best. Precious. Not to be frittered away because of pride. You were right when you said that we are not getting any younger. Why throw away something magical that flows between us. I know you felt it, too. I know that you and I have the potential to be great together."

Ian snorted. Like Eve with a shiny, juicy apple, she was tempting him with the promise of a happily ever after. But the sooner they both faced reality, the better. There was no future for them.

He opened his mouth to rebut when he saw the tears that swam in her eyes. Slowly, they ran over her lips and she pulled a full, wet lip between her teeth.

Ian wanted to leap over the rails of this bed, take her in his arms and comfort her. Kiss her tears away. But that was impossible. He'd never walk again, let alone leap. How could he ever be a real husband to her? He couldn't father her children, and even if he could, he wouldn't be able to play with them the way a normal dad would.

His stomach roiling, Ian was suddenly sick with sorrow. Grief over the loss of a relationship that he'd only just discovered. And the only way he knew how to deal with it was to send Juliet away.

It was the only fair thing to do. She might not understand now, but in time she would. Juliet needed a husband who could give her all the things she wanted out of life.

And him? Well, he needed to start over again. Like some kind of a helpless child, he needed to learn to do everything from scratch.

He was tempted by her sweetness, but knew that he had to be a jerk in order for her to get on with her life and forget him. They didn't have that much invested yet.

Yet.

Taking a deep breath, Ian did his best to harden his heart. "Juliet, I want you to forget what happened between us the other night."

"I know you can't mean—"

He plowed ahead, ignoring her protestations. "What happened between us was a fluke. A glitch in an otherwise normal day. Caused by that foxhole mentality where everything is accelerated and spiritual."

"But—"

The hurt in her eyes was killing him more than the bullet he'd taken. "Go. Just go."

"Ian…"

"Juliet, it's what I want. Go back to your real life. Be happy. Thank you for caring, but really, I don't need the hassle. I have enough to worry about without having to take you and your future into consideration."

With that, fists clenched, molars grinding, he turned his face away and refused to look back. Knowing that he'd hurt her caused more agony than his physical wounds. He could hear the whisper of her coat as she swished out the door.

And out of his life.

The roar of a jet taking off overhead silenced Juliet for a moment and gave her a chance to study

Ian's smiling sister. Juliet was settled in the back seat of Liza's roomy SUV with Ian's sister, Penelope. Her husband, Terry, was sitting in the front seat with Liza. Off in the distance, there were the twinkling lights of suburbia. It was dark out and, blessedly, it had stopped snowing.

When the roar died down, Juliet continued her conversation with Ian's extremely delightful and friendly sister, which was more than she could say for *him*, but she was trying not to dwell. ''How was your flight?''

''A little choppy. I'm a horrible flyer, so Terry's fingers will be black-and-blue by morning.''

''That's okay, honey,'' Terry said from the front seat. ''That's what I'm here for.''

Penelope reached out and took Juliet's hand. ''So you were the one hiding in the closet with my brother. You must have been terrified.''

Juliet nodded and told her a little about their ordeal. And about how they'd gotten to know each other.

Liza snorted and Penelope, sensing some information packed in the none too subtle snort, asked, ''What? Am I missing something?''

''I think Juliet and Ian did a little more than get to know each other.''

Juliet gasped. ''Liza, really. You make it sound so...so...''

"Tawdry?" Penelope asked.

"Yes! It wasn't like that at all. Actually, we discovered we had a lot in common…"

"And?" Liza probed.

With a tiny groan, Juliet rolled her eyes. "And, we discovered that we are very compatible."

"Aaaand?" Liza sang.

"Would you stop?" Juliet shot a sheepish look at Penelope. "It was sort of a hate at first sight, love at second sight kind of a deal, and Ian…" she touched her lips with her tongue "…Ian sort of proposed—"

Everyone in the car whooped with delight.

Penelope threw herself at Juliet and squeezed her in a bear hug that managed to knock both of their snow hats askew and leave a ruby lip print on Juliet's cheek. "Ian? In love? Oh, my! You must be very special."

"Apparently not anymore."

Penelope sobered. "What happened?"

"I went to visit your brother this morning, and he pretty much told me to go away and stay away. Said he was only half a man."

"That sounds just like that chowderhead. He always was an altruistic nerd. Probably thinks he's doing you some kind of big, cosmically correct favor. What a doofus."

For the first time since she'd left Ian's side that

morning, Juliet laughed. Laughed until she cried. The tension release was wonderful. She could tell already that she liked Penelope. A lot. With or without Ian, she would certainly love to consider this woman a friend.

"Listen to me, Juliet. You need to stick with my brother. He can be such a hardheaded cuss. He does that to keep people at a distance when he's afraid. And, I suppose, if you put yourself in his shoes right about now, you'd be afraid, too."

"Terrified."

"And, you'd probably try to send him away."

"Probably."

"But he wouldn't let you. Because he's an altruistic nerd. And you shouldn't let him send you away. Go to him. Plague him. Badger him. Stick to him like glue. This works. I know." Penelope buffed her nails on the placket of her wool coat. "I used to do it to him all the time. He'd finally get so sick of me, that I'd get my way."

Juliet giggled. "You guys sound like my family."

"You have a brother?"

"Oh yeah."

"Good. Then you know what to do."

Indeed, Juliet did.

After Penelope and Terry had visited Ian—who was still in an abominable mood—they met with

Liza, Nick and Juliet for dinner at a restaurant not far from the hospital. In a private conversation between Juliet and Penelope, Ian's sister swore that she could tell Ian's foul temper was a good sign.

"When he thought no one else was listening, he pulled me close and asked me if I'd met you. I told him yes and he wondered what I thought. He was really fishing for information. He wouldn't do that if he didn't give a rat's patootie. I know that. He's my brother. Anyway, I told him you were wonderful and that he should think about going for you. Then he gave me that 'I'm half a man crap' and I said, 'Yeah, you are acting like a child, that's true.' Of course, that made him roar like a wounded lion and the nurses drove us out of there."

"Oh, no!" Juliet pressed her fingertips to her smiling lips.

"Yep. So here's the deal. He's got it bad for you, I can tell. His face has this look just like when he was back in college with—"

"Liv?"

"He told you about Liv? He never tells anyone about Liv! Wow. Well, yeah. She was the love of his life. Until now, I think. Anyway, you need to get back into that hospital room first thing tomorrow morning and make like you thought he was hallucinating when he sent you packing."

Juliet's head fell back on her shoulders and she laughed, loving Penelope. This woman was so very special.

"What the devil are you two cackling about?" Terry demanded.

"Girl talk, honey. Girl talk."

Terry groaned. "Poor Ian. Boy don't stand a chance."

Nick lifted a glass. "To Ian. And second chances."

Everybody drank deeply.

Taking Penelope's advice, Juliet decided to persevere with Ian, in spite of the fact that he'd made it clear he didn't want her company. Though his words had stung, she knew Penelope was right.

Ian was scared.

And he needed a friend.

So, the next morning, she called her office and told her secretary to let everyone know that she could be reached on her cell phone for the next few days. Business was slow between holidays anyway, so Juliet didn't expect much interruption. Then, she packed a bag with some reading material, a few snacks and a bottle of water and with a smile and a wave at the friendly nurse at the desk, slipped down the hall toward Ian's room.

She arrived just in time to see his surgeon enter

with a clipboard. She hovered behind the curtain while they conferred.

"—any feeling in the lower extremities yet?" the doctor asked.

"No." Ian's voice was dull and without hope.

"Give it time."

"As if I had anything else to do."

The doctor chuckled. "True. But I really think your progress is quite remarkable. Vital signs are impressive, the wound is healing nicely, and the swelling is coming down. Frankly two days ago I wouldn't have believed it. When they wheeled you in, you were one hurt cowboy. Since you're exceeding my expectations, I'm upgrading your condition."

"To what? Worthless?"

"To stable." As the surgeon held up his clipboard, Juliet watched him draw a diagram of the human spine. "Just so you'll understand where your body's at—"

Ian harrumphed. The doctor ignored him with good nature.

"The bullet passed through your lower back, missing your spine, but just barely. You were a very lucky man, as the bullet also missed your inferior vena cava and the common iliac vein…very fortunate."

"I feel lucky." Ian's sarcasm caused Juliet to bite back a smile.

"Right now," the doctor continued without missing a beat, "the swelling is compressing the spinal cord, causing the paralysis. With any luck, there is a chance that you will recover partial, or all of the use of your lower extremities."

"And there are chances that I won't."

"Unfortunately, that's a chance." The doctor flipped through the pages on his clipboard. "How's the pain?"

"On a scale of one to ten, ten being unbearable, I'd give it a solid twenty-one."

"I'll go see what we can do to rectify that. In the meantime, try not to worry. I've seen some cases just like yours recover beautifully. And those that don't, given the proper attitude, go on to lead productive, happy lives."

The doctor clapped the side of the bed with his clipboard and with a last nod at Ian, strode to the door.

Juliet walked in the room just as the doctor was leaving. "Doctor?"

"Oh, hi, yes, you're the fiancée."

"Uhh, I'm…" She glanced in Ian's direction and lowered her voice to a whisper. "Right. Anyway, I was wondering if you could answer a few of my questions."

The surgeon smiled. "I'll do my best. Why don't we go have a seat and perhaps you and Ian can discuss the answers to your questions together, when he…er…cheers up a bit." The doctor turned and without preamble, pulled two chairs up to the edge of Ian's bed. He took one and gestured for Juliet to take the other.

Ian ignored her. Treated her as if she wasn't even in the room. No greeting, not even a glance in her direction. Juliet overlooked his rudeness and took her seat.

"How long until we know if Ian will recover the use of his legs?"

"It depends on many factors, but I'd say within the next few days, we might see the swelling subside and some sensation return."

"That's wonderful!"

"Wonderful?" Ian snorted, for the first time acknowledging her presence.

"Ian," the doctor gently admonished, "you should try to share in your fiancée's optimism. Attitude is a large percent of the healing process."

"Fiancée?" Ian asked derisively. "Since when?"

"If I'm going to have two children, I figure they'll need a father."

Awkwardly, the doctor looked back and forth between them, and sensing something far deeper than met the eye, stood. "Well, if I've answered all your questions—"

"I thought I told you to forget all that." Ian turned his face away and waved a dismissive hand.

"You did. I'm simply here to vex you."

"Okay then." The doctor smiled. "I can see you two have some things to talk about. If you need me, I'll just be seeing to his pain medication."

"And don't take all year," Ian bellowed after him.

"My, you're cranky. I think you need a bit of romance to lighten up your days." Juliet plunked her book bag up on the edge of his bed and withdrew a volume of Jane Austen's *Pride and Prejudice* and, without ceremony, began to read aloud.

"'It is a truth universally acknowledged that a single man in possession of a good fortune must be in want of a wife.'"

Pulling his pillow up over his head, Ian groaned.

That evening, Juliet went to the Marriott to visit Ian's sister, while Terry went to pick up their parents at the airport with Liza. She and Penelope had ordered ice-cream sundaes from room service and were busily visiting like a pair of old school chums. Penelope was so personable, Juliet soon felt very comfortable venting about Ian's boorish behavior.

Laughing all the while, Penelope encouraged Juliet to keep getting back in the ring to fight for her man.

"I can't believe you are reading *Pride and Prejudice* to Ian. That's just hysterical."

Juliet giggled. "I know. He claims he hates romance. He turned his face away and ignored me, but I could tell he was listening."

"Too funny. Well, he'll either learn to like it, or he'll have to get well so that he can get away from you."

"That's the plan."

They giggled together and Juliet set down her dish, the first food she'd managed to polish off in two days. "Penelope, tell me about your children."

"I have two. A daughter, Brittany, and a son, James."

"How old are they?"

"Seven and three. Wanna see their pictures?"

"Of course."

Penelope tossed her a sassy wink. "You might get a little idea of what you and Ian's kids will look like."

Juliet hooted. "We're terrible."

"Naw. Just tellin' it like it is. Brother dear is going to have to get used to the idea that he's met his match. Time to settle down."

"But, Penelope, what if he doesn't get better, and he completely rejects me."

"Honey, he might never get better, but he'll never completely reject you. He loves you. Love conquers all. Don't your authors tell you that?"

That evening, as Ian's parents arrived at the hotel after a quick visit with their grumpy son, Penelope introduced Juliet as a very special friend of Ian's.

And hers.

Juliet was incredibly touched.

Ian's mother immediately glommed on to Juliet, clutching her arm and dragging her down next to her on the couch. Barbara Rafferty, an attractive, rather chic woman who draped her well-rounded curves in stylish designer attire, promptly found a photo album in her gargantuan purse and leaned over Juliet's lap.

"Look, sweetheart, he was such a cute little boy. Everyone everywhere just *loved* him!"

Obviously having been subjected to this oration more than once, Ian's sister rolled her eyes.

"Here he is on the first day of school. In those days, the boys wore short pants to private school. Doesn't he have adorable knees? And here he is with his first fish. Twelve pounds. Donald, you remember that? Donald? You remember that? Don? Honey?" Barbara leaned against Juliet. "He's not paying attention. He never does. Okay, here's Ian at the prom."

"Mom," Penelope gasped, "c'mon. Don't show Juliet those geeky pictures of Ian at the prom with Bianca Munson. She'll run screaming."

"What? He looks adorable in that light blue tux. What? That was the style! It was!"

On the following day, December 28th, Juliet trekked back to the hospital, intent on forcing Ian to see that she wasn't going anywhere, and that she loved him, legs or no. She read more Jane Austen to him and though he pretended to be asleep, she could sense him becoming lost in the tale along with her.

"'Of having another daughter married to Mr. Collins, she thought with equal certainty, and with considerable, though not equal, pleasure. Elizabeth was the least dear to her of all her children; and though the man and the match were quite good enough for *her,* the worth of each was eclipsed by Mr. Bingley and Netherfield.'"

With that, Juliet closed the book, thinking that Ian had probably had enough of her voice for one day.

"Where are you going?" he demanded, cranky as a Model T. "You're gonna just leave off there? What's going to happen to Elizabeth?"

Ian's sister and mother hovered in the doorway, watching with twitching lips.

"Are you going to ask nicely?" Juliet asked.

"No."

Juliet frowned. "You know, Ian, your attitude is terrible. I understand that you are feeling sorry for yourself. Who wouldn't in your shoes? But you don't have to treat me like something you stepped in out in the barnyard. I have feelings, too, you know. And I care about you. The fact that some terrorist shot you is not going to change that. So get used to it. Because I'm not going anywhere. Now, if you'll excuse me."

Heels a-clicking, Penelope marched in, as Juliet departed.

"She's right, brother dear. That girl is a jewel and if you let her go, you are a fool."

Hands on her hips, Barbara bobbed up over her daughter's shoulder. "I must agree, Ian, darling. Your sister is not only poetic, she is right. You are a boob."

With that, they both stormed off in a cloud of indignation.

"She said fool," he called after his mother. "Not boob," he muttered under his breath. "Fool."

Chapter 8

For the next two days, Juliet visited the short-tempered Ian, bringing him games and flowers, and cards and movies. He was still cantankerous and in constant pain, but she doggedly hung in there with him, entertaining him, talking to him about their future when he pretended to be asleep and caring for his every need when the nurses weren't around.

From the nurses, she learned to dress his wound so that she could take over these duties when he was released. The nursing staff all loved her because she stayed in the background when they were there, but eagerly jumped in to help whenever they needed a hand.

To anyone who would listen, Ian made caustic remarks about the fact that Juliet wouldn't go away, but everyone could see how unhappy and extra petulant he was when she left for home late each night.

It was about 11:30 p.m. on the third night when Juliet closed her volume of *Pride and Prejudice* and stretched and yawned. Realizing that she was not only perched on the edge of his bed, but also worming her way back into his cast-iron heart, Juliet wasn't surprised when Ian turned away and feigned dozing off.

Sliding alongside him on her elbow, she whispered in his ear. "Good night, you big faker. I know you're not asleep. And I know you love me. And I love you, too."

As she slipped out of the room, Ian smiled in spite of himself.

Ian's mother was waiting in the hallway for a quick good-night kiss before heading back to the hotel. When she saw Juliet, she stood and enveloped her in a huge bosomy hug.

"How is our bear today?"

"I think he's coming along. He's still not very friendly, but I think he's beginning to realize that his attitude is not helping anything."

"Umm-hum. You know, he was like that as a little boy, too. Whenever something would go wrong, he'd act as if he didn't care, but I could always tell he did.

"One time, he and the boy next door spent a week building a rocket ship in our backyard. They were convinced that this thing was going to take them to outer space. Well, they both ended up in the emergency room with second-degree burns and a bunch of cuts and bruises from the bottle rocket they jammed in the rear end of that rickety old thing... Well, my stars, it's lucky they weren't killed.

"And that's not the first time that boy of mine has nearly gotten himself killed, but that's not the point. What was my point? Honey, what was I talking about?"

"You were telling me about how Ian used to act like he didn't care...."

"Oh! Right, right, right, thank you, dear. Yes, well, Ian was devastated that his old rocket was laying in pieces on the ground, but the only way I knew it was by the little quiver in his bottom lip. He told his dad and me that he couldn't care less and that he knew it wouldn't fly to begin with, but you know he cared. He had big plans of floating around in space, don't you know. It was really a cute thing, too bad..."

"Mmm." Juliet nodded, not sure what was required of her in this conversation.

"Oh!" Barbara's bracelets jangled as she tried to gather her point. "Well, anyway, what I'm trying to say is, yes, yes, here it comes, oh, right. Don't believe him. He loves you. I can tell. He has that same look on his face when he looks at you, that he used to have when he'd look at that rocket of his. Pure, unadulterated love. Why the boy is positively goofy. So, you hang in there. If he doesn't get well—" His mother stopped and pressed her hand to her mouth and battled the tears.

Her arm still around Barbara's shoulders, Juliet gently patted her back.

"Well, if he doesn't get well, he's going to need you more than he knows."

On New Year's Eve, Juliet—allowed past visiting hours because it was a holiday—showed up in Ian's hospital room, dressed to kill. Pushing aside a cart with an eternally beeping monitor, she came to the edge of his bed, lowered the stainless steel guardrail and climbed up next to him. Too stunned to protest, Ian simply stared as she lowered her mouth to his and kissed him hard. When she finally felt him respond, she pulled back and whispered against his mouth. "Ian Rafferty, you might as well give up and let yourself care about me, because I am never leaving."

"That's what you said last night, just before you left," he complained.

"You are such a pain in the neck." She kissed him again, nuzzling his neck and tugging on his earlobes with her teeth. "I love you. Legs or no, and I want to make a life with you. Our life. To hell with the car pool. Bring on the wheelchair. We'll make do. And best of all, we'll be..." she kissed him again "...together."

Ian sighed and stared at the ceiling. "But what about children? You want lots of children."

"We can adopt."

"But what about sports—"

"Shhh!"

"But what about your freedom—"

"Shhh!"

"But what about our honeymoon—"

"Shhh!" She silenced him with a kiss, the same way he did her, back in the closet.

"Did anyone ever tell you that you are the most obstinate—"

"Shhh," she murmured and kissed him again.

"About the subject of children," he continued, lipping her lips, kissing her cheek, her jaw and her neck.

Juliet's sigh was audible. "Talk about obstinate."

"I don't…" He swallowed and began again. "I don't think there will be any problem there."

Juliet reared back and looked him in the eye. "What do you mean?"

"Kiss me again, and we'll know for sure."

She did.

"Okay, check this out." He pointed down below his beltline.

Juliet gave a reticent peek, and was shocked to find that his toes were moving. Her shriek of joy could be heard all the way down the corridor.

At that moment, the clock struck midnight and Juliet leaned forward for another toe-curling kiss. "Auld lang syne" played over the in-house music system and a nurse dropped in with a bottle of champagne, poured them each a glass and slipped to the next room, leaving them to celebrate in privacy.

Ian lifted a glass. "Marry me?"

"Are you sure it's not the champagne talking?"

He ran his hand up her arm and closed his fingers around her biceps. "No. Mom was right. I've been a fool. I was lucky enough to fall into the closet with my destiny. I'll take that as a sign from God."

"Then, yes, I'll marry you." Juliet smiled and lifted her own glass to his. "But only if you'll agree to the 'for better or worse' part. Ian, what happened to you could happen to me, or one of our kids. But as long as we have each other, we have a reason to live.''

''Mmm.'' Ian tugged her close for a kiss. ''Amen. So. Where should we go on our honeymoon?''

''Well, you said scenery didn't matter as long as you had your wife and a warm bed.''

''And so I recall, yes.''

''Then I know this little place under the stairs where no one will ever find us...''

Ian laughed and pulled her into his arms for another kiss to seal the deal.

Epilogue

One month later, Samantha and Jesse Colton threw an engagement party for Juliet and Ian in the very same ballroom where the couple had met only a month and a half before. Attending were most of the folks who'd attended the wedding, and the air was festive with celebration for more than just the coming nuptials.

After several hours of eating, drinking and making merry, Jesse Colton was finally persuaded to leave his wife's side and make a toast. A makeshift platform, complete with microphone, had been erected near the fireplace. Samantha—with Ian, who waved at the crowd from his wheelchair—joined Jesse there.

"Ah-hemmmm. Hello? This thing on?" Jesse tapped the mike and, with nods and thumbs-up from the crowd, a hush descended. "Good. Can you hear me in the back? Good. Okay! Welcome, everyone! I've been told that as the host, it is my duty to make a little speech."

The crowd cheered encouragement.

"It's been a heck of a year, huh?"

Applause thundered and when it died, Jesse continued. "As many of you are now aware, Kurt Hoffman, you all know Kurt? Kurt, wave, buddy. There he is—" Jesse pointed him out "—Kurt helped bring George Kartoff, leader of the Chekagovian Freedom Fighters, to justice."

Again, cheers and wild applause erupted.

"Good job, man. Kurt and his bride, Julianna, will be leaving from here for their second honeymoon in Mexico. A well-deserved vacation after what they have gone through to catch George Kartoff. Our congratulations." Jesse nodded at the beaming couple. "Yeah, old George will be spending his golden years behind bars and the music box he stole on Christmas Eve has been recovered and Helmut Ritka will give it to a Chekagovian museum for safekeeping.

"Helmut couldn't be with us tonight, but his daughter, Eva…" Jesse squinted out over the crowd. "Eva? Oh, there you are, Eva. Eva will also be soon joining the Colton clan as she has consented to make an honest man out of my cousin, Billy. Way to go, buddy.''

More cheering ensued, and Billy and Eva smiled and waved from the middle of the good-natured throng. Jesse waited for the well-wishers to calm before he continued.

''I'd also like to introduce to you the latest member of our family, Noel Colton, born on our wedding night, of all things, to Rand and Lucy Colton. He's a looker, like his father and when he wakes up—'' Jesse pointed to a stroller parked in the corner behind him ''—you can stop by and meet him. After you've washed your hands. And taken a crash course in baby handling. And been sand-blasted by our sterilization/sanitation crew...''

Lucy glared at him over the laughing crowd.

''And now, to the reason we are all here tonight. I am so pleased...no—'' Jesse paused and swallowed, emotions clearly getting the best of him ''—make that thrilled, to announce that my sister-in-law Juliet and her fiancé, Ian Rafferty, have set the date for their wedding.''

Jesse motioned for Juliet to join him at the mike. Cheers and whistles greeted her as she stepped forward.

''Hi.'' She offered a shy wave at everyone, and then a special nod at Ian's sister and parents. ''Thank you. Thank you. Yes, we've set the date, and I'd like Ian—'' she had to raise her voice to be heard above the hubbub ''—I'd like Ian to tell you when.'' She glanced back over her shoulder and the cheering reached a fevered pitch as Ian rose from his wheelchair and slowly approached his intended.

While he waited for the noise to subside, he bent Juliet back and gave her an enthusiastic kiss, which did nothing to quiet the masses.

Finally, after what seemed like an eternity, Ian was able to be heard. ''Thank you. Thanks so much. Yes, I'm happy to announce that Juliet and I will be tying the knot on New Year's Eve of this year. You're all invited. We are holding the wedding here, and, being that I'm in charge of security, we are not anticipating a repeat of last year's excitement.''

When the laughter had ebbed, Ian held up a glass of champagne and looked out over the crowd with unshed tears brimming in his eyes. They were tears of love. Of thanksgiving. Of belonging, at last. He ran a hand over his face and cast a tremulous smile at his bride-to-be, who was swiping at her cheeks with the back of her wrist.

''To family,'' he said, his voice thick with emotion.

''To family,'' Jesse echoed.

''To family,'' everyone murmured. And the Colton clan lifted their glasses and drank to the ever-growing ties that bound.

* * * * *

We hoped you enjoyed
A COLTON FAMILY CHRISTMAS.
Please look for the next book in
The Coltons' *series*
about the newfound Oklahoma clan
with Teresa Southwick's
SKY FULL OF PROMISE
(RS#1624, 11/02)
coming in November.

For a sneak preview of
SKY FULL OF PROMISE,
turn the page...

Chapter One

"You don't look like a home wrecker."

The sound of the deep male voice turned Sky Colton quickly from the sales receipts she'd been totaling. She hadn't heard anyone enter the store. Since Christmas the previous month, her high-end jewelry business in Black Arrow, Oklahoma, had been slow. Facing the tall, dark, handsome stranger, she wondered if sales were about to pick up. Along with her heartbeat.

Then his words registered. She folded her hands and rested them on the locked glass case containing her exclusive, original jewelry designs. "Home wrecker? If you're not looking for a demolition company, I have no idea what you're talking about."

"Right. And mermaids can do the splits."

Sky studied him more closely. His worn black leather bomber jacket was at odds with the powder-blue, button-down collar shirt tucked into his jeans. She couldn't help noticing his abdomen was washboard firm. No beer belly or love handles. His dark brown hair was cut conservatively short. It was the dead of winter, yet his olive skin made him look tanned. And she expected his eyes to be warm brown, like hot chocolate. They weren't.

Instead they were dark blue and sizzling with anger. Why? What had she done to him? She'd never seen this man before. She was sure of it.

"I would remember you," she said, then winced. Nothing like nourishing the ego of the man who was looking at her as if he wanted to stake her out on the nearest anthill. "If we'd ever met," she added.

"We haven't."

"It doesn't take a mental giant to see you're annoyed. Is there anything I can do for you?"

"Haven't you already done enough?"

She straightened to her full five-feet-six-inch height, but that didn't do much for her intimidation quotient. He had the advantage of another six inches and pretty much towered over her. Quite an attractive tower, she couldn't help noticing. And if he weren't so crabby, she might have been tempted to flirt.

"Look, Mr.—" She waited for him to supply a name, but he didn't. She sighed. "The only thing I do is design and sell jewelry. I use Native American elements in my designs, which some people find mystical. But I'm not psychic. You're going to have to give me more information if you expect me to undo any injustice you think I've done you.''

''I don't think it. I know it.''

''What?''

He reached into the pocket of his jacket and pulled out two black velvet jewelry boxes, then set them on the glass counter. Curiouser and curiouser, she thought.

Sky picked one up and opened it, noting her business logo embossed on the lid's satin lining. The ring inside was definitely her own design and one of her favorites. It was a gold band that she'd created for Shelby Parker, a wealthy oilman's daughter from Midland, Texas. She'd become engaged during the holidays to a man she'd known a short time and her fiancé had wanted the wedding arranged quickly.

After hearing about Sky's designs from a friend, she'd had her chauffeur drive her from Houston to Black Arrow to personally commission wedding bands. Her fiancé hadn't had time to buy her an engagement ring or to accompany her to shop for this very important purchase. Shelby had returned several times, to make adjustments to the designs and talk about her ideas for bridesmaids and groomsmen gifts. Always, the chauffeur had driven her, making Sky wonder if she were as flaky as a soda cracker or just afraid to fly.

Sky remembered the young woman chattering away while she'd roughed out some ring sketches. Then again when they'd discussed changes to the designs, Shelby had wondered about using gold as opposed to silver or white gold, and possibly adding precious stones. Now Sky struggled to recall snippets of the conversations. Shelby had said her fiancé was a well-known Houston plastic surgeon. His name was—

She could only recall that Shelby had joked about calling him Dr. StoneHeart. Sky couldn't remember his real name and opened the other box, plucking the large men's ring from it. Subtly etched into the gold were the initials D.R. She had the most inane thought about the irony of his initials spelling out his profession. Then, she looked up from the ring in her hand to eyes growing angrier by the second if the darkening blue around his irises was anything to go by.

"Dr. Dominic Rodriguez," she said. She held out her hand. "It's nice to finally meet you. I'm Sky Colton."

"I know," he answered coolly.

"Shelby told me a lot about you." Most of which she couldn't remember.

"Interesting you associate your clients by pieces of jewelry."

Sky didn't much care for his tone. "I've seen enough medical dramas on TV to know that doctors identify their patients by symptoms or diagnosis. Frankly, my way is far more pleasant. Wouldn't you agree?"

One corner of his mouth turned up, but that was her only indication that he was even the tiniest bit amused. "No."

"My sincere and heartfelt congratulations on your upcoming wedding. Obviously you're here because you'd like some changes on the rings. I can—"

"I'm here because there's not going to be a wedding."

Sky blinked up at him. "No wedding? But I don't understand. Have you and Shelby postponed—"

"I believe the words were quite clear. But let me rephrase. The wedding is off. Permanently," he added for emphasis. "I received a bill for wedding bands. And for groomsmen gifts in progress."

Sky stared at him, mortified that she couldn't stop herself from noticing how dangerously sexy he was. She sensed in him a leashed intensity that could change to passion in a heartbeat. If provoked. Or maybe she was overdue for an appointment with a shrink. For goodness' sake, the poor man had just been dumped. Or had he? Maybe *he'd* called it off.

Studying the tension in his jaw and the stiff set of his shoulders, added to the angry gaze and sarcastic tone, she decided she'd been right the first time. Definitely dumped. And he wasn't the least bit happy about it.

For good reason. He'd practically been married. But "almost" wasn't a done deal. Why should that please her even a little bit? Good question, for which she had no answer. Since her own broken engagement, she'd managed to get on with her life by scrapping her girlish fantasies of marriage, husband, children. Now her goal was to build an already fast-growing business. It was counterproductive to be attracted to this man. Technically he might be available, but emotionally he was still attached to someone who was no longer attached to him. While Sky might think the woman shortsighted, or even blind, maybe mentally impaired if not downright stupid, the fact remained, he was hurt and angry.

But what in the world happened? From what little she could recall of her conversations with the bride-to-be, Sky had the impression that Dr. StoneHeart was perfection personified. What had made her change her mind? Why had Shelby blown him off? Then Sky recalled the words that had alerted her to his presence when he'd walked in the shop. *You don't look like a home wrecker.* What had he meant by that?

"Dr. Rodriguez, I have the impression you hold me responsible for something."

"Yes, Ms. Colton." He laughed, a harsh sound and completely without humor. "I do."

Award-winning author

BEVERLY BARTON

brings you a brand-new, longer-length book
from her Protectors bestselling series!

ON HER GUARD

As the powerful head of one of the most successful
protection agencies in the world, Ellen Denby believed
she was invincible. Invulnerable. Until she came face-to-
face with the one man who made her remember what
it was to feel. To love. But would her passion for secret
service agent Nikos Pandarus come at too high a price?

Available in November from your favorite retail outlet!

Only from Silhouette Books!

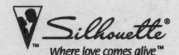

Where love comes alive™